Table of Contents

Bump

Austin Smith

Introduction

The idea of the novel, as you will soon find out, is that everyone has a story. We are all main characters in the book of life. The protagonist of Bump changes based on who is last touched, then changes again with that person's next physical contact. The point of view changes to reveal the lives of dozens of different characters within one novel.

Several genres are included in Bump, and the tone of the novel will change constantly as the story takes on the lives of various characters. There are happy endings, and not so happy endings, and some that are bitter sweet.

Rules

To follow the Bump several rules must first be acknowledged.

1. The perspective can change more than once, including being transferred back to a former protagonist.
2. The perspective does not change multiple times if a character is touching someone while also engaged in hugging, hand holding, etc.
3. A prolonged physical situation will not necessarily indicate who has last been touched, so try to keep up.
4. Tugging on clothing does not warrant a change in perspective.

PS: If you're wondering about the thirteenth chapter I decided to omit it from being listed, much like the thirteenth floor of so many great hotels.

Chapter 1

The mother collected her son's homework from each of his teachers. One teacher in particular caught her eye, Mr. Freud.

He leaned casually on the edge of his desk, facing the mother. She stood across from him, holding a handful of papers.

"Thank you so much for this," the mother said. "He's not a bad kid, in fact I think you'll love to have him in your class. He's one of those kids to always raise his hand and give the answer, but that doesn't mean he's a know-it-all or anything because—"

"I'm sure he's a great student," Mr. Freud interrupted.

She blushed a light pink color. "Sorry, sometimes I babble on and on about nothing."

"Most people do that when they get nervous." He stood from his desk and walked closer. "Are you nervous, Mrs. ....?"

"Kavinski, and no, I'm not nervous." Her face blushed harder.

She looked down at Mr. Freud's hand, then back at his face. "There's no ring on your finger," she said.

He tilted his head. "But there *is* a ring on yours."

She covered her ring hand with her other hand. "Yeah.... I guess there is."

He smiled at her, it might've been too big of a smile, but he didn't realize.

Mrs. Freud, Kathy Freud. It had a nice ring to it, much better than Kathy Kavinski.

"Well," she said. "I'd better get home so Chris can start his homework."

"How many days was he suspended?"

"Just two."

He smiled again, this time less intensely. "Then I guess I'll see you tomorrow."

The drive home gave her too much time to think. Every red light and stop sign gave her the opportunity to think about cheating on her husband, yet no time to think how it would affect Chris.

It's not like he's never done it before, she thought. *I just haven't caught him yet.*

The inside out collar, the smell of one too many drinks on his breath after work, and she could've sworn seeing a faded smear of lipstick on his face once. Although, it could've been ketchup or some other sauce. Ben always *was* a messy eater.

Kathy's hands were shaking as she approached her house. She didn't do anything wrong, but her subconscious plagued her, sort of like a guilt alarm.

And rest assured, Ben was sitting in his chair, waiting for the second she came through the door.

"What took you so long?" he asked contemptuously.

"I told you already, I was getting Chris's homework."

He stood from his chair and slowly advanced toward her. "It takes ten minutes to get there, maybe fifteen to get his homework, then ten minutes to get back depending on the rush hour." He stopped moving just a few feet from her.

"They had to explain how to do the work."

"On the first day of school? He couldn't have had that much homework."

She lifted the stack of papers to his face, waving it a little.

"Geez," he said. "It gets worse every year, doesn't it?"

Ben shamefully retreated back to his chair. They locked eyes. Kathy gave him a very particular expression. It was the same expression she made when he lied about his after-work drinks.

"I'm sorry," he said, his eyes now avoiding Kathy's

glare. "I'm sorry I didn't trust you. I was mad about having to leave work early so I could watch our son get suspended. We need more money, and I'm tired of living paycheck to paycheck."

Kathy abandoned her thoughts of cheating completely. She walked over to Ben and sat down on the arm of his chair, crossing her legs.

"I'm so damn tired, Kathy."

"Me too Ben. Who would've thought one kid would be so exhausting?"

His eyes shimmered. "Would you have wanted another kid?"

"You know we can't Ben."

"You know *I* can't, Kathy."

"It's just how you are. Besides, kids are expensive, and we've already got our hands tied with one. One beautiful, gifted child."

She put a hand on Ben's shoulder. He shivered a bit, embarrassed at his wife's comforting words. He was supposed to be the comforting one. He was supposed to be *the man*.

Ben stood up. "I'm gonna go for a walk."

"I'll go with you."

"I'd really rather go alone, clear my head."

"Oh. Well, I'll go upstairs and give Chris his homework. He's probably driven himself crazy waiting for it. If you want some company, give me a call."

"Sure."

If Ben would've said, "I'm going for a drive", Kathy would've known he meant, "Go out for a drink". Ben *wanted* to go for a drink, but taking the car would've been too obvious. Still, the nearest bar or liquor store wasn't for at least eight miles.

He was somewhat of an alcoholic, not a heavy drinker, but if he went to a bar anywhere downtown, he would know the staff by name, especially the bartenders. He'd stay just for a couple of drinks (usually), then head home to Kathy. Nothing too bad…. usually.

He wasn't a violent drunk, and Chris hardly noticed his drinking at all. Most of it was done away from home and away from Chris. Ben liked to call himself, and often did, a "social drinker".

He opened the door. It was getting dark but if he made it to West Central Park in time, he could watch the sun go down. One of the many things he and Kathy did before they had Chris.

He didn't want to be gone for too long, Kathy would think he was out drinking. He left his car keys on the key rack for Kathy to see but he *could* still call a cab.

If Chris knew he'd been drinking he would inevitably blame himself and get distracted from his schoolwork. And that was the last thing Ben wanted.

If he couldn't save his marriage, he could at least save his son.

He started walking to his right. There was no particular set destination but West Central Park was in that direction. He'd most likely sit on a park bench and watch the sun go down with the nice old ladies who fed the birds at this hour. No harm done.

As each car drove by, he counted their colors. By the time he arrived at the park he'd seen two blues, one yellow, four reds, and six grays.

The park changed since he was a kid. He grew up around West Central Park and watched it slowly change over the years. The metal structures had been replaced by less dangerous plastic ones. The slides were now plastic and spiraled as they descended toward the ground. He couldn't think too much about it without frowning. The new park wasn't bad per se. In fact, it was an improvement from the metal that'd burn him on a hot day. But it was different. Not his childhood park anymore.

The old ladies were there, just as he predicted, but they weren't tossing bags of seeds to the ground, they were just sitting and laughing. It was the usual kind of

old person laugh, the kind when they would laugh so
hard they'd cough halfway through and cover their
mouths.

Years of cigarette abuse, he guessed.

He sat on a bench in the middle of the park, facing
opposite the sunset he came to see. Staring across from
him was a fake rock with a sign attached that read:
Please Don't Feed The Birds.

Come to think of it, the park had been crowded with
birds lately. They probably kept coming back wondering
where the old ladies were with their bags of bird seeds.

Ben spread his arms over both sides of the bench's
backside, deterring anyone from wanting to sit there. He
rested his ankle across his knee and stared up at the sky.

Chris was most likely doing his homework right now,
starting off with math and finishing with English.

Chris always announced what he learned from
homework over the dinner table, trying to teach his mom
and dad a thing or two. The way Chris saw it, his parents
were done with school but school wasn't done with
them.

Ben tried to remember the things he'd say, although
sometimes he'd go to a bar and drink those thoughts
away.

"Excuse me," said a voice in front of him.

He bent his head. One of the usual old women stared
at him. She wore a polka dot dress and a sun hat with a
bow tied around it.

"Could I sit there?" the woman asked.

Ben lowered one arm to his side and the woman sat
next to him. She opened up her purse and pulled out a
thick paperback novel. She opened it and started to read
before Ben could see the title. Chances are he didn't need
to think hard to guess what it was. She was reading
whatever old women read in a public park, probably a
romance novel.

She shifted around, almost bumping Ben in the
process. He moved over a foot to give her extra room.

"So no more feeding the birds I guess," Ben said abruptly.

"What?"

Ben pointed to the sign on the fake rock. The old woman took a pair of glasses out of her purse, unfolded them, then put them on her face. Even still, she leaned forward and squinted her eyes, trying to read the sign.

"Oh, well, I won't take out my seed bag then," she said.

"Did I disappoint you?"

"Rules are rules. I suppose you can't have too many birds flying around." She grinned.

The woman's smile surprised Ben. Would he be that happy when his face was as wrinkly as hers? Would he still be with Kathy?

"You still have your book?" he asked.

"My what?" She looked down at her book, like she heard him anyway. "Oh right, yes."

"What're you reading?"

She closed her book and stuffed it back into her old lady purse. All this happened too fast for Ben to read the title.

"So what brings a young man to the park on a weekday?"

"My son got caught with a pack of cigarettes. I didn't want to leave work but the principal insisted on speaking with *both* parents."

"That's nice."

Ben knew the old woman wasn't really listening. Or maybe she didn't hear him. He looked at her ears but found no hearing aids. He assumed she only heard what she wanted to. Selective hearing.

He could use this to confess his wrong doings. He needed to tell someone but he didn't need them to judge him or give him one of those painful lectures he gave his son…. and his dad gave him.

She probably had Alzheimer's too. She looked about that age. Anything he'd tell her would go in one ear and out the other.

"I also came here to think about my marriage," he said. "Thinking about telling my wife how I've slept with other women."

"Well at least you're trying to fix things."

Dammit! She was listening!

"I'll pay as much as a marriage counselor wants if it means fixing my marriage. Not just for me, or my wife, but for our son. Kathy deserves to know the truth, and Chris does too."

"How old is he?"

"He's fourteen."

"That's tough for a thirteen-year-old to go through."

"Fourteen."

"And how long have you been married?"

"Seventeen years. Thirteen of those were the best years of my life."

"And then what happened?"

"Alcohol, money, temptation, the usual."

"But you're fixing it now?"

"I have to tell her first. Tell her everything."

"I'm sure it'll work out for the best."

A shadow cast over him, it made Ben uncomfortable, even cold. How long had someone been listening to his conversation, eavesdropping.

It was a young kid, about twenty, and smiling at the woman. He had the same exact nose as she did.

"You ready to go grandma?" the boy said.

"Is it that time already?"

"Sorry," the kid said. "I do have work tonight and I can't be late again."

"Yes of course," she said, standing up and picking up her purse. "Young people have their priorities. It's easy to forget that when you've been retired for as long as I have. Good luck with your troubles sir, I'm sure it'll all work out fine."

Ben extended his hand to the woman but she turned away before she could see it. The grandson took notice and shook it to save Ben from embarrassment, and Ben laughed at this.

The grandson leaned in slightly and talked in a soft voice. "She's old," he said.

The man nodded, and the grandson and grandma left the park.

"Did you have fun grandma?" he asked, offering his assistance, and her not noticing.

"Yes. I walked around and saw some old friends and met some new ones."

The grandson was skeptical she had "made new friends", but he humored her. "Who was that man you were speaking to?"

"I don't really know," she replied. "But it sounded like he was having a hell of a bad day."

The grandson laughed. "Poor guy."

When they approached the grandson's car he walked ahead of his grandma and opened her door. She smiled and shakily crawled into the car. It felt about time she bought herself a cane or maybe a walker. He closed the door for her, walked around to his door, opened it, and stepped inside.

"Back to your place?" he asked, closing the door.

"That sounds good."

"It's a plan."

He started the engine and drove out of the parking lot and onto the road.

"I haven't seen you around so much lately." his grandma said. "Or heard from you."

"I'm sorry you couldn't stay and chat grandma, there's so much work for me to do lately."

"I know you kids always have some work to do. Though, I won't be around forever you know. I can't even remember what I ate for breakfast."

"Neither can I. Please don't talk about that stuff when I'm driving."

She didn't respond. She used the more effective strategy of an awkward silence, a strategy her grandson was all too used to.

He pushed a few buttons on the radio and set the channel to a station he thought she'd like. Something with Jazz. He made a mental note to change the station before his not date tonight.

His grandma had a cat named after him, David. Not a good name for a cat but she named all of her cats after her grandchildren, usually based on their personalities. She thought they would find it flattering — they didn't.

She'd have conversations with relatives and say things like "Marion died last week". They'd go insane thinking it was one of her grandchildren until she explained that it was their feline counterpart. Now whenever that happens the relative asks, "Which one, the kid or the cat?"

She'd never admit to it, but whenever one of her grandkids misbehaved she'd stop giving their corresponding cats treats or toys for a while. A cynical way to live, but it was all she knew.

They pulled up to her house.

It wasn't exactly a nice neighborhood, but it wasn't a bad one either. Good enough for a retired woman her age. All that could be said for sure was that it was quiet, and that's what mattered.

"Give me a quick hug before I go inside," she said.

David hugged his grandma, trying not to squeeze too hard.

"Do you need help getting inside?" he asked.

"No that's all right. I may be old but I'm not *that* old."

She left the car door open as she crawled out and walked to her house. The driveway was an almost flat incline but she still walked slowly up it. When the grandma closed her door David shut the car's.

He double checked his grandma being safe in the house then called his not girlfriend, Alexa, putting her on speaker phone, then pulled back to the road and drove.

"What's up?" she said.

"I'm coming to get you, don't make me wait an extra

fifteen minutes when I get there."

"You know I have to. What kind of not girlfriend would I be if I didn't?"

David hated when she called herself that. Not girlfriend made him sound…. cheap, undeserving.

"Where are we going on our not date?" he asked.

"Either see a movie or just go out to eat. I don't have that much money right now."

"Well whatever you buy you pay for, that's the rule for our not dates."

"I'll pay you back!"

"If you knew we were going out why didn't you check your wallet?"

"I didn't know what we were doing."

David let out a sigh so big it almost seemed like it blew through his phone and into Alexa's ear.

"Or we could watch a movie at your place," she said hopefully.

"Nope. My parents think I'm at work. I even had to lie to my grandma."

"Well we can't stay at my place, my parents are home and you know they talk to your parents."

"I'll take you out to eat, my treat."

"You sure?"

David wanted to sigh again, but then it wouldn't mean as much. He had to save them for something else, a real disappointment. "Yeah, what the hell."

"See you in twenty?"

"Sure."

End call.

David knew his not date would end the same as it always did. They would go to some public place where every guy within eyesight come running to her, since it was of course, "not a date", she would accumulate a vast amount of phone numbers.

Of course David couldn't go around and flirt with women because his not girlfriend would throw a fit, make a scene if she wanted to. She only allowed him to get a woman's number if *she* walked up to *him*. And the chances of that were slim to none, especially since every girl who saw them together assumed they were dating.

Not one guy who flirted with Alexa ever made it to boyfriend-hood. There was always something wrong with them. Somehow, some way, there was something wrong with them. But she liked the attention. And David liked giving her attention.

Not girlfriend and not dates was a loophole Alexa used to get attention. It also saved her the pain of watching her not boyfriend get the same affection. She didn't love David, but he was always an option.

It was seven in the afternoon.

Alexa walked out wearing a glittering silver dress that ended just above her knees. It was far too nice for either a movie or a cheap meal. The dress wasn't for David though, it was worn for someone else. She didn't know who, but she hoped to find him.

If David found his someone else, great, but she didn't want to know about it.

Alexa stepped into the car and shut the door. David knew Alexa thought she had him figured out pretty well. Same boring David, doesn't talk back, no real opinions on anything.

What she didn't know is that David had considered suicide dozens of times before. They were mostly just thoughts although he *did* recently buy a six shot revolver, which he kept on an ankle holster he covered with his jeans.

He was on the border of suicide and had been for weeks. Not once did David talk to anyone about it. No one even knew he had a gun.

If it was found on his ankle he'd tell them he had a license to carry a concealed weapon. Obviously it wouldn't work with the police, but he hadn't counted on them, or anyone else finding out.

If someone found it lying in his sock drawer, he'd say he wanted to go hunting. If it was his dad, who knew very well he'd never gone hunting a day in his life or even expressed interest in the idea, he'd say, "Surprise! I bought you a gun. I was saving it for Christmas. I know it's months away but I saw it and I just had to buy it."

David stared at the crease between Alexa's breasts, then at her face. She didn't wear makeup, and she didn't need to. Still, she liked to take as much time as she needed before going out.

"Where are we headed?" David asked, feeling ashamed to ask that sort of question, as he was the one driving.

"You're the one with the car, you pick."

David raised his eyebrows. "We could go to the mall. I think Big Baller's Burgers is still open there."

"That's perfect. I could browse around, do some shopping while I'm there."

"And I could stand next to you looking like an idiot."

"Don't tell me you couldn't do any shopping. You *definitely* need new shoes."

Twenty minutes passed and they arrived at the mall. It was the biggest one in town, lots of good looking guys were there, trying to find someone to end the night with. They parked in a parking structure far from the actual mall itself, Alexa complained about the walk every hundred feet.

David held the glass mall door open for Alexa and followed her inside.

"Well I got my daily workout," she said.

They walked to the two sided directory map and searched for Big Baller's Burgers, or as they liked to call it, B-B-B.

You are here, **ENTRANCE**. They searched further on the sign. **Food Category, Big Baller's Burger's, 2E.**

They walked onto the escalators, letting it carry them to the second level. Alexa stopped three steps up from David, avoiding his eye contact as if he were a stranger. When David climbed a step further Alexa would do the same, acting as if she was doing it subconsciously. Sometimes David thought she was purposely distancing herself so no one would mistake them for a real couple. Still, David would take a not girlfriend over nothing.

They walked down the long crowded hall and inside B-B-B. A pretty hostess greeted them almost immediately, smiling at them from behind her podium.

"Just you two?" she asked.

"That's right," David said.

She picked up two menus, carrying them close to her chest as she sat them at a nearby booth. It was a slow day and few people were dining.

An even prettier waitress walked to their table with a pen and notepad. An extra pen was wedged between her ear and the side of her head. David thought it was cute. This is the woman he wanted to be with. If she was a good waitress too he'd be sure to leave a big tip she'd brag about to her coworkers.

"Can I get you any drinks to start off?" she said. "Any appetizers?"

Alexa looked down at her laminated menu and made a disgusted face. Then she flipped the page. "I'll have…. the curly fries…. and a water."

The waitress scribbled on her notepad and turned to David. "And for you?"

David didn't look at the menu. "I'll have the same."

She wrote his order and walked away, her hips swaying.

"Are you coming to work tomorrow morning?" Alexa asked.

"Yeah. I can't afford to miss two shifts in a row."

"Not while we have Jason as our boss anyway."

David bounced his knee spastically under the table, as he usually did when he was nervous. He couldn't think of what to say. Not that it made a difference. Alexa was there to eat, not to talk.

She ran her fingers through her long dark blonde hair and looked around the room, no doubt hoping to catch someone checking her out. The dress she was wearing made it seem like she'd walked out of a party or a wedding reception. David wanted to mention it, why he was wearing a t-shirt and jeans and she was wearing a sparkling attention grabber. He could picture what she'd say, "A girl's gotta look good".

An awkward barrier of silence rose between them. His eyes shifted around the room, trying to find something to talk about. *Anything!*

"Do you like the food here?" he asked.

"It's not bad," she replied. "My dad used to take me here when I was a kid."

The waitress came back holding a tray flatly with her wrist bent, the standard waitress hand position. She carefully placed their waters in front of them and even put their straws in for them.

"And I'll be right back with your curly fries," she said.

She wasn't lying. Before another uncomfortable silence arose, she swayed back to them, holding a tray with two baskets of curly fries. She set them down and walked off.

Alexa grabbed a bottle of ketchup sitting on the edge of the table and squeezed it over her fries. She started eating, first one at a time, then two at a time. David did little eating of his own. He spent most of the time actually watching Alexa eat, amazed.

She had a terrific body for someone who ate as much as she did. David wasn't too surprised, her mom had a great body too, not as thin as a twig, just fit. Her dad was built like an ex-wrestler. He could remember getting arguing with him once over the way Alexa dressed for school. Looking back, he wished he'd sided with her dad.

Alexa raised her head and frowned when she noticed the still full basket of fries sitting in front of David.

"I'm starving," she said.

"I'm not hungry."

"After all that walking? Seriously? You really could use some weight on you."

David picked up a curly fry and rotated it between his

fingers. The grease rubbed onto his hands, giving them a gross, shiny appearance. Revulsion ripped at David's stomach. He had to force himself to eat half the basket.

Two more people walked in, and David figured he'd rather be talking to either one of them.

It was an older couple, late sixties maybe. Apparently neither one of them had anywhere better to be.

"You guys have enough time to think?"

David jumped a little in his seat. The waitress appeared next to him, seemingly out of nowhere.

"I'll have the double BBQ bacon burger," Alexa said, folding her menu and handing it to the waitress.

"And I'll have the same," David said, he started to close the menu, then Alexa spoke.

"Don't you have any of your own opinions?" she snapped.

"It's a good burger," the waitress retorted.

David eyed the nametag on the waitresses' shirt. **HELLO, MY NAME IS JUNE**.

David folded his menu and handed it to her. Alexa said nothing more but crossed her arms and legs. It reminded David of a turtle hiding in its shell, away from its problems outside, and suddenly, David felt like a hungry fox.

"Thank you," he said to June.

June stacked the menus together and shot a quick judgmental glance in Alexa's direction. A wave of heat radiated across David's chest. He smiled, but quickly hid it for Alexa's sake.

June walked off.

"You don't actually think she's pretty, do you?" Alexa asked.

"Actually, I think she's very pretty."

Alexa leaned across the table and brought her voice to a near whisper. "She looks skanky."

David shook his head. There was no use in arguing. He'd never win.

They almost finished their burgers when a man

wearing tattered jeans and a white tank top walked into the restaurant.

"Brett is that you?" Alexa said.

Brett flashed a smiled. "The one and only. I saw you guys sitting here so I thought I'd pop in and say hello."

David was always amazed at how Brett could smile almost as widely as his face.

Brett pulled out a neighboring chair and sat on it backwards, pointing it towards Alexa. David knew when Brett sat down their not date was over.

"Do you still skateboard?" Alexa asked.

"Longboard now. It can't do as many tricks, but I still like it better. I was actually going to Simon's to look at some jackets. You wanna help me pick them out?"

Alexa turned to David. "Do you mind? I mean, you were going to pick up the check anyways." She starting standing up, already anticipating David's approval.

"Would it matter?"

She sat back down. "If you don't want me to go, then I won't go."

"I don't want to make you feel guilty or miserable. Just go."

Brett rolled his eyes. Then he mouthed the word "wow" inaudibly.

"Fine," she said curtly.

Brett and Alexa walked out together, David thought she might look back to check his reaction, but they walked until David could no longer see them.

June walked to David's booth, this time without swaying her hips.

"Do you want the check or do you need a minute?" she said.

"There's no point in staying, I'll just take the check."

Frowning, June removed the extra chair and slid it under its original table. She walked to the hostess' podium, grabbed his check, walked back and handed it to David. He paid in credit and ripped off a blank space on the receipt.

On the space he wrote his phone number and pulled out an extra ten dollars from his wallet. He didn't care if she called him, but he wanted to hope, he missed that feeling, hope.

She raised her eyebrows when her fingers felt the receipt.

"What's this?" she asked, although it was obvious she knew what it was.

"Read it and find out."

She looked at the number, then back at David.

Her kind eyes gave him an answer before even opening her mouth.

"I get off at nine when the mall closes," she said with no distinct enthusiasm, more of an obligation, really.

After David walked out of the store, he glanced at June through the glass window. She looked at the money he handed her. It wasn't a one or a five, it was a ten. A ten-dollar tip for a twenty-two-dollar check.

David walked to Simon's. There was no trace of either Alexa or Brett. He felt embarrassed trying to meet with the same person he came with. He could take out his phone and ask Alexa where she was, but what would be the point? If she wanted to talk to him and tell him where she was, she would have.

If David were a betting man, he'd say both Alexa and Brett were in a bathroom stall. The public mall bathroom was a less than ideal place to have sex but that wouldn't faze Alexa, not when she was with Brett. And knowing Alexa, she'd probably be the one to suggest it.

He could go back to his car and drive home, leave Alexa there and force Brett to take her home. Brett would probably end up taking her home anyways. But David wanted to be out of the house. If he went home and sulked, he'd just want to get out of the house again, meet another terrible woman to get his mind off the last terrible woman, get blown off, rinse and repeat.

There was still something. The six-shooter revolver strapped to his ankle. He had it loaded with one bullet.

He only needed one, he couldn't miss.

Sure, there was June, but chances were she'd never call him. A girl like that probably gets dozens of numbers every day, and she never actually *said* she'd call him. She said she got off at nine, but did she *really*? With his luck she got out at eight or eight thirty and would already be long gone by the time he got back.

David tried to think of more depressing, mind numbing thoughts, but he couldn't. Not with the sound of the indoor merry-go-round.

There was only one small child riding it. His mom was standing next to him, cheering him and holding onto a safety bar while he sat next to her on a big plastic lion. The music was making it difficult for David to think about anything else. The song was catchy. David hummed along as he searched for the escalators.

He followed the flow of the crowd to the corner of the mall and took the escalators down, still trying to spot Alexa before he left. Something in the core of his stomach told him she never went to Simon's at all.

He waited on the cold stone bench outside, not sure what he was waiting for, just waiting. How many times had he been in this same situation? If he counted it with his hands he'd run out of fingers. There might've not been enough toes either, if he counted after ten.

What was he waiting for? The revolver was in his pant leg, loaded and ready to go.

Sitting on the cold bench made him depressed. Thinking about Alexa made him depressed. He needed to *do* something.

Screw Alexa.

David stood up and started toward the mall. The glass doors swung open and Alexa burst out, crying into her hands.

David narrowed his eyes, trying to focus them on the person before him, to make sure it was not an illusion. "Alexa?"

If she had been wearing mascara it would've smeared

her face.

"David!" She threw her arms around him and buried her face in his chest.

"What happened?" he asked.

"Brett's a jerk, that's what happened! I'm sorry for leaving you, can we please just go home?"

He took her hand and led her where he thought the parking structure was, hoping Brett wouldn't run into them.

He'd probably try to reel her in again with an "apology" then do the same thing (whatever it is he did) in a couple of weeks.

Alexa hid her face from the people walking by. It didn't stop them from glaring at her and then quickly look away.

Two people walked by and gave David a sour expression as they passed. David assumed they thought he was responsible for making Alexa cry. He let go of her hand, only for her to immediately grab it back.

Alexa made more noise coming back to the car than she did complaining about the walk inside. She kept crying, inhaling small breaths of air as she did. Her shoulders bounced up and down with every breath she took. She tried to limit her sobbing to be as quiet as possible but couldn't help wailing a few times.

David loaded her into the car, walked around, and crawled in. He thought about turning on the radio. Alexa could tell he wanted to fill in the awkwardness. She wanted to grant him that wish. But David talked.

"Do you want to tell me what happened or do I have to guess?"

"I c-can't talk right now."

"You were gone for what…. ten minutes?"

She tightened her hands into fists and threw them at the side of David's seat. "I said I don't want to talk about it!"

The traffic only accentuated the problem. Alexa

wanted to go home and text everyone in her contacts list, making sure everyone knew Brett was a jerk (if they already didn't). She wished David would drive more aggressively, swerve through cars, speed through yellow lights, something. But *noooo*, he took his sweet time as usual, acting as if she wasn't in an emotional crisis at all.

Alexa wiped her eyes as they approached her house. Her tears had dried completely.

"Despite everything that's happened," she said. "I did like our not date tonight." When she said, "not date" she raised her hands to eye level and used an air quotes gesture, something David had never seen her do before.

David nodded and she blew him a kiss, something she'd only done once before. When Alexa left the car, David leaned over the passenger seat and tried to grab her. But he was too late. She'd already closed the door and started toward her house.

He rolled down the passenger window. "I bought a gun."

She turned around and stared at him, incredulously.

"Why, David?" The color of her face drained away. Her own problems suddenly vanished, if only for a moment.

He thought for a moment…. "I don't know, but sometimes I bring it with me."

She walked to him, reached through the open window, and put a hand on his shoulder.

He turned away, staring at the road in front of him, remembering his revolver.

"I'll see you at work tomorrow, okay?" David said, removing her hand.

"Do you want to say something?"

"Not really." His face was blank and serious. It was probably as white as a ghost, but it was too dark for Alexa to tell.

She blew him another kiss, this time slower and more sensual. He lifted his hand and caught it, still frowning, then drove away.

Alexa's head was spinning.

David wouldn't really do anything, she thought. *He's just having a low point.*

She opened the door and stepped inside, standing motionless by the front door. She couldn't find a place to sit soon enough so she rested her back on the front door. The stairs were too much of a challenge now.

Dammit David! Why couldn't you just drive home and call it a night? Why'd you have to say one more thing? I probably won't be able to sleep tonight, and I have work tomorrow morning. Thanks!

"Alexa are you home?" a voice called from upstairs.

"Yeah mom! It's me!"

"You're home early, is everything okay?"

"Yeah mom!" There was something in her voice that sounded disingenuous. Alexa started climbing the stairs, using the handrail as a support. Her sweaty hands made it hard for her to grasp it.

Her mom walked out of her room and watched her struggle up the stairs.

"Are you drunk?" she asked.

"No mom!"

"Then why can't you walk right?"

"I've had a rough day."

"It's some boy you've been seeing, huh?"

"No mom, and if it is it's none of your goddamn business."

Her mom made no reaction, hearing her daughter curse at her was not a rarity. "What about that David kid. Why don't you like him? Or is he the who made you feel like this?"

"It wasn't. Actually, I think he might be the only boy I can trust right now."

She was at the top of the stairs. Her mom stood by, watching closely, her bedroom door open behind her.

"Go to bed, Alexa."

From the mix of crying out her energy, thinking about David, and having a long day, Alexa snapped.

"Is there something you want to say to me?" Alexa didn't think her eyes had any more tears to give, she was wrong.

"I just think you need some sleep is all."

"I heard what you said. But I don't think that's what you *wanted* to say."

"We'll talk about this in the morning," her mother said as she retreated to her room, closing the door behind her.

"I have work in the morning!" Alexa yelled through the closed door.

Chapter 2

Alexa couldn't remember the dream she had last night, but she knew it was horrifying. It had something to do with David…. and his gun.

The morning air was cool and her bed was warm. She was like a caterpillar in a cocoon, and she wanted to stay a caterpillar.

But there was work to do.

She brushed her hair, put on work clothes, and omitted her morning makeup routine. The headache she had could've been mistaken for a hangover. Nothing she did that morning could make her forget about David. Seeing her at work later would no doubt make things better, awkward too, although she could set her mind at ease knowing he lived to see another day.

When she opened her bedroom door she listened for her mother, hoping she wouldn't talk to her. Her parent's bedroom door was completely shut, it didn't appear to have opened since the night before.

She walked out her room and down the stairs, holding her shoes so her footsteps could be relatively silent. At the bottom she sat on the first step and put them on. There was no way she could eat breakfast without waking up her mom, so she skipped it, and walked into the garage.

There, waiting patiently, was a 1973 Camaro. Not bad for a nineteen-year-old.

Alexa pushed a button on the wall and the garage door opened, it was loud, and didn't move quickly enough for Alexa's liking. Her mom would wake for sure.

She stood still, stunned by the noise the garage made. When no one came out Alexa started up her car and set off to work.

Her mind was at ease when David walked into the diner. He was working in the kitchen cleaning dishes when she first saw him that morning.
They must be low on busboys, she figured.
As much as she wanted to walk up to David, leave her work area, and confront him about last night, she refrained herself knowing she would be fired. She was already in deep water on account of all her "sick days".
David didn't seem sad, which was the worst part. He was catatonic. His eyes were without their usual warmth. If only he'd show one small sign of human emotion she might be able to calm her noisy mind.

Everything was normal that morning, slower than usual actually, until ten' forty exactly.
The bells tied to the front door jingled as the next customer walked in.
He was an older looking man. A scar ran down his left cheek, his hair was graying, and he came in with his hand stuffed into his jacket.
He walked with quick strides to the hostess' podium and pointed a gun at her face.
"Give me…. everything you have," he said shakily.
David was nearby.
The gun, David, use your gun. I know you have it, she thought.
"I want everyone's wallet! Take them out *slowly*!" He didn't speak to the store at large but only to the hostess shaking behind her podium.
David ducked behind a table and Alexa cringed. She didn't think the gunman saw him though because he still had his gun pointed at the hostesses' face, and she was glad David evaded his attention. David came back up.
He aimed his gun at the robber and the robber turned

toward him instinctively. David was too quick for him. He shot his revolver and hit the robber in the torso. A stream of blood shot out from his chest and hit a close patron. She screamed in horror, her once white shirt was splotched with red. Her boyfriend, or maybe her husband, grabbed her from behind, preventing her from fainting onto the floor. Obviously, he knew she was prone to do so because her eyes rolled back and she fell into his arms.

David dropped his revolver and ran through the diner to where the robber was lying. His gun had been ejected from his hand and landed on the ground close by. The robber reached towards it but David stepped on his hand.

Alexa grabbed the revolver and pointed it at the gunman. She pulled the trigger. There was a rapid clicking noise, empty. Before the fifth click people had already swarmed around the unarmed robber and held him down.

The manager called the cops immediately. With all the attention diverted to the robber Alexa took advantage and walked over to David.

"What were you doing with that gun in the diner?" she asked him.

David answered with the same words, in the same voice he used the night before. "I don't know."

"David," she said gravely. "One bullet in the gun means ending business. More bullets means starting business."

He laughed. "Well it looks like I'm still open."

Alexa laughed in a nervous, psychotic manner. David laughed too, trying to match her energy. They were the only ones in the diner that were laughing. Everyone else was either yelling or crying. They were too busy to give judgmental looks to either of them.

The cops arrived, followed closely by an ambulance.

Two paramedics ran inside with an unfolded stretcher. They lifted the robber onto the stretcher. He writhed and screamed as they lowered him down and rolled him outside to behind an ambulance.

As they were rolling him outside to behind the ambulance someone yelled, "I hope it hurts!"

Alexa stole a glance through the glass windows. The robber was losing a considerable amount of blood. A deep red soaked through his sheets, which made Alexa cringe and almost look away.

A cop approached him and slapped a handcuff around his wrist. He cuffed the other end to the metal stretcher, then did the same to the other hand.

Alexa turned back to David, two arms wrapped around him from behind. It was a girl, about two years younger than him, blonde, and wearing a red baseball cap. Her ponytail was sticking out from under it.

"Thank you! Thank you! Thank you!" she cried.

A heating anger rose within Alexa. At first she tried to fight it. She didn't know why, but she didn't like the blonde girl, especially when she touched David.

"Get off of him!" Alexa yelled, running behind the girl and prying her arms off David. "He's just had a traumatic experience! He doesn't need some random stranger sneaking up on him!"

Alexa tugged on her shirt and the blonde gave up. She released her arms and staggered back a couple steps before falling on Alexa. She grabbed the closest table and helped herself up.

Alexa didn't get up immediately. She stared at the girl, upset at herself for what she'd just done. The blonde didn't yell back, although the look on her face suggested she clearly wanted to. With all the cops around they might think they were starting a serious fight.

She readjusted her shirt and tucked it into her pants incase Alexa thought about going for her again.

"I'm sorry," Alexa said, her eyes turning glassy from tears. "I can't think straight right now, I need to breathe."

Alexa pulled herself up and sat on a chair. She grabbed her head with both hands and rested her elbows on her knees. She bowed her head, deep in thought.

The blonde patted her shoulder, but her offender showed no reaction.

People were staring at them, unsure of what to say.

The ambulance turned its sirens on and drove away, being followed by two police cars, their lights were flashing, but their sirens went unused.

The seriousness of the situation hadn't sunk in, but she feared it would hit her on the drive home.

"All right," an officer said. "We're gonna need everyone to step out of the diner. Please watch your step and walk around the evidence. Keep in mind that there is some blood near the front of the diner."

The blonde and the rest of the crowd left in an orderly line and police officers walked in to replace them. She didn't realize how many cops had arrived, and how soon, too.

Two more police cars parked diagonally in the parking lot. She frowned. All she wanted to do was go home. None of this was worth getting pancakes for breakfast.

Have you been questioned yet?" a voice asked from behind her.

An equally blonde police officer carrying a pen and notepad walked toward her.

"Oh, no not yet."

"Okay." He clicked his pen. "You wanna tell me what you saw here today?"

Not really, she thought.

"There was a man in a red jacket that came in and pointed a gun at one of the hostesses. Then one of the —"

She couldn't think of her next words. Telling the story, *out loud*, made the memories come flooding back — the blood…. the screaming. The situation had sunken in.

"Do you need a minute to think?" the officer asked.

She swallowed. "I'm fine."

"What happened next?"

"One of the waiters shot the robber in the chest, at least I think it was a waiter. Everyone swarmed in after that and then it got too hard to see."

"Can you tell me who the waiter was?"

The blonde turned around and spotted the waiter within a few seconds of searching for him. She pointed. "Him."

The officer looked behind her. Three officers were already dealing with him.

"Can you remember anyone screaming, any words being said?"

"Just 'give me your money'. Then the man got shot and the screaming started. I'm sure you'll find this on the security cameras."

"I'm gonna need you to give me your name, address, and phone number so we can contact you if we need to."

"Savannah, 5270 Brooklyn Lane, 840-555-0114."

The officer scribbled away on his note pad. "Thank you for cooperating and we'll contact you if we need to."

Savannah walked slowly to her car and stepped inside. The air was suffocating, her childhood asthma was returning.

She scrambled through the glove box for her inhaler. *Come on, I know I left at least one of those in here!*

She shuffled through papers, receipts, and pepper spray. Only at the back of the glove compartment did she finally find her inhaler. Her vision was turning blurry. The inhaler in her hand turned into blotches of bright colors.

There was no time to shake it. Savannah closed her eyes, put the inhaler in her mouth, pushed the button, and breathed deeply. When she opened her eyes again her vision had returned clearly.

She rolled down her driver's side window to breathe fresh air. Everyone outside was making her nervous, all the voices, panicking in unison.

She backed out of her parking space and left the lot

entirely. As she drove away she glanced in the rear view mirror, officers were setting up police tape.

The worst part of everything was figuring how to tell her parents. How would they react? Or would the local TV news tell them before she could?

Her mom watched the news quite often and she didn't have anywhere else to be except sitting in front of a television.

Savannah didn't look forward to her mom's excessive tears or her dad's bear hugs. Once her mom started with the waterworks she was like an unstoppable force. She'd cry and cry until she was out of tears, and then she'd fall asleep. Her dad would be more upset than concerned, certainly less sympathetic than her mother.

Savannah didn't like confrontation. She remembered having a particularly difficult time telling her parents she wasn't ready to go to college. Her mom was mortified and her dad didn't speak to her for at least a week. A diner shootout would put them both in a coma.

If she didn't go home now then her mom would never feel right again. At the very least she could try and soften the story to make it sound less frightening. Then later the news would come on and make it sound *worse* than it actually was.

She sat in her car parked in the driveway of her house for over an hour, trying to convince herself the diner robbery was a dream. Her mind drifted off for a while but shot back to reality like a spinning boomerang.

Her mom came out. Her face was unconcerned. She hadn't heard the news. She walked to the garden hose and began to water the plants, stopping only to wave at Savannah. She'd seen her now. She *had* to say something. Savannah rolled down her window, mentally bracing herself for the reaction.

"There's something I need to tell you mom."

"Can it wait till I finish watering the plants? And don't you have work later today?"

"I don't think I'm going in today."

Her mom stopped the stream of water. She set down the hose and walked to Savannah. For a moment Savannah considered telling her mom then drive away immediately. But that was a useless fantasy.

"When I went to Eddie's Diner to eat breakfast a man walked in and tried to rob the cashier."

Her mom gasped and simultaneously raised a hand to cover her mouth.

"I'm okay!" Savannah wished she'd started with that. "One of the waiters had a gun and shot him in the chest before he could do anything. As far as I know, he's still alive."

"Why didn't you file a police report?"

"I did." Then Savannah thought her eyewitness account wasn't much of a police report. "I talked to one of the cops and gave him our address and phone number. There were lots of other people there too, and a security camera. I don't think I was in any danger personally, he just wanted the money."

Her mom didn't cry like she thought she would. She opened Savannah's door, kneeled beside her, and gave her a strong motherly hug. Savannah wanted to cut it short but she let her mom have it. It was one of her motherly instincts, so why fight it?

"I'm so glad you're okay," her mother whispered. Her voice sounded broken, like the onset of tears. But she held herself together, pulling away and rubbing her eyes in little circles.

Savannah's eyes filled with tears. She often cried with her mother.

They walked together into the house and settled in the family room. Savannah didn't want to talk, only to cry.

"Are you hungry?" her mother asked.

"I lost my appetite."

"Well you have to eat something. Your brain is tricking your stomach into thinking it isn't hungry, but it really is."

"Can I just have a banana? Something easy on my stomach."

"You got it." The mother smiled, then walked to the family fruit bowl, picked a banana and started peeling it.

"Mom, can I ask you a question?"

"Of course." Her mother walked back to her, ready to hand over the banana.

"Where do you think people go when they die?"

Her mother froze just as she offered the banana. She hadn't thought of that in a long time. She'd never had a near death experience but she understood why her daughter was asking.

"I don't know for sure, but…. I don't think there's any more pain where you go."

Savannah stood up and took the banana from her mom. She smiled weakly. "Thanks, I think I'll take this to my room and go lie down for a bit."

"Don't forget to call into work and tell them you're not going," her mom said gingerly. Then she kissed Savannah on the cheek and watched as she walked away.

Savannah finished the banana and left it lying on the desk not two feet from the trashcan. Then she walked to the far wall and turned on the ceiling fan. The blades rotated slowly, like they were being woken from a long nap.

Savannah lied on her bed, the overhead fan blades spun progressively faster. Its extreme repetitiveness made her think of hypnosis.

What about self-hypnosis? Her life would be better if she forgot this day ever happened. Why wouldn't it? But could it even work? Staring up at the fan and thinking, *you did not witness a shootout today, it was only a dream. When you wake up you will forget it ever happened.*

It was worth a try. She stared at the fan for ten minutes, hardly ever blinking, repeating those words in her head. She closed her eyes.

Come on. Work dammit!

When she opened them again, she could remember

everything even more vividly than she had before. The smell of the diner, the food on people's plates.

No dice.

Maybe if she tried again, *really* focusing, repeating the words out loud instead of in her head.

She closed her eyes. "You did not witness a shootout today, it was only a dream, when you wake up — you will — you will."

She laughed in the empty room. Her words reminded her of some phony carnival hypnotist who'd make people snort like a pig or think they could fly.

Her stuffed teddy bear sat in the corner of the room, watching her with black glossy eyes, judging her. Then she laughed again.

I guess some things are meant to be remembered. An endearing experience.

The day had just begun and she hadn't actually done anything productive. Her dad came home every day and asked what she did. If she couldn't say college then she could at least say work.

Not today though. Savannah almost thought a diner shootout wasn't an excuse enough for her dad.

She grasped her bed covers tightly. Her head hurt just thinking about him coming home. With her luck, he'd stare blankly at her and say, "That's nothing, do you know how many times I've had a gun put to my head? Barely a shot was fired. The news just twists everything to make it sound cynical. Do you think skipping work is going to change anything?"

Then her mom would yell at him, or cry, or both. They'd get into a big argument and it would be all her fault. It was her fault for getting caught in a predicament and her fault for letting it get to her head enough to miss work. Savannah didn't have to worry about putting her dad in a home, ever. He was going to work until the day he died.

He was clear on where he stood about what happens when you die. Lights out, party's over. She was glad she'd asked her mom instead. She liked the way she said it, "I don't think there's any more pain where you go."

Savannah jerked from her thoughts. She took out her phone and dialed her work. It picked up on the third ring.

"Hello?" her manager answered.

"Hello, this is Savannah. I'm sorry I can't come in today I got caught in a shootout at a diner and I —"

"What? A shootout! Are you okay?"

"Yes, I'm fine. The only one that who shot was the person robbing the place, and I think he lived. You'll probably see it on the news later."

"Well good riddance to him. And Savannah, take all the time off you need."

"Thank you, but I think I'll just take the day off. My dad wouldn't be happy if I took *two* days off. He's gonna have trouble with just the one."

"You tell your dad you don't have to worry about your job."

"He doesn't care about money he cares about working."

"Oh. Well either way, if you don't show up tomorrow just call in."

"Thanks, Jared."

He hung up first.

Savannah wished she hadn't used the word "shootout". Jared had somewhat of a crush on her, even though he was married. He was known to overreact to news, especially when it came to Savannah.

He once fired an employee for hitting on her, and that was a woman. Despite Savannah being a heterosexual, Jared believed his improbable fantasy was being threatened.

His unwarranted infatuation would've made Savannah quit a long time ago if not for the fact that he gave her constant raises from out of nowhere. And for the fact that her dad would force her to start applying to college.

Savannah had dated guys on and off since she started working there. Not once did she mention any of them to Jared. She liked allowing him to have his fantasy.

Oh, she made good money for someone who never went to college, and it only made her dad angrier. She hadn't even been working long and had already been given three raises, each for some made up reason.

Her dad never got by on his looks though, far from it. In fact, he often questioned why his wife was with him.

The room was suddenly spinning, and Savannah thought she was having another asthma attack. She stood up so fast her legs trembled, and she almost fell to the ground. There was a spare inhaler somewhere in her messy dresser, but she couldn't tell her dresser from her window.

She twirled around thinking she might be walking straight and bumped into what could only be her wooden dresser. When she opened the drawer she could see normally again. Fearing it would happen again she pocketed her inhaler and closed the drawer.

"Happy thoughts," she said out. Then, there was a knock on her door.

"Savannah? You okay in there?" her mother said through the closed door.

Savannah panted heavily, caught her breath, then said, "Fine mom."

"I heard bumping around in there."

"Just an accident."

"Your dad will be home in twenty minutes. I called and told him to leave work early. Do you want me to tell him what happened or do you want to?"

Her head was spinning again, in full force. She felt her pockets but couldn't remember which one had the inhaler. Between her phone, wallet, car keys and inhaler, both her pockets felt like two big lumps.

She started hyperventilating full, deep breaths, which meant breathing was not an issue. Still, for some reason she couldn't shake the belief that her inhaler would stop her head spinning. The sensation reminded her of stepping out of a winding roller coaster.

For a moment she doubted her legs were strong enough to support her.

"Fine!" she yelled.

Her mom didn't answer. A second later there was only the noise of her footsteps, which got quieter as she walked away.

Savannah woke with her face glued to the floor. She wasn't sure when she woke up but her dad hadn't yet come home, so it couldn't have been more than fifteen minutes. Her head felt heavy and her muscles were soft and weak. When she stood up she lost her vision for a brief moment, her head pounded like a hangover.

She stumbled to her bed and fell backwards with all her weight, making a thud when she hit the mattress. The weight of her fall made the bed bounce a few times.

The scenario played in her head. The shine of his gun, the look on his face, the blood splatter when he was shot. She couldn't help but feel sorry for the man, why he felt the need to rob a diner and traumatize innocent patrons. Still, better him than her.

There was another knocking on the door, but softer, and more spaced than before.

"Honey, it's me," her dad said. He sounded quiet and sympathetic.

"Come in."

The door squeaked open. Savannah bent her neck to see her dad. He stood in the doorway staring at her with sunken eyes.

"How you hanging in there?" he asked. The way he talked suggested her mother had already filled him in.

"Just trying to forget it. Listen dad, before we talk I need to tell you I'm taking the day off. I might even take tomorrow off too."

"Take as much time as you need."

Savannah sat up quickly with a straight spine. Her eyes widened and eyebrows raised. "What? What do you mean? Where's the dad I know?"

She thought he'd laugh at this, but he kept a steady expression. "I know it's a traumatic thing to have a gun in your face. And while I still think you need as much work experience under your belt as possible, I do believe you need to rest. You can't be a productive worker if your mind is a million miles away."

There's the dad I know.

Her dad walked to Savannah's bed and sat so close to her that his weight made Savannah sink awkwardly closer towards him. He put his heavy arm around her shoulder, consolingly.

"Savannah," he said. "You have to believe that I only say the things I say because I know they'll help you."

She couldn't look at him, she turned her head and fixed her eyes on the corner of the room. "I know, dad."

"Life's not always fair, but someday, hopefully sooner than later, you'll be over this. You'll move on and your life can start where it left off."

"Dad I'm not going to worry. You shouldn't either."

"I'm hoping this will be a wakeup call for you and not— "

Savannah shrugged her dad's arm away and stood up.

"Dad, do you think I'm not doing well? I've gotten three raises in a year and I might be up for a promotion!"

He threw his hands into the air at eye level. "And I'm very happy for you but you've gotta realize not every employer is gonna give you a raise just for looking good."

Her face turned brick red. It frightened her dad enough to stand up and slowly walk away from her, not turning his back on her, the way a lion tamer would.

"Get out!" she yelled.

He scrambled out of the room without hesitation, making sure to close the door behind him. Savannah hated her door open.

The father hoped his wife didn't hear the yelling. She warned him not to make things worse before he went in there. He told her he wouldn't.

He walked into the kitchen to see if she had heard. She was waiting for him, standing in the kitchen, hands on hips. The look on her face told him he wasn't sleeping in his own bed tonight.

"Alan, I told you not to make things worse," she said in an angry but hushed tone, in case Savannah might be listening.

"I didn't know how she'd react. At first we were talking about the robbery, then work, then it went off the rails from there."

"Your daughter has just suffered a traumatic experience. The last thing she needs to hear is that she has to think about her job."

"She'll forget about it tomorrow."

She stomped. "That's not the point."

"I'll just go back in and straighten this out." He started toward the hall but his wife ran in front of him.

"You'll only make things worse. Right now, your daughter needs time and space. I'll check on her before she goes to bed, but you don't say a word to her, got it?"

Alan hung his head and licked his dry lips. "Yeah."

"Do you know where you're sleeping tonight?"

He raised his head and started towards his wife, towering over her, staring straight into her eyes. "I'm going to a motel, or a hotel, anywhere's better than here."

Alan wasn't about to spend one more night on the couch, then having to lie to Savannah about it the next day, pretending that everything was okay when in fact it was pretty fucking far from that. Not one more fucking night.

His wife blinked, then staggered back a few steps. He watched her, then noticed Savannah standing in the hallway with her door open behind her.

"I'll go back to work tomorrow dad, I promise."

Alan lowered his shoulders.

"We weren't talking about you sweetheart, try and relax. Get some rest."

"Please stop fighting, it's not worth it whatever it is."

"Now look what you did," the mother said. "You've upset Savannah after she just got home from a life-threatening experience."

"It's not that bad really," Savannah said. "The news always makes it sound worse than it is, but I barely even saw it. It was over in minutes."

The mother hustled to Savannah and gently grabbed her shoulder.

"Mom, I'm *fine*."

The mother guided her back to her room, kissed her on the cheek, and shut the door behind her. She hurried back to Alan to confront him, but he was miles ahead of her.

Alan walked to meet her, distancing his face mere inches from hers and said, "I'm going to stay here for a few hours, and when Savannah falls asleep I'm checking into a hotel."

She smiled. "Wow, it's almost noon and I can't smell alcohol on your breath."

Alan stared at her, hoping she'd back down, but she didn't. Every time she didn't yield to his outbursts was a small victory to her.

She grazed a hand on the side of his check and smiled mockingly. A tickling sensation arose in the core of her stomach. It was enough to almost make her laugh. He grabbed her hand and yanked it away.

Alan was one step above his dad simply because he did not hit his wife. His dad's dad was even worse, he'd have hit her at the first sign she was giving him trouble.

Alan knew those genes would be a problem but he tried to ignore them, thinking they'd only be a problem when he drank too much. It didn't stop him from drinking though.

But his drinking was justified, oh yes. Long days of work, only to come home to a wife like his.

He walked into the family room and sat on the big leather couch that brought the room together. He switched the TV on to something hopefully nonviolent.

What better channel than the local news?

The nice-looking anchorwoman stared at the camera with a serious face, speaking in a monotone voice. The headline at the bottom of the screen read: **Robbery at Eddie's twenty-four-hour diner**.

He grabbed the remote and pointed it at the screen, clicking it to raise the volume.

"Our top story today, a shootout at Eddie's Diner when a man tried to rob the diner with a loaded pistol when one of the employees fired back at him. The only injured person of the robbery seemed to be the robber himself. No word yet on whether or not the employee himself will be charged. The police have collected the footage taken by the diner's surveillance camera but have not yet disclosed it to the public."

Although it'd been hours since the actual incident, Alan couldn't stop mentally putting Savannah in that diner, seeing her huddled in a corner praying she would be spared from injury. That was how he envisioned it happened, how Savannah acted in an emergency.

He couldn't watch anymore. Alan clicked the remote again and the TV made a swishing noise as it went black, leaving nothing on the screen but his sad reflection.

But what could he do? He'd already tried talking to Savannah and his wife, it only made things worse. No matter what he did it would only make things worse.

He took out his phone and stared at its blank screen.

Better take advantage of only making things worse before I do anyone some good, he thought.

On his phone, like any phone owned by someone his age, was a long list of contacts. Most of these contacts were business related, family, friends, etc. Two of them were not like the rest. One of them was probably a hooker and the other one was *definitely* a hooker.

He thought about calling definitely a hooker then put

the phone face down on the arm of the couch.

If I'm going to sleep in a motel tonight, I might as well have some company, he thought.

He picked up his phone again and texted definitely a hooker.

"I'm gonna need your services tonight."

He waited. Less than five minutes later she texted back, "The usual rate?"

"Three hours," he replied.

"Where at?"

"That one motel on the corner of Oakmont and Applewood, eight o' clock." There was no point in having both a fancy hotel *and* a hooker.

"See you then."

Alan tapped on the back of his phone, anxiously waiting for the night to come. As he waited in his chair, with nothing except his thoughts, he tried to trace back every decision of his life that led to this moment.

I don't want to have sex with this hooker, I need to, he thought. *Somehow, I need to do this.*

The sunlight flooding the room reminded him that it was a long time until eight o' clock. Then he remembered the words his wife said earlier, "Wow, it's almost noon and I can't smell alcohol on your breath." He wanted to prove her wrong, but he wanted to drink away his problems even more. With any luck, he'd meet another definitely a hooker there, get her number, and add her to his list of problems.

His hookers weren't added to his phone as hookers, obviously. They weren't even female names. He listed definitely a hooker as Robert, and maybe a hooker as Davidson. Both were categorized as work contacts.

Alan picked up his phone and sighed.

Hunney, he thought. *Why are you making me do this?*

He stepped into the garage and started up his SUV. He liked his old two-seater Corvette but his wife sure hadn't. Said it wasn't "family friendly", whatever that meant. It never really hit him that he was a dad and a husband. It was more important to him to just keep being Alan.

And why not? It was easier that way, living his own life.

While all his other friends were getting married and telling him they couldn't go out because they had a list of prior commitments, he was sitting at the bar, drinking the day away.

He drove away from his house, away from his wife, away from his recently traumatized daughter and into the city. There were lots of bars to go to but he was drawn to Malone's.

Malone's was a seedy, dimly lit dive bar. It had no open mic night karaoke, no dancing, and everyone there was as miserable as him. It was Alan's kind of place. His home away from home.

He sat in his SUV, windows rolled down, stopped at a red light, and admired the cars around him. His once new SUV used to shine in the sunlight on days like this. Years of wear and tear had turned it to a dull bleak color, and to make it worse, there was mud on its underside.

A kid in his twenties was next to him driving a red mustang. He pulled down his visor and flipped open the mirror then checked his spiked hair from all angles, making sure there were no flat parts.

Even though the kid strongly reminded Alan of himself at that age, he couldn't help but hate him.

"Just wait till you're my age, buddy," he said under his breath.

The kid looked at him from his low to the ground Mustang, as if he'd heard what Alan said. Alan wasn't sure if he really did hear him or if he was just looking around as people so often do when they sit idly at a red light. Alan turned his head in the direction of the intersection.

When the light turned green the Mustang eased off its brakes and pressed on the gas simultaneously. The car made a loud screech, then speed off. Alan could smell the burning rubber left from it.

His old Corvette could've outrun that punk, no problem.

He casually drove forward, not nearly catching up to the speed of the Mustang. Four more turns and fifteen minutes later he was parked at the edge of Malone's parking lot, facing the street. Before rolling up his window he heard dogs barking from the distance, paired with domestic arguing he had become all too familiar with.

Three girls walked by, two of them were definitely hookers, the third one was debatable. Each of them wore fishnets stockings. He couldn't smell them from his car, but if he could, he'd bet they smelled like sweat and piss.

They stopped at the corner and shared a cigarette between the three of them. One of them pressed the crosswalk button. Alan stopped watching them. It would be too late now to chase them down and see if any of them were definite hookers.

Alan left his car and went into Malone's. It was exactly how he remembered it. The pool balls made loud clanks as they bounced off one another, people high-fived each other and other people cried at their bar stools, hunched over their drinks.

He walked over to join them, pulled out a stool of his own, then seated himself. The bartender immediately turned his attention to him. Before the bartender said anything, he ordered.

"Scotch on the rocks."

The bartender nodded his head and poured him a drink.

Alan gazed at the man sitting next to him, a man with a scruffy beard and brown hair down to his shoulders. The sad bastard looked like he'd been drinking for hours and his beard had had crumbs stuck to the top of it.

"Hey," Alan said to him.

The man barely turned to him and muttered something that Alan interpreted as a mutual hello.

A baseball game played on a TV hanging above the bartender's head.

"You like the Mets?" Alan asked.

"What?"

"The New York Mets," Alan pointed at the TV but it had now changed to a toothpaste commercial.

The man scoffed, then took another shot of whatever he was drinking.

"You didn't answer my question," Alan said irritably.

The man stared at his empty drink, then said, "They're okay."

Some time passed, and after a few more scotches, the man spoke again.

"I almost played for them," he said.

"Really? How's that?"

"I was playing in college and I was up for consideration but I broke my leg in a skiing accident."

"Sounds like you were living life to the fullest."

He sighed, and Alan knew he was in for a long sob story.

"And now I'm here," the man said. "Drinking until every last one of my brain cells retires."

"So baseball was the only thing you knew how to do?"

"It was all I cared about…. for years." He bent his head back completely and finished his drink in one sip, then he tapped the bar aggressively to signal for another drink. The bartender refilled his glass almost immediately, his face impassive to the drunk man's rude way of requesting another round.

Alan realized that since he'd sat down not once did the man smile. He thought about shaking his hand but the grime on the man's palms made him think otherwise.

"What's your name?" the man asked.

"Alan, and you?"

"Collin."

"Did you mean what you said? About the Mets."

He leaned closer and the smell of his last drink travelled to Alan's face. Collin raised an open hand close to his face. "I promise."

He had a look that said, please trust me, it's all I have, it's all I've done with my life. Alan still wasn't sure if he trusted him, but having nothing better to do, he was willing to humor him, hoping some poor bastard might do the same for him someday.

"If you died right now," Alan said. "How do you think people would remember you?"

He expected the man to be offended, even drunkenly violent. But the alcohol had probably suppressed his emotions, if anything.

"I think my mom and dad would remember me how I was growing up. My friends would remember me for my college baseball days, everyone else would remember me for the drinking."

His words didn't sound like they came from an alcoholic. They sounded articulate, like they came from a poet, someone down on his luck.

"Wife?" Alan asked.

"Divorced for twelve years. I don't know what went wrong. It was either my lying, living in the past, or cheating on her," he laughed. He leaned so far back the front two legs of his bar stool hovered off the ground for a moment, then his arms swung in circles like an injured bird trying to flap its wings, he managed to lean forward and save himself.

Alan studied Collin's arms. They were covered with tattoos but only two of them grabbed Alan's attention. They were dates, January 12 and September 16.

Alan pointed to the first one. "What's that?"

"What's what?"

"January 12, on your arm."

"It's a date."

Alan grimaced and narrowed his eyebrows. "I know that dammit, but what does it mean?"

Collin shrunk in his chair at the sound of Alan's words, like he was being interrogated.

"The-the first one's my anniversary and the second

one's," Collin hesitated, apparently embarrassed. "The second's my wife's birthday."

Alan laughed. "Why do you need tattoos to remember them? Ever hear of a calendar?"

"I thought if I had them tattooed to my arm I'd never forget, guess I was wrong.

Alan's eyes widened, he was intrigued. "Why didn't you just get them removed?"

"When most people ask me that I just tell them it'd hurt like hell, but to be honest." He leaned in closely again, like he was telling a secret. "I still love my wife." He pulled his head away and took a small sip of his drink.

Alan looked at Collin's hand. The wedding ring shined even from the dim lighting of the bar. It looked brand new.

"Did you remarry?"

He shook his head. Alan didn't ask any more questions. He didn't need to. It was clear to him; Collin loved his ex-wife too much to take that ring off. Either that, or his fingers had grown too big to slip it off.

They pounded more drinks and talked about things they wouldn't remember. Only Alan would remember most of what they talked about there. Collin's memory could not hold onto that conversation, as far as he could remember, he'd never met Alan.

Alan walked out of the bar. He wasn't drunk, but he was beyond tipsy. He was a man who could usually hold his liquor but he had to rest his arm on the outside wall for support, his head resting on his forearm, his body slouched. After a moment of regaining his composure Alan pulled away from the wall.

A pregnant woman stood on the sidewalk just outside the parking lot, next to Alan's car. She appeared completely normal to Alan, except she was smoking a cigarette.

"You can't do that," Alan said, as he approached her.

The woman turned to face him and opened her red

stained lips. "Piss off!"

She turned back around and inhaled another lungful of smoke. The length of the cigarette diminished significantly with one inhale. Alan tensed and tried to control his heavy breathing.

"You know you're killing yourself *and* the baby, right?"

The woman didn't bother to look at him. "I'm not keeping it anyways," she said before taking another inhale.

Alan wanted to push her into the busy street and watch the cars throw her body across the pavement.

"How many months?" Alan said calmly.

"Eight," she snarled.

"That's a pretty late term abortion."

"I'll find someone, maybe in Mexico."

"Let me guess, the dad left you? Or you do you not know him at all?"

She flicked her cigarette on the ground and stomped it out, twisting her foot as she did. The woman stared at him, taunting him. She slowly brought another cigarette to her lips, held it in her mouth, then she sparked a match, which she held closely to, but not touching the tip of the cigarette.

Alan knew not to give her a reaction. She *wanted* him to react.

Realizing nothing else was going to happen, she flipped Alan off and walked away.

Alan flipped her off too, but to her back. He hopped in his SUV and started the engine.

It was almost eight o' clock. He had to check in and give definitely a hooker his room number before she arrived there and started waiting around the motel looking suspicious.

He showed up at the motel a quarter to eight and checked in at the lobby. He tossed his credit card on the counter.

The man at the front desk took the card and swiped it. "And how long will you be staying here?"

"Just one night, I think."

"You're in room 22. Check out time is at ten in the morning, so unless you plan on staying an extra night show up here before ten."

"I know how it works."

He smiled as he handed the card back to Alan. "Well then, enjoy your stay."

Alan half-smiled back. *'Enjoy your stay'*. He didn't believe the man even believed he could do that, not with all the bloodstains and semen covered bed sheets he'd seen while staying there previously.

Alan walked back outside and texted definitely a hooker, "Room 22", then he walked up the suspended staircase and into his motel room. He hadn't even closed the door when definitely a hooker texted him back, "Be there in ten."

Alan took off his shoes and put them by the door. He flicked on the lights and hopped on the bed.

The room's lighting was dim, even with the overhead light and the lamp turned on. The floor was a dull white color, and felt irritating to his bare feet. If Alan only had a black light he could expose what might be contaminating the room he'd soon be sleeping in.

After fifteen minutes Alan started looking out the window periodically, lightly pulling the curtains aside as he did.

Thirty minutes passed. Alan was sitting on the bed reading a complimentary magazine when he heard a knock on the door. He put the magazine down (it was an old issue of a magazine he wasn't sure even still existed), walked over to the door, and gazed through the eyehole.

There was a dark, shadowy figure with a feminine looking body standing outside his door.

"Who is it?" He had to be sure.

"Who do you think? It's cold out here!"

Alan opened the door. She walked inside the second the door opened wide enough for human passage and took the liberty to quickly shut the door behind her. She hadn't lied, her legs were shaking in her fishnet stockings and her teeth were chattering a little. Seeing her shaking that way reminded Alan of a shaved lamb on a winter night.

"So where should we start?" she asked.

"Where do you think?"

She took off Alan's shirt, then his pants, then boxers, throwing each of them wildly behind her. Alan took her shirt off and threw it into his pile of clothes. She kissed him from his lower abdomen up to his neck.

Alan held a groan in the pit of his throat. His eyes rolled into the back of his head.

Definitely a hooker wasn't satisfied, not until Alan had his big finish. She had pride in her work because there was little she *could* do. After years of giving it away to strange men she met on the streets there was little pleasure she could feel.

Alan slipped on a condom and lied back while he let definitely a hooker do her job. She thrusted into him repeatedly and he found it hard to hold back his moaning. When he let out his first groan of pleasure there was an aggressively rapid knock on the door.

Probably a complaining neighbor, he thought. But his heart beat rapidly nonetheless.

He put on his boxers and shirt (the bare minimum of what he thought was legally required to censor himself to a knocking stranger) and peaked through the eyehole.

It was dark, too dark to make out any of the stranger's facial features. All he could tell was that the stranger (whoever it was), was for sure a woman.

The motel did have lights outside but due to poor maintenance most of them were burned out. Alan opened the door a crack. It was enough room for the stranger to force it open the rest of the way. He was too surprised to react, he staggered back from the door, almost falling down.

The stranger stepped into the light. It was the last person in the world he wanted to see…. his wife.

"Judy!" he yelled. "What the fuck are you doing here?"

"I followed you, Alan! From the house, to the seedy bar, and back to here!" Definitely a hooker sat on the bed, naked, except for her fishnet stockings. "Oh that's nice, a hooker."

Her cover was blown. The hooker stood up and gathered her clothes, putting them on in a hurried mess.

"Yeah, so what?" Alan said. "Don't think I haven't noticed the way you've been looking at other men lately. Who'd you fuck first, our mailman?"

Judy slapped Alan as hard as she could, leaving a red mark on his cheek. Alan covered the injured cheek with his hand and frowned at his wife. Judy's eyes filled with water but Alan wasn't sure if she was sad or just mad at him. He didn't know what to do except keep being an asshole, at this point it was all he knew. He didn't know anything about fixing a marriage. It didn't work for his dad, why would it work for him?

Judy went for another slap but this time Alan was prepared. He blocked it with his arm, then stepped back.

He pointed a finger at Judy, stabbing the air with it as he spoke. "You mean you waited in your car, *spying on me*, like a fucking police steak out?"

"Don't try to turn this on me, Alan!"

Definitely a hooker finished dressing. She ran behind Alan to use him as a barrier from his wife, barely grazing his elbow as she inched her way out the room.

She knew where this was going. One of the neighbors would get scared and call the motel management, or worse, the police.

She hadn't collected the money Alan owed her, or her pimp, more specifically. Sex first, then pay. That was the deal. She would still collect from him when the opportunity rose.

The hooker ran down the stairs and crawled into her car. Aside from the violence this was the worst part of her job, breaking marriages. She wouldn't mind it so much if it didn't happen right in front of her. The mere fact that Alan called her meant his marriage was in trouble. If it wasn't her, Alan would call some other hooker and *she* would get his money.

She ruffled through her purse, took out a piece of mint gun, then put it in her mouth and chewed. If this didn't get the taste of Alan's body from her mouth nothing would.

This time tomorrow, she'd be deep throating another married stranger. Never knowing their lives beyond when she fucked them, never knowing whose wife was getting the raw end of the deal. All for sixty bucks an hour.

Chapter 3

She woke at two in the afternoon. She couldn't remember much from the night before, except that she'd been drinking. Something sticky was in her hair.

Please let it be gum, she thought.

Raking her fingers through her hair, she picked out the mint green gunk and showered the rest of it off. As she stepped onto the bathroom mat she grabbed a towel off the rack of the sliding door, dried herself, then went to the bathroom. It hurt when she peed. It *always* hurt when she peed. Too bad hookers don't get health insurance, they need it the most.

It took nearly half an hour to put on makeup. That was relatively light, most hookers take longer.

Her parents hadn't seen her in years, and she preferred it that way. She was no less than two hundred miles from them, and in her case, the farther the better. If her dad saw her loitering on a street corner she might die of embarrassment. If that wasn't enough to do it she'd finish herself with the switchblade she kept in her bra. It had come in handy more than once, and she wished she'd started carrying one sooner.

Her phone buzzed on the coffee table, moving it an inch as it vibrated. She picked it up and read the text. "Be at my place at three."

The microwave clock said it was half an hour till three already.

Geez, Rob wants it early today, she thought.

Rob, to her, was actually a Rob. Most clients didn't use their actual names, but his sounded genuine. Her own name varied from client to client. Sometimes it was

Bubbles, sometimes Glitter, Sparkles, Trixie, Cassie, or whatever first came to mind. To him, she was Claire.

Claire walked to her car in a hungover, uncoordinated fashion. The searing pain in the back of her skull intensified. She grasped her head tightly, cradling it in her hands.

Through most of the drive Claire's mind was occupied with the image of Rob's fat sweaty cock, and given his track record, he was asking for a blow job.

On the bright side, given his track record, it wouldn't take long.

She parked down the road, making Rob's house barely in sight. Discretion is a hooker's best friend, Rule 17.

It was a family neighborhood, and Claire had no business being there. She'd stick out like a sore thumb the moment she stepped out of the car.

It was three o' clock. Kids had just come home from school and were playing basketball in one of their driveways. The hoop they used was adjusted much lower than normal to accommodate their shortness.

Claire opened the door and stepped onto the sidewalk. The kids' basketball bounced away from them and rolled over in Claire's direction, stopping at her feet. No parents were supervising.

Claire sighed in relief. She picked up the ball, her knees trembling with difficulty in her high heel stilettos, and threw it back to them. One of the kids caught the ball but none of them resumed playing. They were all staring at the sore thumb in front of them.

One of the kids cupped his mouth and yelled, "Hey baby, how much for an hour?"

Claire was shocked at how young they were and that they knew what she was. She hadn't figured they'd been exposed to that kind of stuff yet.

Her stilettos echoed as she walked across the pavement. The sound of them drew even more eyes in her direction. A woman walking on the sidewalk grabbed her child's hand and crossed the street with him. Claire winked at the small child. The mother's face riddled with disgust as she turned her son's head away from her direction.

She came up to Rob's house and knocked on his door. A minute passed. Claire rang the doorbell just to be sure, twirling her golden hair as she waited.

She had naturally curly hair, the kind her young clients really liked. Her morning showers did little to straighten it out.

"I'm coming!" a strained voice yelled from within the house.

Claire rolled her eyes.

Here we go again.

Rob opened the door. He was a short man, shorter than her in fact. His head was so bald she could almost see her own reflection in it. Outside of the prostitution industry she wouldn't have looked twice at him.

"Hi," Claire said.

Rob held out a beckoning finger. "Get inside before more people see you."

Claire walked into the house and took in the new atmosphere. She walked into the living room and over to a family picture propped on top of a nightstand. She picked it up and studied everyone in the picture.

"Cute kid," she said.

"Put that down," he yelled, walking to her in sudden quick strides, his arms swinging.

Claire thought about what might happen if she didn't put it down. If she held the picture high above Rob's head, just out of reach, then lowered it enough for him to grab it only for her to raise it again at the last second. She smiled, but decided against her plan and put it back down in its place.

"You ready?" she asked.

"We're going to the bedroom."

Claire followed behind Rob as he led her there. He started undressing early, making a trail of clothes scattered down the hall. Claire frowned as she looked at the family pictures draping the walls, Rob's half-naked body leading her past them. They walked inside the room and Rob closed the door behind her.

Claire took care of business. She was in and out, ten minutes flat.

Rob paid Claire her forty dollars (that was in blowjob hours, not the usual rate), and saw Claire out the door.

"We should do this again sometime soon," Claire said on exit.

Rob didn't say anything back, he just slammed the door. He was disgusted with himself, not just with what he did, but with everything. He often wondered if his wife knew how much of a sad little man he really was.

His legs were weak from earlier, and he was still out of breath. He wasn't sure if it was from his physical exertion or from his almighty conscience scolding him for what he'd just done.

He rolled his head in a clockwise motion to relieve the leftover tension in his neck. He resented the fact that it was too early to get drunk, to drown away his problems. He gave his neck one more crack then walked into the living room.

His wife and daughter would be home in the next two hours. There was a reason he scheduled "Claire" so close to their arrival. He liked the excitement, the possibility of them walking in on him. He'd be caught red handed and his wife would have to divorce him.

But Claire was gone now. They'd arrive home to find no traces of his infidelity. He'd wince when she'd open up the door, anticipating another night in bed with that woman, snoring next to him as he tried to get through another restless night. All the beer in the world couldn't change that.

His insomnia made his cheating worse. With hookers he'd sleep with them, but he wouldn't *sleep* with them. That way he could get off and still have his peace and quiet. He might've been able to sleep earlier in the day if his wife could shut her mouth for one damn minute.

Everyday she'd go off and collect things to say to him when she came home. There was no limit to what she would talk about, clothes not matching, hair not straightening, anything he didn't want to talk about.

And the hair. He might be able to get through her rants if she'd stop talking about her hair, reminding him of a time when he had a full head of hair…. before he met her.

Come to think of it, his hair disappeared around the same time they met.

His eyes travelled to the picture of his family sitting on the nightstand. He walked over to it and held it in his hands.

"What do you want from me?" He screamed at the picture, spit flying onto its glass frame. He wiped it off with his fingers and put it back on the table.

"I'm not perfect!" he cried. His legs gave out and he fell to his knees. He grasped a table edge with one hand and cried into his other hand.

A scratching noise echoed through the hallway, followed by a loud barking. At once Rob knew it was his dog.

"Cliff," he said to himself. Rob locked Cliff in her room an hour ago to prepare for Claire's arrival

He rushed through the hallway and opened the door to his daughter's room. The dog came rushing out, his tail wagging behind him. Rob bent down and patted him on his round little head while Cliff panted into his face. His doggy breath made him sick and he turned his face away, laughing at his dog's enthusiasm.

"You need to go outside don't you? Huh, boy?"

Cliff ran past Rob, down the hall, and out the kitchen's doggy door leading to the backyard.

Cliff had a hole by the fence, which he'd dug for half a week. Rob neglected to fill the hole because he hadn't seen his backyard for at least a week. The grass was reaching the height of a jungle's and had started losing its color.

It wasn't the first time Cliff had fun digging holes and it wasn't uncommon for his neighbor, Derek, to stomp over to his house and reprimand his owner for it.

Rob would nod his head but he rarely ever did anything about it. To him, Derek was just another nuisance, a nuisance with a full head of hair.

Cliff ran straight to the hole like his life depended on it. He crawled down with his butt in the air, tail still wagging from before, and dug. Cliff finished digging when he saw the sun's light from Derek's backyard. He squeezed through the underside of the fence and climbed into Derek's yard.

Cliff ran excitedly in little circles. He was going so fast it almost looked like he was chasing his own tail. After a while he tired and lowered his head onto the grass to chew it. This is what Derek hated the most.

Derek planted tall fescue grass a year ago and he often bragged about it during his backyard parties. His latest party was in a few days and his boss would be there to see it, or not, depending on how much Cliff ruined.

"No!" Derek shouted from across his yard.

Cliff lifted his head, startled from Derek's voice. His tail stopped wagging.

Derek ran towards Cliff, waving his hands in the air sporadically. The dog still didn't move, he was frightened, clearly, but his animal instincts hadn't kicked in yet. Lost perhaps, from years of domestication.

Derek stopped three feet from the dog and gently pushed its chest.

Cliff took off and dove back into the hole.

Derek didn't know where to channel his anger. So he went back inside to complain to his wife. She was cleaning the dishes by hand, scrubbing in little circles with a soapy rag.

"That damn dog just dug up another hole."

His wife dropped the dishes into the sink, then turned

around and frowned. "Again? You need to be a man and make Ron do something."

"Ah," he grunted. "He'll probably just pretend to get mad at the thing then it'll go right back to tearing up our yard."

She stared at him, hands on hips, as if to say, "That's not good enough Derek."

He thought about his response, placing a hand on his chin. "You know what." He raised a finger in a sort of rushed epitome. "The neighbors talk an awful lot about how strange women go into his house when his wife and kid are away. I'll bet his wife has no idea about it. I mean, it's not like we've heard any yelling from over there. I think if I hold it over his head he'll finally do something about that damn dog."

His wife's eyes lit up, the whites of her eyes dominated most of their color. "Now that's thinking like a man!"

At that moment Derek thought she'd have sex with him right then and there next to the kitchen sink. Imagine that, Derek getting to have sex with his wife.

Derek put on an extra thick coat hanging from the rack by the front door. It broadened his shoulders nicely and its dark color gave him a nice men-in-black appearance.

He walked out and strode to Ron's house, then knocked on the door and waited.

The door opened slightly, Ron knew what Derek wanted.

"Yes, Derek, what is it?"

Derek pointed an accusing finger. "You know goddamn well what it is. Now are you gonna do something about that dog of yours running around destroying my property?"

"If it bothers you so much why don't you just fill it up with soil?"

Derek pulled his head back and blinked. "Because it's your fucking dog! Get that thing declawed so it won't dig up any more holes. Now it's your fucking problem. Don't make me call someone about this."

Ron opened the door a little more, he was curious. "Who would you call?"

"You know who'd I'd call. I have half a mind to take you to court over this. I've had to deal with your dog time and time again, and I'm sick of it. My wife's sick of it too."

"Is your wife making you do this, Derek? Is she making you talk to me?"

"Don't you change the subject!" Derek made an advance towards the door. Ron shut it abruptly, and there was a clicking noise immediately after.

"Oh yeah!" Derek yelled. "And does your wife know what you're doing when she's out of the house?"

For a moment Derek though Ron wouldn't answer. Would he really risk Ron's marriage just to win an argument?

The door clicked again and slowly opened just wide enough for half of Ron's face to show.

"How do you know about that?" he asked.

"Actually," Derek sighed, ashamed of having to use that as a defense. "I think…. the whole neighborhood knows about it. Word gets around, you know?"

"Yeah, I know."

"So will you?"

"Will I what?"

"Do something about that dog?"

"Yeah, I'll fix it," Ron said, sounding defeated.

"Then I guess we won't have a problem."

Derek walked away, and never heard the door shut. Ron was probably watching him walk. He could feel his eyes following him.

It's only a matter of time before Ron digs up dirt on me, he thought. *It doesn't matter, I've got nothing to hide.*

When Derek arrived back home he barely opened the front door when he yelled, "Honey! I think we got him!"

"Finally!" she yelled back. "I was wondering when you'd take back your manhood.

Derek's face contorted, his jaw tensed. He hurried to his wife in the kitchen, making loud thumps across the tile with every step.

"You know," he said. "It's comments like that that make me not want to have sex with you."

She leaned forward, putting all her weight on one leg, her other leg almost off the ground. "Let's get one thing straight! I decide when you have sex! Okay? Not you, me!"

"Maybe Ron's got the right idea. I wonder how much one of his hooker's charges. I think I'll go over there and ask him."

Derek started towards the door. His wife caught up with him and blocked his exit.

"Why take the risk?" she said seductively. "With some disease riddled sewer rat."

"I'll take my chances." He tried for the doorknob, but she knocked away his hand with her hip.

She giggled and bit her lower lip as she slid her back down the door. As her back slid down, her shirt stuck to the door and revealed a shiny belly button ring.

She sat down and ruffled her hair to make it look messy. Derek liked it messy and dirty.

He kneeled so that his face was level with hers, and he kissed her upper lip. She put his hands around his neck and brought his torso closer to hers.

With their lips locked they rolled across the tile and onto the soft carpet.

Derek struggled to remove his belt with his wife on top of him.

She pulled back from him. "I'll take care of it."

She unbuckled his belt and threw it carelessly behind her.

He unzipped his pants and slowly smiled. "I'll show you how much of a man I really am."

Her hair dangled in his face. She took a hair scrunchie from her pocket and put her hair up in a sporty ponytail.

She took out Derek's cock. He left his pants mostly still

on to prevent rug burn. She unzipped her own pants, leaving just enough room for her privates to show.

Derek split her downstairs lips with his fingers. This was going to be a quickie, Derek knew it. Not just because his wife had desperately important things she needed to do, but because he doubted his own endurance. Still, all the more motivation to work with the little time he had.

His wife stayed on top of him, dominating.

"Natalie! Natalie!" he chanted.

Her legs spasmed. Natalie was starting to doubt her own endurance.

In fifteen minutes Derek came and so did Natalie. Derek stood up and re-dressed himself.

"You want anything from the fridge?" he asked.

"Beer please. And I'm gonna have to wait a minute before getting up, just put it down next to me."

"Okie dokie."

Derek walked out of the room, smiling triumphantly.

Sweat dripped down Natalie's forehead. She stared at the ceiling, panting and yearning for a cigarette. She'd given up years ago but if ever there was a time to start smoking again, this was it. Too bad Derek never loved them as much as she had or they'd both be smoking right then. Still, she was glad they fought as much as they did because it always made for great makeup sex.

Sometimes she'd invent arguments just to get Derek going. He'd channel that energy into their love-making, and she was fine with that. It seemed to keep their marriage alive, and fresh.

Derek returned holding two bottled beers that seemed to be sweating as much as they were. Derek handed it down to her and she smiled when she saw that it was already opened.

"Do we still have birth control pills?" she asked.

"Uhh." He looked up at the ceiling, trapped in his own thoughts, then back down at her. "Yeah."

"Derek, are you *sure*?"

He cleared his throat. "No, I'll go to the store and get some more."

She sat upright. "No, that's okay, I'll go."

Natalie tried to stand up but fell backwards. Derek grabbed her hand and picked her up.

When she was steady on her feet she kissed his cheek and went to the pharmacy.

The lady at the counter was old, sixty maybe. She was dressed in a white pharmacy coat, her hair was tied in a bun. Dark circles surrounded her eyes and she looked one work shift away from going postal.

"I'm here to pick up a prescription," Natalie said.

"Name please," the pharmacist said.

"Natalie Carpenter."

The pharmacist pushed some buttons and grabbed the prescription. She put the prescription on the counter and peered at Natalie from under her eyebrows, judging her.

Not my fault you're not getting any, Natalie thought.

The pharmacist pushed some more buttons. "Thirty-nine dollars and ninety-nine cents."

Natalie paid by credit card and the pharmacist bagged her pills along with a folded paper manual listing the side effects.

The pharmacist forced her next words. "Have a nice day." But she couldn't force a smile to go with it.

Natalie nodded, took her bag, and went off.

She made a mental note to complain about the pharmacist's attitude when she saw Derek. If she'd taken the time to read her nametag she'd complain about her name too.

The evening sky was cold and dull. A kid was crying as her mother dragged him into the pharmacy. Natalie smiled at this and the woman politely smiled back. But Natalie wasn't smiling at the mother, she was smiling because she was glad she didn't have kids.

Come to think of it, maybe they *couldn't* have kids. There'd been several close calls when that could've been a reality. Forgotten to take the pill, lost spermicide, broken condom. Not once had she become pregnant.

She'd known at least three people who accidentally got pregnant and every time she was glad it wasn't her. Now, maybe she wasn't so glad.

Natalie got in the car and stared at her full packet of birth control. They stared back at her, each one carefully aligned in its see-through plastic sealing.

Maybe I just skip this one, she thought. *See what happens. Maybe I could surprise Derek for his birthday.*

Reality gave her a swift kick in the head, and she snapped from her train of thoughts. Before she reconsidered it she popped out one of the pills and put it in her mouth, letting her saliva carry it down her throat.

Crisis averted.

She melted in her chair and breathed a sigh of relief. Then a knocking on her window. She screamed in a high pitch as she instinctively reached to her purse to find her pepper spray.

It was a homeless man, at least, that's what it looked like. He had a wool beanie cap, a thick beard, and the hand he used to knock on the window was about as filthy as the dirt under the car itself. He flinched when he saw Natalie reach for her purse.

She rolled the window a crack.

"I'm— sorry to scare you," he said. "I just wanted to know if you could spare some change. I'm real desperate."

Natalie shook her head. "I don't have any change."

The man frowned, unconvinced.

"Please," he pleaded. "I don't like askin' people, I just really could use some change right now."

She thought for a moment. "Hold on."

Maybe she had some in her glove compartment.

She reached over and pulled it open, feeling around inside for any loose coins. She grabbed whatever her hand caught as she dragged it inside.

"It's all I have," she said, rolling the window down

further, just enough to hand it to the man. She made a disgusted face when her hand touched his. It rubbed off a little grease onto hers and she planned to wipe it off the minute the man turned away.

" I 'preciate it."

The man went back to his street corner where he left his cardboard **NEED MONEY, ANYTHING HELPS** sign. As he picked it off the ground his back made an audible cracking noise. A car went by, driving through a puddle that splashed him and his cardboard sign.

He was cold enough already without the help of road water.

He wanted to cry. He was too old to be begging on the streets. But he didn't have enough water in his system to produce any tears.

The man pulled change out of his pocket and counted it in his hands along with the money the last woman had already given him. He had two dollars and nineteen cents total. Not even enough for a combo meal at a fast-food restaurant. He'd need to beg to get some more.

He'd tried the army veteran routine, but that wasn't cutting it anymore. Most people now only gave money if someone was missing an arm or a leg or both.

To them, he was nothing more than a bum wasting space on the side of the road, waiting to die on the sidewalk. They'd step over his corpse like they did when he was sleeping, acting like he was just a crack in the pavement.

His throat weakened and his eyes started tearing up.

I guess I am hydrated enough, he thought. *But what little water I had left is going out my damn eyes.*

His body was so numb he could no longer feel his feet. He was too scared to take his shoes off because he was afraid they would be purple or blue, and he couldn't bear to see that now, no more bad news.

He ringed out his beard and the water droplets fell to the ground. A man and his girlfriend were walking by. If they would've seen him sooner they'd have crossed the street to avoid him. But they were deep in conversation, and the homeless man was quick.

"Spare some change?" he asked, holding out his hands, supplicating. He knew a man with his girlfriend was an easy target because nine out of ten times the guy would try to look sensitive and sympathetic.

The young man reached deep into his pockets, past his wallet, hoping to find only loose change. But when his hand came out it held two rolled up dollar bills. His girlfriend even fished out fifty cents. They handed him the money and in return the homeless man offered a handshake to get some human compassion.

The young man was closest, and therefore, the duty was his to shake it. He tried to look at his girlfriend but she was too far behind for him to look at her without it being awkward.

He hesitantly shook it and the homeless man's hand trembled. His hand was colder than the young man thought was possible.

"Thank you," said the homeless man, his voice sounding hoarse.

The young man smiled, eyes shimmering. Then he and his girlfriend walked off to a better path than his.

Chapter 4

They were headed to the Downtown Moonlight Theatre. The young man had a car, but he thought they'd take the scenic route, get some exercise. Also, he was low on gas.

They were six blocks from their destination. Five of those blocks were a pool of gangs, stray dogs, and rusted car parts lying on peoples' front lawns. Then, past the border to the sixth block, there would be smiling faces, fountains, nice restaurants and shopping malls.

The young man kept his girlfriend close, grabbing her waist from time to time or holding her soft hand.

The sound of dogs barking ringed in his ears. One dog on a leash tried to lunge toward the young man but its owner yanked it in the opposite direction.

"He's friendly," the owner assured. The young man doubted him, yet smiled all the same.

Most everyone who walked by either had sleeves of tattoos or piercings over every hole on their face.

This would also describe Liz, (his girlfriend walking next to him), when the young man met her. There was nothing actually wrong with her, only that the young man had a prejudice towards people covered in tattoos and piercings.

There were a lot of things, and a lot of people, Liz used to do before the young man met her. Now Liz dressed to cover herself down to her knees. She rarely wore skirts and almost never miniskirts. If she did, it was only in private, to turn the young man on.

They were two blocks away. The Moonlight Theatre was peaking over the buildings around it. Liz pushed the button to cross the intersection. When it didn't instantly turn into a little glowing white man she pushed it again, repeatedly.

The young man laughed. "You only need to push it once for it to work."

"I know," she sighed. "I'm just impatient."

He took her hand and kissed it. She blushed and giggled, it reminded her of a knight from the Middle Ages, or a lord, or a prince.

She punched the young man's arm playfully. "What is this, the eighteen hundreds?"

He smiled. "Call me old fashioned."

The crosswalk light gave them the go ahead and they walked. They were just a few minutes from the Moonlight Theatre. They were going to see some shark movie they hadn't bothered to find the name of. The Moonlight Theatre sometimes played classic movies, but this was a rarity. One more thing that made the young man — old fashioned.

He'd picked a horror movie on purpose. Liz was what he called a jumper. And when a scene didn't make her jump in her seat she'd bury her head into the young man's chest. She couldn't watch that sort of stuff. He loved when she did that, and she knew he loved it too.

"How old is this movie?"

The young man pushed the button on the cross walk, it was the last one separating them from the theatre.

"It was made in the eighties, I think."

She laughed. "Adam, why do you always pick old cheesy movies?"

He smiled but said nothing.

A gust of wind blew and Adam crossed his arms to warm his chest. His girlfriend shivered, and Adam surrendered his jacket. He hated seeing her look like a newborn calf.

"Thanks babe," she said, zipping it up.

"We're almost there anyways."

"But won't it be cold in the theatre?"

"You'll have to fight me for it in there," he said. "All bets are off once we're inside."

The little man glowed on the crosswalk sign. "You'll

have to take it from me," she said, jocularly. She ran away with only a three second head start.

Adam deliberately slowed his steps to give her more time. In high school, he was top of the track team. He could catch her if he wanted, even with a *ten* second head start.

Adam caught up with Liz in the middle of the ticket line. He was slightly out of breath but hid it completely so Liz wouldn't think he'd lost his athleticism, which was a touchy subject for him. Call him lame, call him dumb, but never *ever* call him unathletic.

"What took you so long?" she said playfully.

The light coming from the sunset hit Liz at an angle that made her look angelic. It made him love her more. Suddenly that piercing covered punk rock girl he'd once known turned into a lovable teddy bear.

"Look at the sky," he said, pointing behind her.

She turned around, unknowingly whipping him with her long brown hair.

"Wow," she said, genuinely in awe. "It makes the clouds look pink."

"Hello?" said a feminine voice near them.

Liz and Adam turned simultaneously and noticed the gap between them and the front of the line. They were next.

"Two for the shark movie," Adam said, approaching the front of the line.

The woman studied their faces intently. "How old are you?"

Liz's face loosened and she looked at Adam with a bemused expression.

"We're both twenty. I have my ID with me," Adam said, digging into his pockets.

"That's sixteen dollars and fifty cents," the woman said curtly.

Adam out his wallet and paid in cash. She placed it in the cash register, pushed some buttons, and a machine spit out two tickets from its metallic mouth. She ripped them out and handed them to the couple, along with Adam's change.

"Enjoy the movie," she said.

Adam took his girlfriend's hand and led her into the theatre. He handed the tickets to the usher with his non-Liz holding hand, he ripped the tips of them and handed them back.

"Number twelve on you're right," he said listlessly.

They walked past him and into the main lobby. The roof was a big dome with beautiful artistic designs lining the sides of the ceiling. The lines at the concession stands were packed all the way out of the aisles.

"Popcorn?" Adam asked to Liz.

"Nah, I'm trying to cut back."

"You? Really?"

She blushed. No matter how long they dated he still talked to her like he was on a first date, hoping to get a second one.

"We should get there early so we can get good seats," Adam said.

"Kay."

They walked out the lobby, through the hall, and into a large dark room only lit by the movie projector and some LED rope lighting along the walkways. A cool draft blew into their faces, making Adam wish he'd kept his jacket.

They climbed up several gradual sets of stairs and squeezed their way into a higher back row. Adam pushed down the retractable seat and sat down. Liz started unzipping her jacket when Adam stopped her.

"Keep it," he said. "It looks better on you anyways."

It was too dark to see but Adam figured Liz was blushing again.

Two dark figures moved towards them. When they got closer it became apparent it was a man and a woman.

"Liz? Adam?" said the dark figure of a man, he said their names in a question, but he sounded very sure. They recognized them before they knew who they were.

Adam recognized the voice, it was, oh no please not….

Liz bolted from her chair and the retractable seat shot back up. "Keith! Jamie!" she shrieked. Two people one row ahead turned around, Adam thought they would shush her, but they only stared for a moment, then faced back around.

Liz hugged them, wrapping her arms around them both. Adam didn't like Liz saying Keith's name first. They were together once, and seeing them together made Adam's stomach turn.

Keith, like many guys before him, encouraged Liz to run around and try different drugs. Liz's family had an intervention and said the root of the cause was Keith. He had encouraged Liz to do any and every drug she could get her hands on, nagged her about a three-way, and made her think she was worth nothing more than the vile crap she shot into her veins.

Adam was glad, however, when Jamie sat next to Liz, thus separating her from Keith. Relief washed over him in an awesome way. It was clearly Jamie's decision though, not Keith's.

They talked through most of the previews. Keith was having trouble talking to Liz with Jamie sitting in between them so he gave up and settled for his phone instead.

Later, a tall man and his girlfriend sat directly in front of Liz and Adam. The tall man obstructed a portion of the screen, enough to make Adam sit on his feet, and even then he had to rest his head on Liz's shoulder to see around him. And Liz laid her head on his.

He hoped Keith was watching them, his head on her shoulder, all cuddled up.

The tall man's girlfriend, who sat in front of Liz, was awkwardly shorter than her boyfriend and Adam couldn't make out how they could have sex. He'd have to bend his neck a full ninety degrees to look at her during missionary.

The movie started.

Only after the opening scene did Keith stash his phone back into his pocket. To Adam's surprise, no one behind them complained.

Adam wrapped his arm around Liz's shoulder and she rested her hand on his, gripping it tightly. He hoped Keith would mimic him, show Liz he wasn't single, but he kept staring straight at the screen, not moving an inch. Adam could see Jamie watching them from the corner of her eyes. After what sounded like a frustrated exhale from Jamie, she put her arm around Keith's shoulder.

"I have to go to the bathroom," Keith whispered quickly.

He stood up and Jamie's arm slid to the bottom of Keith's chair. Liz and Adam politely pretended they hadn't noticed. Jamie scrambled to regain her composure. She shifted awkwardly in her seat, making rubber friction noises.

More than twenty minutes passed before Keith returned to his seat.

"What took you so long, are you okay?" Jamie asked.

Keith scowled at her, looking offended, like he couldn't take a damn piss without her getting worked up.

"I'm fine," he said.

Liz and Adam exchanged looks of discomfort. Liz shivered in her seat, and Adam figured she remembered how Keith used to treat her.

"You cold?" Adam asked.

"No, I'm okay."

He laughed. "You'd better be, you've got my jacket."

Liz laughed too, but it was a fake, courtesy laugh. She pulled out the sleeves of Adam's jacket to cover her hands, only her fingertips were visible.

Keith whispered something to Jamie and Jamie leaned over and whispered something in Liz's ear. Liz whispered something back then turned to Adam.

"They want us to go hang out at Keith's apartment."

"And?"

"Do you want to?"

"I don't really think I can stand that guy for another moment."

"I understand," she said, a hint of regret in her voice.

Adam knew she didn't understand, she was only being passive aggressive. She couldn't let go of her past no matter how bad it was. She preferred to remember the good in Keith despite how little there actually was.

Liz stood up and started away.

"Where are you going?" Adam whispered.

"The bathroom."

"You can't leave now, this is the best part."

A shark on the screen took a large chunk out of the boat and swam back into the ocean. Two women in the audience screamed, everyone else jumped in their seats, a minority of people clenched their armrests tightly.

Liz sat down for the rest of the movie. There was a thought in the back of Adam's head that told him if Liz were alone, walking to the bathroom, Keith would follow her and try to get her to do the things she used to do to him.

The movie ended. The overhead lights turned on and the credits rolled. People stood up from their chairs and grabbed their belongings. Liz, Adam, Jamie, and Keith weren't one of those people.

"So?" Jamie said. "What do you guys wanna do?"

"I think we're gonna pass," Liz replied. "It's getting kinda late and we've got things to do."

Jamie's eyes glinted and fear ran across her face. She seemed afraid to be left alone.

"Well," Liz said. "We could stop by tomorrow maybe, Adam?" Her expression resembled that of a puppy dog, complete with wide eyes and pouted lips.

"Yeah, sure," he agreed. "Are you guys living together?"

"Just moved in," Jamie said, not so enthusiastically.

"How long have you guys been together?" Liz asked.

"Three months," Keith interjected.

Adam and Liz jumped at the sound of Keith's sudden voice. They had almost forgotten he was sitting next to them.

Adam leaned forward enough to see Keith.

"Sorry," he said. "We're gonna take a rain check tonight but maybe some other time."

Jamie turned to Keith. "Is tomorrow okay?"

"If its later in the day, sure."

Adam inhaled sharply, unconsciously gripping the sides of the rubber seats. If there was one sure way to ruin Adam's day it was to put Keith and his girlfriend in the same room and then watch Keith passive aggressively flirt with her.

They walked out together, splitting in different directions out the front door. Adam feared Keith would offer them a ride but he walked away with little more than a goodbye to Liz, and not a word to Adam.

The outside had turned to night. Adam's eyes were glad to not have to adjust.

They travelled together in the dark city streets, taking wrong turn after wrong turn. In the daytime, Adam remembered the directions from the scenery and landmarks but it had all turned hazy since the night came rushing in. And it was getting darker.

The streetlights were on and their shadows were barely visible.

They were still downtown. The only people on the road besides them were four hooded men blocking the sidewalk. Keith pulled Liz close to him and hurried across the street with her. The four hooded men moved as they did, following them across the deserted street, boxing them in.

Adam knew he could outrun them. But what about Liz? She couldn't outrun all four of them, and even if she did she'd never be able to keep up with his lead.

It was a residential street. No stores were within a two-minute run from them, although he couldn't be sure they weren't mostly closed anyway, he hadn't checked the time.

Adam lifted a hand to wave hello. The nearest group member slowly mimicked him, holding a hand in the air as Adam did. Adam didn't think it looked as friendly as his.

"What do you guys want?" Adam yelled. His words echoed, filling the silent, empty street.

"Give us your girl and we'll bounce," said the one nearest to them.

Adam reached behind his back and pulled out a shiny metal object that was wedged between his boxer's and his jeans. The man looked at it, and because of his background, he recognized it immediately. Even in the dark night the reflection of the gun shined, and the man back-stepped. The gun was warm in Adam's hands after being tucked against him for so long, almost comfortable. He and his friends ran in the opposite direction, into the darkness. And just as they faded from Adam's vision, he pulled the trigger.

From the end of the gun popped a small fire that lit Adam's smiling face. He laughed to himself, almost hysterically.

"That's not funny Adam!" Liz said as she walked ahead of him.

"You need me to light a cigarette?" He laughed, catching up to her.

"Can we call a cab or someone, you know, for a ride?"

"Who? Like Keith?"

"I didn't say that. But…. since you brought him up," she paused, allowing Adam to brace himself. "He might be the only one to know where we are."

"Liz, I don't even know where we are. I'll look up a cab, we'll walk to a crowded street and wait in a well-lit area and then take a cab to your place."

Liz's lower lips quivered and her eyes started to fill with tears. Adam quickly hugged her, and tightly. His own arms were shaking in the cold air.

The street was covered in an eerie silence only interrupted by the occasional gusts of wind that blew through the tree leaves. Adam couldn't be sure they were still alone.

He wiped the tears from Liz's face, grabbed her chin, and angled her face towards his, staring into her eyes.

"We need to keep going," he said.

He looked into his phone and found the directions home. Liz didn't want to take directions though. She was done walking on deserted streets. Adam agreed, and they took shelter underneath the roof of a bus stop station.

The fog surrounded them but a streetlight hung directly over their heads. Adam ordered a cab and they waited.

"Hey Liz?"

Her eyes were sunken and her face pale. "Yeah."

"What do you have that they could've taken?"

She stared at him. Her mind was still trapped in the deserted street. "Let's look."

She emptied her pockets and took out a lighter, a phone, a wallet — twenty-three dollars and fifteen cents, and a single wrapped stick of gum.

"A lighter?" Adam said, taking it from her. "I thought you didn't smoke."

"You never know when you'll need a lighter, Adam," she snatched it back from him. "And why do *you* need a lighter?"

Adam raised an informative finger to his face. "Remember it doesn't *look* like a lighter. I had it for the exact reason I used it for tonight. If anyone confiscated it I wouldn't be in any real trouble though. It's just a means of intimidation."

They turned their attention to the street, hoping for their cab to arrive.

"Can I ask you something?" Liz said.

"Shoot."

"What do you think they were going to do if they had

me?"

"You mean if I hadn't scared them off?" Adam said conceitedly. "I don't want to think about that, but I think it's pretty clear what they wanted."

Liz frowned.

The cab pulled up. Its headlights cut through the fog, barely showing its details enough to look like a cab. Its once bright yellow coating had now faded to a dull color from years of picking up strangers.

Liz and Adam walked toward it. Adam walked ahead of Liz, still unsure of the legitimacy of the cab. He stepped inside it first.

The cabbie was tan, most possibly ethnic, and he smelled strongly of cigarettes.

"Hey there," Adam said, sliding into the farther seat.

"Hey yourself," the cabbie said. Liz got in and slammed the door shut. The cabbie flinched from the noise it made.

"So where to?" he said.

"Four—one—seven—eight, Westview— "

"Don't you think we should go to a police station?" Liz interrupted.

"Why?" the cabbie asked.

"We've just been mugged," Liz explained.

The cabbie angled the rearview mirror to examine them. "You don't look like two people that's just been mugged."

Liz leaned back in her seat, crossing her legs and arms. "Well thankfully Adam here scared them off. We weren't beaten or anything if that's what you think."

Adam locked eyes with Liz. He hated when she gave his real name to strangers. She mouthed the word "sorry" and looked back at the cabbie.

The cabbie's eyes reflected through the rearview mirror, then turned to Adam, sizing him up. He didn't look like someone who could fend off a mugger, not one from this part of town, anyway.

He shrugged his arms and readjusted the rearview

mirror. "So," he said. "Where to?"

They looked at each other again.

"Look," Adam said. "There were no witnesses, no cameras, and we have no evidence. Did you even get a look at their faces?"

"No, but if we don't tell the cops they could do it to someone else. How could you sleep knowing you could have done something?"

"The cops aren't gonna do shit," the cabbie said.

Adam lifted an agreeing hand and pointed it at the cabbie. Liz slapped her own leg defiantly.

She shot Adam with the all too familiar "death stare". Then finally, the cabbie cut them both short of an argument.

"I get paid by the mile, not by the hour," he said.

Liz crossed her arms and peered out the window. "Fine," she scoffed. "Let's just go home and pretend it never happened."

"That's my girl," Adam said, rubbing her back. "That's four—one—seven—eight Westview River Drive."

The cabbie punched in the address to his dashboard GPS and they drove off.

"You can stop here," Adam said, his hand almost touching the cabbie's shoulder.

The old taxi came to a screeching stop. "That's…. thirty-five dollars and sixty-eight cents," the cabbie said.

Adam handed him a debit card, the cabbie swiped it, then handed it back along with a receipt. Without another word, Liz left the cab and Adam followed.

Liz walked up to the apartment's gate and pushed 5-5-6-7 #. For a moment nothing happened. Then the mouth of the two gates slowly opened and they walked through. The cabbie watched the gates close and sped off into the now fog-less road. Adam waved to the leaving cab, doubting he could see him.

Liz and Adam walked through the walkway and up

the stairs to apartment 40 C. It was Liz's apartment, hers was the name on the lease, but she knew Adam liked to think of it as his second home. Half his belongings were there, including a toothbrush, spare apartment key, some extra clothes, and of course, condoms.

Liz took off her jacket and threw it on the couch. She let out a heavy sigh as she dropped her body weight onto the seat cushions.

Her recent half-traumatic experience left her in need of a shoulder to cry on. Adam sat beside her and ran a hand up her spine, rubbing her neck when it got there.

"Adam," she said. "I'm not in the mood to fool around."

He kept rubbing. "We don't have to fool around, it's just a back rub. You deserve one after the night we've had."

"I still think we should've gone to the police."

"I have to agree with the cabbie, unless someone got robbed, or brutally beaten, or killed, they wouldn't want to hear about it. It's done with. Over."

"Promise me we'll never go back there."

"If we do we'll have to take my car."

"Do you think we should've gone with Keith and Jamie?"

He stopped rubbing abruptly. "*Keith* and Jamie? No, I don't."

"Why'd you say it like that?"

"I especially wouldn't let Keith drive us to his apartment knowing we had no car to leave with."

"Why would we want to leave early?"

"Because the idea of having you in a confined space, trapped with Keith, makes me sick to my stomach."

Liz stood up from the couch and faced Adam. Her face was cherry red. "Jamie would be there too, Adam. I can't believe after all this time you still don't trust me!"

Adam sprung to his feet and matched Liz's vocal level. "It's not *you* I don't trust. Do you remember what Keith did when Jamie tried to put her arm around him? He tried to distance himself, like he didn't want you to think they were serious."

"Maybe he wanted some space. She could've been distracting him. Even when I dated him he didn't like getting all lovey dovey in public."

Adam stepped closer to Liz and brought his voice down to a quiet, but intimidating tone. "Do you miss him?"

Her next words were shaken, her throat struggled to breathe them. "N-no."

"Admit it, you miss the excitement, not tonight excitement, but you liked taking care of someone, didn't you?"

Liz started walking around the apartment with no particular destination in mind.

"It's true," Adam continued. "You miss taking him to the emergency room to get his stomach pumped. Now someone's taking care of you and you don't know what to do with yourself. That's it, isn't it?"

By the time Adam ended his sentence Liz made it into the bathroom and slammed the door so hard the framed pictures hanging adjacent to the door shook an inch from the wall.

Liz's sobbing could be heard from outside the bathroom. Her crying echoed a little from the bathroom's atmosphere.

Adam knocked on the door. "Liz, I'm sorry."

He wasn't completely sorry. He was sorry for making her cry, he wasn't sorry for his words.

The crying continued, making Adam knock louder to compete with it. "Liz, can you open the door so we can talk about this?"

Adam stepped back until his back was against the wall of the hallway, opposite of the bathroom door. Liz's crying turned choppy, broken up, like she was running out of breath. It stopped completely for a moment, then continued.

Adam rolled his eyes, exhausted. He walked back to

the couch and grabbed his jacket. It was going to be a long night.

He put his jacket on and zipped it up completely. He could still smell Liz from when she had worn it. He grabbed his face with both hands and dragged them through his hair.

His stomach growled. The fridge in the corner of the kitchen was calling to him, but he didn't think he deserved to eat. Not Liz's food anyway. He couldn't bear to eat when she was crying, whether he was the one to make those tears or not, he couldn't eat a bite.

Adam walked to the bathroom, then held a fist up to the door and paused. He sighed, then banged on the door.

"Do you want me to make you a sandwich? You've gotta be hungry after what we went through tonight."

There was no reply, no crying, no noise at all.

"Look," he continued. "I just got paranoid. It's been a weird night for me too, you know? You just asked a simple question and I overreacted. I'm sorry. Now could you please come out here and eat something?"

Again, there was silence. Adam bowed his head and pressed it against the bathroom door.

Then, the door opened and the sudden lack of support almost caused Adam to fall onto Liz. He waved his arms, trying to find his balance, then regained his posture. Liz chuckled, covering her mouth with her hand.

Adam was glad to see her laughing again. He made her favorite sandwich, a simple PB&J with the crusts cut off. He handed it to her as she lied across the couch, her legs dangling off the edge of the armrest. Adam turned on the TV to make some noise then joined her on the last unused couch cushion. He had to lift up her head then lower it onto his lap so he could sit down.

Together they watched a marathon of a show's name they never learned, they talked over it for hours.

It was two o' clock in the morning. Liz and Adam were now cuddling on what little room the couch had to offer. Their voices had been reduced to a soft and sensual pillow talk.

"Hey Adam?"

"Yeah?"

"I think I'm ready to let go of Keith."

"That's great," said Adam's tired voice. He questioned how long he had until he drifted off to sleep.

"I thought you'd be happier," Liz said, equally as tired.

"I am happy," he yawned. "But I'm also ready to sleep."

Liz shifted around Adam's comforting grip. "But I'm not giving up Jamie, okay?"

"Okay," he breathed.

"Goodnight Adam."

"Goodnight Liz."

Chapter 5

Adam woke up with morning wood, and it woke Liz up too.

"Up and early?" she said.

They were in the same positions they fell asleep in. Adam's jacket was draped over them in place of a blanket.

"Did you put my jacket over us?" he asked.

"I was cold, I did it after you fell asleep."

There was a knocking on the door. But the knocker didn't wait for a response. There was a jingling of keys, then the door unlocked and swung open.

It was a girl. She looked very similar to Liz, but younger, and with shorter hair. Adam knew at once who she had to be.

"Lucy!" Liz cried out as she got to her feet, ran forward, and threw both her arms around her sister.

"Liz!" she said back, trying to push her sister away enough for her to breathe. But her sister's grip was strong. It'd been too long since they'd last been together.

Adam rushed to them and pried Liz off her sister just as her face turned a dark red color.

"Thanks," Lucy said, trying to catch some air, her back hunched.

"What are you doing here?" Liz asked.

"I just wanted to see my big sister," she replied, catching her breath and standing straight again. "And I take it this is Adam?"

Adam got in between the sisters (in case of another bear hug) and shook Lucy's hand.

"Nice to meet you," she said, her face now turning a full, healthy color.

"You want to sit down?" Liz asked.

"I do. Now where can I sit where you guys haven't had sex?"

Adam laughed, a little too hard for Liz's taste. She frowned, and Adam ceased his laughter, clearing his throat uncomfortably.

"You can sit anywhere," Liz said.

She took the leather chair. Liz and Adam took the couch they slept on. Then Adam wrapped an arm around Liz's shoulder.

"Nice place," Lucy said, looking around admiringly. "Hope you don't mind if I crash here sometime."

Liz was caught in a spotlight. Her mouth opened slightly, then shut when it became blatantly obvious she was hesitant.

"What do you mean by *sometime*?" she asked.

Adam knew Liz valued her privacy and had mentioned very little about her sister. And for good reason. Lucy was everything Liz used to be. All the lowlife abuse she used to do to herself, she didn't do it alone, they did it sister and sister, under the watchful eye of Keith. Then Adam came into her life and all that stopped. But Lucy never got her Adam.

"Mom's making me pay rent now, and I need some place to crash. I *promise* not to get in the way and keep to myself."

"When is she kicking you out?" Liz asked.

"End of the month."

"What you need," Adam said. "Is a job. She's not kicking you out she's making you pay rent. How much is she asking for?"

Lucy's cleared her throat. "Two hundred a month."

"That's nothing!" Adam said. "You could make that on minimum wage!"

Lucy's ears turned red and she crossed her arms. "So," she said. "Where do we go from here?"

The heat of the awkwardness radiated the air around them. Lucy was sweating but Adam suspected it wasn't from her nervousness, but instead from withdrawal. Her sweat was sticking to the leather couch.

Realizing this, Lucy wiped her forehead then stood

from the leather chair. "Well?" she cried.

"Let's put a pin in it for now," Liz replied, placating her sister. "There's still time left before the end of the month."

"Tell me something," Adam said. "If I could get you a job, right now, would you take it?"

Lucy curled her fingers and tilted her head. For a moment the hairs on Adam's arms stood up. Then she gritted her teeth and spoke without opening her jaw. "Yes."

"And you will agree to that job's drug testing policies?" Adam pressed.

Liz quickly covered Adam's mouth. "*Okay*," she said loudly, standing to her feet. "Lucy, I'll text you later about the job, right now I think me and Adam need some time alone."

Adam removed Liz's hand from his mouth, feeling offended to be treated like a child.

Lucy sighed. "I'm sorry Liz. I messed up again, didn't I?"

Adam frowned. He walked to Lucy and shook her hand again. "It was nice meeting you. I'm sorry it was under these circumstances."

Lucy looked away.

Liz walked over to guide her sister to the door but Lucy saved her the trouble and showed herself out, avoiding any additional pity Liz might show her.

After leaving, Lucy couldn't shake the feeling that they were talking about her. She didn't want to leave the way she had, once again pushing her sister away. Now she'd have to go home early, face her mother, and try to make an excuse as to why she couldn't stay longer. And her story would have to match with Liz's because her mother would undoubtedly check with her.

Lucy stood in front of her house, already playing different scenarios in her head of how her mother would react to her news. Not one of them ended in her favor. It seemed no matter what she'd say her mother would be disappointed. However, if she led with her trying to get a new job it might soften the blow.

She opened the door. There was a loud, continuous mechanical noise. Her mom was vacuuming. She stopped cleaning to look at Lucy then back down at the carpet she was vacuuming. Lucy immediately knew something was wrong. Normally, her mother would interrogate her about every detail of her day.

"I'm home!" she yelled over the scream of the vacuum.

"Almost finished!" she replied.

Her mother vacuumed the edges of the floor where the carpet ended and the tile started. Long trails of lines followed the vacuum as she did. When the last inch was finally covered, she turned the vacuum off, and the mechanical noise progressively died.

"Can you talk?" Lucy asked her mother.

"Actually," her mother sighed. "There's something *I* need to tell *you*."

Lucy walked to her mother, preparing her puppy dog face. Her eyes widened and her lips pouted as her mother's eyes locked with hers.

"What is it mom?"

"You remember your cousin Martin?"

"Yeah," she said timidly.

"A car hit him in the middle of the street as he was trying to cross the road. His mother just called, I could barely understand what she was saying through all her crying."

Lucy's face froze.

She didn't care about Martin, she'd only met him a handful of times. Still, she put on an emotional show for her mother.

She bowed her head and let her hair dangle in front of her face like curtains covering windows. Her mother patted her back consolingly.

She was crying herself. It was her sister's son for

goodness sakes. She thought of her own daughter, running through the streets, all alone, and then, *bam*! She was gone.

And what about Liz? She'd finally gotten her life together, the mother would cry for three weeks straight if anything happened to her.

She straightened her back, trying to be strong for her daughter. She didn't want to think about Martin, or Liz, or Lucy, or anyone else for that matter.

"Wh-when's the funeral?" Lucy sobbed.

The mother hadn't seen her daughter cry in a long time, not real tears anyways, only those fake one's you might find on reality television. This time was different, however, she could swear Lucy's eyes were turning red.

"Day after tomorrow," she said, wiping her own tears away.

"Does dad know?"

"I already called him. He'll be back from Florida the morning of the funeral, maybe the night before if he decides to get an early flight instead."

Two days went by. Lucy's mother had hardly left the house, not even to get groceries. The only reason she stepped outside was to breathe fresh air and to soak up her daily dose of vitamin D.

She had a soft spot for Martin, even though no one else in her family did. He was a bit of a trouble maker growing up, stealing thing then lying about stealing those things. But no matter how much he stole he was still her nephew dammit.

She drove Liz and Lucy to the funeral. Her daughters hardly said a word to one another the entire drive. She'd forgotten to ask Lucy about her visit to Liz in the midst of all her grieving.

Lucy was wearing a beautiful black and white dress and a fake gold necklace around her neck. Liz, on the other hand, wore an all-black dress Adam had bought her the day before.

"Where's Adam?" the mother asked.

"He wanted to go but his boss wouldn't give him the time off."

"Having troubles with his job, is he?" Lucy muttered under her breath.

"At least he *has* a job!" Liz barked.

"Will you two stop fighting?" the mother said. "Good Lord, if you two start up at the funeral we're going to have some serious problems. This day isn't about you two, it's about remembering Martin and being there for Suzy and Luke."

Suzy was her sister and Luke her brother-in-law, both parents to the late Martin Gregory.

Martin was only sixteen when he died, which made losing him all the more difficult. When Suzy called her sister about Martin it took two and a half hours for the conversation to come to an end. She constantly had to catch her breath from all the crying and even when she spoke her words were difficult for her sister to understand.

Her mind drifted back to when Lucy mentioned Adam, Liz's knight in shining armor.

Why couldn't Lucy find an Adam of her own? she thought. *Maybe there was an Adam already at the funeral, waiting for her.*

The chapel was drawing near. The mother's husband's flight was delayed and he planned to meet her at the funeral.

The cross at the peak of the chapel was the first thing the mother saw as she drove close to it. A Cadillac Hearse was parked next to the chapel, its trunk hanging open. Four men were lifting the casket from the car and loading it onto a cart. People stood in two parallel lines, making a clear path for the pallbearers as they watched them wheel it into the chapel. It was a small casket, almost child sized. Martin never grew like the rest of his classmates and was often made fun of because of it. This did not, however, keep Martin from picking fights with people twice his size. One of the things the mother remembered fondly about him…. he was a fighter.

Together the mother and her daughters left the car, each of them closing their doors as quietly as they could.

It was a relatively small chapel. High on top was a stained-glass mosaic of the Mother Mary. She was smiling at the ground as if to greet everyone walking inside, happy to see them.

The mother and her daughters walked inside. They signed their names on the sheet sitting on the podium.

Suzy was sullenly greeting guests as they walked into the main seating area. The mother didn't know what to say. What does anyone say to someone whose just lost a child?

The mother and her daughters walked to her, putting on their sad faces as they approached.

"Karen," she said in a soft-spoken tone.

Karen opened her mouth to speak but Liz hugged her before she could get a word out. Lucy followed in her sister's actions, then their mother.

"Karen, how are things?" Suzy said to her sister. She talked to Karen as if she was the one to have lost a child.

"Things are fine, Suzy, but how are things with you?"

"I just don't know how I'm going to face this tomorrow."

Suzy's makeup was smeared from her earlier cry spells and her thin veil did little to conceal it.

"I saw they already took Martin into the chapel," Karen said.

"Yes, we asked the funeral director if we could. It would be too hard to watch him being taken in there."

"Where's Luke?"

"He's already inside, the service is about to start."

"Where do you want us to sit?"

"Family sits up front."

"We'll sit now then."

Karen, Liz and Lucy disappeared with the crowd

moving into the chapel. Suzy continued to greet people and thank them for coming until no one was left.

When Suzy entered the room she knew eyes were following her. She knew they weren't trying to watch her, but they were, nonetheless. No one wanted to watch a mother mourn over her son, but they did want to, in a way.

She took her seat in the front row of benches, next to Luke.

Halfway through the service Suzy stood before her mourning audience and gave a speech about how Martin was "a handful, but also full of love". The audience made a sympathetic "awww", and Suzy sat down, a pastor taking her place at the podium.

"Is there anyone else who'd like to share their feelings about Martin? A funny story, perhaps?"

Everyone who'd known Martin well enough had already given a speech. Most of them were kind enough to ask her in advance if their speaking was okay.

Then, from deep within in the audience, stood a girl a little older than Martin's age. She'd caught Suzy's attention when she entered the room but she didn't think much of her. She'd never seen her before.

The girl eased through her crowded row. People pulled back their knees to let her through, but she seemed almost too anxious to wait for them.

Suzy didn't know what to think of this girl or her impending speech. She actually squeezed her eyes shut to perform some sort of reality check. When she opened her eyes, sure enough, the girl was standing at the podium, in the flesh, and adjusting the microphone to fit her height.

"I knew Martin around high school and was shocked, *shocked* to see so few of his classmates have come to see him." She paused to let the audience sink in the effect of her speech. Their faces were blank. Some of them even leaned to the edge of their seats, wondering what she could possibly say next to get her removed from a funeral. Imagine that. Removed from a funeral, none of them had seen that before.

"Well," she continued. "I only knew Martin for a short time but I could tell right away he was someone I'd remember. Even when we first met he was always cracking jokes as I'd pass him in the hallway. He'd find anything to talk about, from the weather to what kind of car he dreamed of buying. And let us never forget his smile, smug, yet with an unclear warmth to it."

The girl talked in a preacher voice, like she knew what she was doing, and gave her eulogy. She looked more comfortable doing it than she did sitting down, waiting. Her speech seemed unrehearsed and was without a paper to read from.

People sitting near Suzy gave her looks that seemed to say, "Who is this girl and what is she doing at that podium?" and, "Is this her idea of a joke?"

The same looks were given to the girl herself but none of them seemed to faze her. She kept ranting like nothing was to worry about.

"I recently went to my older brother's funeral not three days ago and I had to drag myself to come here, because well, Martin deserves it. It's been hard dealing with all this loss but then I remind myself that if Martin was looking down at me he'd want to see me at his funeral, talking here to you. Thank you for listening and before I go I'd just like to tell Martin thanks for helping me through Chemistry when times were tough. He was the best tutor anyone could've asked for."

The girl paused again, then went back to her rows of seats. She looked like she could go back and talk for another ten minutes.

The preacher walked back to the podium but the eyes of the crowd were glued to the girl as she took her seat in the back rows of benches.

The preacher tightened his collar nervously. "That was, um, powerful. The Lord welcomes all who want to share their grievances."

The rest of the funeral went as planned. No more strange speeches were given, nothing out of the usual happened. After it was finished, Suzy wanted nothing else but to talk to the strange girl and find out more about who she was.

"Thank you," she said to her, following her to the lobby. "How long did you know Martin?"

"Since the beginning of the school year. I always passed him by his locker on the way to Chemistry and one day we talked about tutoring and he helped me ever since."

"He never told me he was tutoring anyone. I would've thought after meeting a pretty girl such as yourself he'd want to tell me right away. Can you think of why he wouldn't tell me?"

The girl frowned. Suzy felt she knew she was interrogating her rather than asking a harmless question to fill in small talk.

"I don't know why he didn't tell you about me," the girl said. "Maybe he didn't want you to know he had extra money coming in. He did talk about you sometimes though, said you were a terrific person, and a wonderful mother."

This was of course, a lie, and Suzy knew it. Martin would spend days talking poorly about his mother, even avoiding her whenever he could. Suzy couldn't decide whether or not this girl was genuinely trying to extend her condolences, or if she was trying to cover something up.

"I didn't catch your name," Suzy said.

"I'm Maddie." She put her hand out for Suzy to shake it. She did, but hesitantly.

"I'm Suzy," she said. "That was a great speech you gave, really unexpected."

Maddie couldn't sense her sarcasm. "Thanks. I meant every word of it. I'm gonna miss him."

"We all are."

"I can't imagine what you must be feeling right now, losing a son."

Suzy shrugged. "Pretty much how you'd expect."

There was an awkward silence between them. The crowd stopped flowing past them, they were alone.

"Are you going to the burial?" Suzy asked.

"Of course. Green Acres Cemetery, right?"

"That's the one."

"Then I'll meet you there."

Maddie walked off to her car and Suzy walked closely behind. They had parked two spaces from each other. Maddie waved goodbye, then drove off.

The burial was less chaotic. No speeches were given, just lots of crying as the small coffin descended into the ground to join the bodies around it, six feet under. He was the worms' problem now.

Maddie paid her condolences to Martin's immediate family, then drove away. Her memory of death now was not occupied by Martin, but by the face of her recently deceased brother. He was a nice-looking man and always wore some sports gear supporting his favorite teams. That's what kept him going, sports. Until finally, cancer's grasp took hold of him and never let go. He was dead within two years of his diagnosis, which was surprising, considering the doctors only gave him eight months, at best.

Maddie drove down the twists and turns of the streets, cursing at every red light she encountered. She sat in traffic, her elbow lying on the armrest, her hand on her face, thinking about her next move.

She was a high school senior and planned to go to college in San Diego with her late brother Marcus. One million, three hundred fifty thousand people where she lived and every face there reminded her of Marcus. His stupid toothy smile, his curly hair that never straightened, no matter how much he brushed it. God how she missed him.

The road turned into an on-ramp, which turned into a highway she rode for three miles, then took her to the next exit. She exited the exit, turned three lefts, then a right, then a left, and there she was, staring at a nice, well cared for building that she called home.

Her mother hadn't fully recovered from the death of Marcus. His room now was a shrine to his memory, completely untouched from when he passed away, down to the dust in the corners of the room to the sheets over his bed.

Maddie had cried over him too but her grieving period was brief. The way she saw it, Marcus wouldn't have wanted her to mope around the house all day wishing she could change the past. She'd said everything she wanted to tell him. Her last words were "Good luck", and he was gone.

Maddie parked and entered the house, expecting to hear someone crying. But it was silent. She guessed no one was home and walked upstairs and into her room.

On the desk was her faithful laptop patiently awaiting her arrival. The overhead light in the room bounced off the laptop making it shine brand new, highlighting it, like it was telling Maddie to turn it on.

She answered its call, flipped her laptop open, and pushed a button. The machine hummed to life and the screen dimly flickered on. She cracked her knuckles, readying her fingers for the typing they were about to endure. Maddie logged into her online profile and checked if anyone had mentioned Marcus in the past hour. Two people had, she read their comments.

She clicked on Marcus's profile (she kept it online so that people could write their condolences), and browsed through his pictures. Friends, birthday parties, college parties, drunk mistakes, they were all there like an online profile should have. But as Maddie clicked and searched through more and more of Marcus's pictures she realized how few of them had her. She wondered rather or not most people knew he had a sister at all.

Maddie pulled her phone from her bra and wrote a text.

"Do you think Marcus liked me as a sister?"

She checked two names in her contacts then sent the message. She put the phone face down on the dresser by her bed then laid her head on a pillow. Within ten minutes her phone dinged twice, she crawled to the dresser and turned over the phone. Both her friends had answered, and then, a third text came to her screen.

The name that appeared made her hands tremble almost enough to make her drop the phone. It was her brother, Marcus.

Calm down Maddie, she thought. *It's probably some sort of a prank. I don't know how they did it, but someone must've hacked his phone.*

She opened the text and read it: "Who's Marcus?"

Maddie wanted to slap herself. Marcus died just before his next phone payment was due. Obviously Marcus didn't pay it himself and the phone number must've gone to someone else. But still, that was only three days ago, what were the chances someone else picked his number so soon? Or maybe her mother alerted the phone company earlier. Martin died three days ago but he'd been *dying* for a long time.

"Sorry," she wrote back. "Marcus was my brother who died a few days ago. I must've checked his name when I sent that text."

Her phone made a ding noise and the text was sent, gone into cyberspace. Maddie expected the reply to say something like, "I know, it's me, your brother."

The phone dinged again and she read it without delay. "I'm sorry to hear that. I'm sure your brother loved you very much."

Maddie's head filled with both anger and flattery. *How the hell does this guy know whether or not my brother liked me?*

She wrote back: "Why do you think he did? You don't

even know me." The text flew.

She sat upright, her back resting against the bed's headboard, staring into her phone screen. This was her body's way of saying she was serious.

Her phone dinged again, she read it. "Just a feeling. Call it a brother's intuition. I have a sister too and even though sometimes it looks like we don't like each other, I can't help but protect her whenever she needs me."

Tears stuck to Maddie's eyes, she blinked, and they streamed down her face. In that moment she could've believed Marcus *was* alive, and he was talking to her right now.

"What's your name?" Maddie asked.

"Elliot, and you?"

"Guess."

"Haha, there's literally thousands of names and you want me to pick one?"

"Yes, I'll make it easy for you, it starts with an M."

"Morgan, Megan, Madison, Maddy, Molly, Martha?"

"Maddie."

"Close enough."

"What do you look like?"

"You first."

Maddie didn't want to go first. If she did, she'd give up all the power of the conversation. She could at least send him a casual picture, nothing too revealing. That way, if he was some perverted old man he wouldn't get too much.

She went through an archive of pictures in her phone and picked one from a year ago. She was looking up at her phone when she took the picture. A setting sun was in the background, beaming light through her long brown hair. She sent it.

Her stomach dropped. For all she knew she'd never hear from this guy again, his name might not even be Elliot.

Sure enough, he messaged her back. One picture was added as an attachment.

This was it, the big unveiling.

Please be an older guy, she thought. *But not too old.*

It was nothing less than what Maddie could've hoped for. Clearly Elliot worked out. He was shirtless, and had a six-pack running down his midsection. There was also what looked like the beginning of an eight pack.

His eyes were a navy blue, his hair was clean and styled. There were small waves in his hair that curled upward at the bangs.

Maddie remembered her brother's hair. He'd always tug at it when he was really angry. After he was diagnosed with cancer, the resulting chemotherapy caused his hair to fall out. Even so, he'd try tugging at his bald head, instinctively trying to grab a handful of hair. Sometimes when someone caught him in the act, he'd rub his head nonchalantly to make it look like he meant to do it.

Maddie smiled faintly.

It was fate. It *had* to be fate.

"How old are you?" he asked.

Maddie's fingers froze before she could answer. She was eighteen, but didn't know if that was old enough for him. From the look of Elliot's picture, he was twenty, same age as her brother. She couldn't tell for sure.

If she guessed wrong, she could scare him off, and then she'd be alone forever.

Oh for goodness sakes Maddie, who really cares about two or three years anymore? Your own parents are four years apart.

"I'm eighteen, senior in high school. What about you?"

Better to get the truth out right away, she thought. *Get it out in the open.*

Three minutes passed without an answer. Maddie's heart sank and goosebumps ran down her arms. *Please answer.*

Twenty minutes went by, no response.

Great!

She'd scared away what seemed like potentially a

perfect relationship, and when she needed it most. Was she ugly? Maddie re-examined her picture. It was crystal clear, no fuzziness, no slight facial hair, perfect angle. It couldn't be the picture, Elliot kept talking after she sent it. It must've been her age.

She didn't want to seem desperate but she also couldn't let him go. If she stopped talking to him now he'd forget her. "That picture was taken over a year ago, I look much older now."

The phone dinged again and her goosebumps returned, this time stemming from excitement rather than fear.

"It's not that, I was taking a shower. You look beautiful Maddie. I'm nineteen, twenty in a few more months. I don't know if it's too soon to talk about but would you mind telling me about your brother?"

Maddie's fingers hit the screen so fast her smartphone could hardly keep up. "He was great, I miss him sooooooo much. He died of cancer about three days ago. I watched him go through so much before he died, radiation, chemotherapy, and a bunch of other stuff we thought might work. I'm sure you would've liked him, he was about your age."

"Well if he was anything like you I'm sure I would've really liked him a lot." Maddie smiled, then continued reading. "Listen, a conversation like this shouldn't happen over the phone. Do you want to meet up sometime and talk about it while we get something to eat?"

"I'd love to. When did you have in mind?"

"Someone who just lost their brother shouldn't wait too long to talk about their feelings. How about tomorrow night at 8:00?"

"Where at?"

"You pick."

Maddie instantly thought of the mall, it was a public place. No, that wouldn't work. If she started crying at the mall (and she knew that was a strong possibility) she wouldn't be able to stop. People would stare at her, judging her, it'd only make things worse.

However, if Maddie *did* cry there wasn't a doubt in her mind that Elliot would offer her a shoulder to cry on.

"Green Road Mall?" she said.

"It's a date."

Maddie wanted to jump on her bed and wave her hands jubilantly in the air. But she hadn't done that since she was a twelve and excited that her breasts were coming in. Elliot wanted a mature *woman*, not a girl. A girl would giggle at every word he said, empty her brain whenever he talked to her, as if she had no thoughts of her own.

She put down her phone and went to the bathroom. When she returned her mother was sitting on her bed, Maddie's phone in her hand, and beckoning her daughter to sit next to her.

"Who's this guy you've been talking to and why's his name in your brother's place?"

Maddie sighed as she walked toward her mother, who put the phone on the bed and stared at Maddie with a stoned, expressionless face.

Here comes "the talk", Maddie thought.

She sat down by her mother, staring at her, waiting for her to make the first move.

"I don't like you talking to strangers," she said. "It's dangerous, and guys his age only want one thing."

"But mom, it's fate!"

The mother rolled her eyes. "Girls your age always think everything's fate. Believe me, I did when I was your age, and — "

"No mom, really," she said. "I didn't even mean to text him, I checked his name by accident and he's *my age*. Now you look me in the eyes and tell me that's not fate."

Maddie thought for a second her mom would roll her eyes again. She didn't. "How do you even know this guy's who he says he is?"

"He sent me a picture."

"I saw that. Nice looking guy with a six pack. Do you really think he couldn't just pull that off the Internet? This guy could be much older than he says he is."

"I'm well aware of perverts on the Internet, mom, and under normal circumstances I wouldn't— "

"That's it," she interrupted. "You miss Marcus." She sprung up from the bed, struck by her own epitome. The idea was almost too strong for her to handle at once. She pointed an accusing finger. "You're missing Marcus and now you're turning to guys to make you feel better."

Maddie knew her mother couldn't actually stop her from seeing Elliot. She had a policy of letting her children make their own mistakes. It worked for Marcus, maybe it'd work for Maddie.

"What does his age matter? You and dad are four years apart, right?"

"Yes, but we met when we were much older than you and this…. Elliot."

Maddie's face turned red. She was losing the argument, but she couldn't let her mom see that.

"Are we finished here?" Maddie said, standing up, her eyes were shiny and they looked like they would fill with tears.

Maddie had the urge to scream, but then again, she was a woman, not a girl. The mother reached for Maddie's shoulder but her daughter was too quick. She grabbed her phone from her bed and ran out of the room, slamming the door behind her.

Her mother called her back but she didn't want to listen. She raised both her hands and clasped them over her ears. All sounds now were muffled whispers to her.

She didn't know where she was going, somewhere far from her mom seemed nice. The worst part of it was, Maddie knew her mom was right. Yet still, if she let it go, and never met Elliot, she might regret it for the rest of her life.

What could go wrong? If Elliot wasn't who he claimed to be they'd be in a public place and she could leave whenever she wanted. Elliot's phone number had the same area code as hers since it was her brother's old number, which meant Elliot couldn't live too far away.

He might not be everything Maddie dreamed about but he was better than nothing, and right now, Maddie was dangerously close to that in the boyfriend department. She couldn't hold onto a guy for more than a few months. She figured no one could handle her quirky attitude or her spontaneity. She never considered changing herself for some guy. Elliot, however, wasn't just some guy. For him, she was willing to be a woman.

Senior prom was just over the horizon and with Elliot's arms around her she'd set all her friends jealous. With him, she might even be voted prom queen.

Maddie strode out the house and circled around the neighborhood several times to make it seem like she was walking far. She would've taken her car but she knew her mom would stop helping pay for gas, and that was something Maddie couldn't live without. Nothing wrong with taking an angry stroll through the neighborhood, though. She might even get mugged, then her mother would *have* to apologize and let her date whoever she wanted.

Her legs were getting tired. She wasn't sure how long she'd been walking or how far she'd walked. She could do the math if she added the distances, but she was too tired for that.

Her mom called her several times that hour but she ignored every call.

Let her worry, she thought.

She stopped at an intersection and watched the cars go by. Several of them ignored the stop signs and simply rolled through them. Did people drive this reckless when children were around?

She checked the time. It'd been two hours since she left the house. The day was ending and darkness was overpowering the light.

Better turn back, she thought. *She's worried enough. You've made your point.*

But which way was home? She stopped knowing the streets about thirty minutes ago.

She changed her direction and backtracked until she came across a main street. She walked along the road until she crossed Jefferson Street, then followed the recognizable streets home.

She came home to the smell of pasta. The way her mom made pasta was something you might find at a five-star restaurant. It was her favorite, and her mother knew it too. She figured it was a sort of a "Sorry for getting into your life" dinner.

Her mom heard the door open.

"Maddie? Is that you?"

"Yeah mom."

"Come in and take your seat."

She didn't sound like she wanted to scold her, but she didn't sound like she was apologizing either. But why make the pasta then? That was an apology on its own because her mom only made it on special occasions, and apologizes were one of them.

Maddie walked into the kitchen and pulled out her chair. She took her seat and slid her chair closer to the table. Her mom winced at the screech it made dragging across the tile.

"Sorry," Maddie said.

She ignored her. "Your dad will be home any minute."

And at that last word, like magic, the garage door opened. A moment later, the back door opened and they could still hear the automatic garage door closing as it systematically lowered to the ground. Maddie's dad entered the kitchen, frowning.

Maddie knew at once that the dinner was for daddy. Surely her mother wouldn't tell her dad what happened between her and Elliot *now*. No sense feeding the fire. At that thought Maddie leaned back in her chair and smiled.

When her dad glanced at her face her smile faltered, then faded completely.

"I made pasta," the mother said, placating him. "I know it can't fix things but I thought it might help."

The mother put a streaming plate of pasta at her husband's place at the dinner. Without saying anything the father sat down and hopped his chair toward the table.

"Tough day at work, dad?" Maddie asked weakly.

He grunted and picked up a fork, using it to twirl the pasta so that it wrapped around it. Maddie and her mother watched as he brought the fork to his open mouth, he blew on it cautiously. When he took his eyes off his pasta he caught his wife and daughter staring at him. He could tell by their expressions that they were afraid to speak.

"Look," he said, dropping his fork with a loud clank. "I didn't get the promotion. I'm overqualified and I lost the position to someone that's not even here legally!" His throat made an audible sound as it struggled to swallow. "But I don't need your special treatment. Unlike the guy who *did* get the promotion, *I-don't-need-special-treatment!*"

Maddie thought her dad was going to stand up, grab his keys, and drive someplace else. She wanted him to. She couldn't stand to see her dad lose his control.

Instead, he picked up the fork and scarfed down his meal. His jaw made little crushing sounds as he aggressively chewed his food.

The rest of the dinner was spent in silence, only broken from the clanking of silverware to plates. Maddie wanted her dad to pass the spaghetti sauce but didn't dare to ask him. She thought he'd tell her she'd already had enough.

After the dinner Maddie helped her mom collect the plates and hand wash them at the sink. Her dad had gone to bed early, isolating himself from everything but his thoughts.

"How long do you think till dad gets better?" Maddie

asked her mom, as she cleaned the dishes.

"A week, maybe," she replied. "Depends on how often he remembers it. He'll be fine just as long as he keeps himself busy."

"Are you gonna help keep him busy, mom?"

The mother stopped cleaning. She thought she heard a sexual undertone in her daughter's voice.

"Madison!" she yelled. Her voice didn't seem to match her expression. Her face was blank and pale, like she was thinking of something else and only yelled as a reaction.

"Not like that, *mom*! I mean are you going to distract him? Help him see the silver lining?"

"Oh. By the sound of your voice I-I thought you meant something else."

"Well if I've got a dirty mind I'll know where I got it from, and it isn't dad."

The mother broke her blank expression and allowed a smirk to pass across her face. Her laugh came in the form of a loud breath through her nose.

"Still," the mother said. "I don't think your dad will ever be happy until he runs that company so he can cut out everyone he doesn't like."

"Like the guy that took his promotion?"

She smiled. "I'd like to think by that time he'd cool down. But if he could fire anyone he'd be the first to go."

"Or he'd make his life miserable. Make him *want* to quit."

Maddie and her mother shared a sadistic laugh and finished cleaning the dishes. She hated to see her dad struggle but it made her happy that it distracted her mother from Elliot.

Her mind drifted back to him. His chiseled abdominals, his broad shoulders. The more she thought about him and that picture, the more details she added. Dimples, long eyelashes, freckles in all the right places.

She took a deep breath and reminded herself to breathe. She squeezed her thigh enough to hurt slightly and jumped out of her trance.

She had hours left until meeting him.

Don't let yourself get too invested, she thought. *Lots of things could happen before then. He could get in an accident, you could get in an accident, or worse…. he could cancel.*

Maddie took a hot shower then went off to bed.

Tomorrow will be better, Marcus is still gone but nothing can change that. Nothing I can do.

Maddie curled up in her bed, various blankets wrapped around her, and she slept a dreamless sleep.

Chapter 6

Maddie was awoken by the sound of her phone dinging. With her head still on the pillow she reached for the phone and examined it. One new text from "Marcus". She read it.

"Sorry to wake you if you're not already up. But I couldn't wait to talk to you— "

Good so far, Maddie thought. She continued reading.

"I've had a change in my schedule. Is it all right if we change our date to 7:00 instead of 8:00?"

Seven? Maddie's heart dropped. Nothing romantic ever happens at seven, the later in the night, the better. Elliot couldn't kiss her goodnight if the date ended at nine. She'd have to kiss *him* if it came down to that.

"That's fine." And she left it at that, because Maddie knew, that Elliot knew, when a girl says "that's fine" there's always a deeper meaning.

"Does that work for you?" Elliot asked. She could sense the concern in his written words.

She knew she had him. Still, maybe Elliot really could only see her at seven. She let him have it.

"No, really, that's fine, see you at 7:00, and if you have to change again let me know."

Check mate.

"Thanks for understanding. My parents are out of town and I have to take care of my grandma until 5:00, she's sick. Then I have work tomorrow morning. I'm just going to be exhausted if I stay out too long."

Bastard turned the tables on me, she thought. *He's trying to pull the sympathy card. I can play mind games too.*

"Aww, that's so nice of you," she wrote. "That reminds me of how I took care of my brother during his last days on earth."

Maddie stared at her screen, waiting for a reply. When her phone didn't ding she gave up.

I went too far, comparing our situations. Please answer me, even if you get mad just say something — please.

"I'm sure he appreciated it," he replied.

"Yeah, a lot of things remind me of him. I think my mind just makes those connections, you know? Like, he won't leave my mind."

"He died recently, it's natural to think about him constantly. I don't really want to talk about this over the phone though, lets save it for tonight. Then we'll talk as much as you need to."

Maddie wasn't sure what to think of this. She knew he was right. It was difficult to tell what he was really trying to say over the phone. Text has no tone. No pitch. She read his words clearly but didn't know what to make of them.

Maddie ran his words through her head, trying to make sense of them. "Then we'll talk as much as you need to."

I don't need to, she thought. *I'll get over Marcus with or without you. I don't need anything. I want to talk about it, but only for your sake, so you can comfort me, lend me a helping hand. I want to make things easier for you, Elliot.*

The clock was ticking.

It was six o' clock already and Maddie's mother tried twice that day to convince her not to meet Elliot.

The first was in the morning.

"Now that you've slept on it do you still think you need to see Elliot?"

She kept her answer short and without emotion. "Yes mom, I have to."

"I wish you'd listen to me but you need to learn from your own mistakes. I just hope he's everything you think he is."

"We'll know tonight, won't we?"

Then again that afternoon, at five o' clock. Maddie was in the hallway bathroom, the door left halfway open.

She looked intently into the mirror as she applied her makeup, her face close to her reflection.

"You getting ready to meet with Elliot?" Her mother asked, standing from just outside the bathroom.

"Sure am," she said with a monotone inflection, still staring at her own face.

"I guess there's nothing left to say."

"Guess not," Maddie said curtly.

The mother walked down the hall and out of Maddie's sight. Maddie wanted to chase her down and give her a reassuring hug, tell her she was going to be okay.

But then she'd give up all her power, letting her mother know she was at least partially right to be worried. It would be much more satisfying to walk through the front door at two in the morning with a smile on her face.

She'd tell her she was wrong, that Elliot took her into his arms and listened to her talk until the sun came up. And if her mother was right, and Elliot was some pervert she'd met by accident, she'd still tell her she was wrong.

Maddie went back to the bathroom and allowed herself one more self-checkup before leaving. She stood with as much distance between her and the mirror as she could manage without touching the wall behind her. She wore a white blouse and a knee length black skirt to contrast it. Perfect for an indoor shopping mall. Her makeup wasn't overdone and she only used enough to highlight her best features. She twirled and watched herself as best she could from all angles.

It was almost seven and Maddie heard no word from Elliot. She grabbed her keys from on top her dresser, as she was leaving her bedroom her phone dinged. It was Elliot.

"What's your address?" he asked.

"Why?"

"So I can pick you up. I realized it doesn't make much sense to go separately."

Her stomach tightened. "No, that's okay. Besides, if you come here my mom will want to meet you."

"What's wrong with that?"

"She was skeptical about me seeing you."

Maddie instantly wanted to remove her text from existence. The last thing Elliot would want to hear is that her mom didn't like them seeing each other. Unfortunately, her coded words had flown into the airwaves, gone from her palpable reach.

"Well of course she is, I'm some stranger you met over the phone. I could understand her not trusting me. If I meet her I think I could set her mind at ease and she wouldn't have a problem with me seeing you."

Relief washed over Maddie so fast she collapsed onto her bed. She tossed her keys back on her dresser.

"You'll be here at seven?" she asked.

"It's a date."

"Thank you," Maddie said out loud. She pocketed her phone and smiled at the ceiling, taking in the warmth of the moment.

She stood from her bed and told her mother of the change in her plan. When Maddie finished talking her mother smiled in a way she hadn't seen in a long time.

"He sounds like a true gentleman," she said. "Actually, he kind of reminds me of how your father used to act when we first started —." She cut herself short and lowered her head.

"Is he still mad about the promotion?"

"He's a little better now. I try not to talk too much about it." She leaned forward and bent her knees a little to shrink to Maddie's height. She lowered her voice and looked around, thinking her husband might come home any moment. "You wanna know a secret? Here's a few key words to watch out for so you don't accidentally set him off. Immigrants, border, job, jobs, promotion, rank, levels, and rising."

The doorbell rang. "Thanks for the tip mom."

Maddie's hair bounced up and down in perfect wavy

motions as she skipped toward the door. Maddie didn't have eyes on the back of her head, but if she did, she'd swear her mom was still smiling. She couldn't remember a time her mom saw her so happy either.

A blurry image of Elliot projected through the textured glass by the front door, a sort of preview. A series of tingles crawled up Maddie's spine. Her hand nearly froze as she reached for the doorknob and she had to force enough strength to grasp the cold metal and turn it. It took all her mental energy to pull the door open.

Elliot stood before her. The muscles in Maddie's face shut down completely.

Say something, she thought. *Say something or you're going to look like an idiot.*

"Maddie?" he asked, almost like he'd shown at the wrong house.

She cleared her throat. "Y-yeah, sorry, it's me."

Elliot revealed all his teeth in one sweeping smile. "You didn't act the way I thought you would when you saw me."

She rubbed the back of her neck. "I'm sorry, it's just been a weird day."

Elliot looked over Maddie's shoulder. Her mom had joined them, and Maddie could feel her breathing down her neck, perhaps as excited as Maddie was to meet Elliot.

"Hi," she said to him, walking around Maddie and extending a hand to Elliot. He shook it. "You must be Elliot."

"Very nice to meet you, I wish it was under better circumstances."

The mother frowned. "What do you mean?"

"Didn't Maddie tell you I got her brother's phone number? It's how we met."

The mother's face widened, and she clapped her hands in sudden remembrance. "Right! I'm sorry my mind's been so occupied lately. Do you want to sit down inside, maybe stay for a snack?"

Maddie wasn't completely sure if her mom wasn't flirting with him. Ridiculous, but possible.

"Actually mom, we've got to go before the mall closes."

"That's okay," Elliot said, stealing glances at Maddie's mother. "The mall was just a suggestion, I could stay for a while."

Maddie looked at her mom with sullen eyes in an attempt to persuade her. Her mother pretended not to notice, but she got the message.

"No, no," her mother said, waving them away. "I don't want to ruin your date before it starts. Go have fun, just have her home before midnight."

"*Mom!*"

"Midnight will be fine," Elliot said. "It's been nice to meet you."

Maddie followed Elliot to his car, a blue 1996 Corvette with a white stripe spread from the hood to the trunk. Elliot opened the door and Maddie stepped in, having to stoop down to enter. Elliot walked around and stepped in too.

Elliot started the engine and drove off slowly. Maddie had the feeling he was resisting the urge to peel out. Her mother was watching them leave, waving to them.

At the first stop sign Maddie spoke.

"Why did you want to stay? I thought you were here to see me. I just lost my brother and— "

"And she just lost a son," Elliot interrupted. "It's not easy on anyone when someone close to them passes away."

Maddie sank into the leather seat. She looked away and hoped Elliot would be more concerned with the road than her facial expression.

"I hadn't thought about my mom until you mentioned that."

"Well," he sighed. "Sometimes when stuff like that happens people only think of themselves. Can't say I wouldn't have."

Maddie wasn't sure if she wanted to kiss him or leave a big red smack mark across his face. He spoke very noncommittally, still, she had a feeling it was his way of comforting her.

Their car ride conversation was mostly small talk — the rain, Elliot's car, Maddie's car, movies. Elliot was an expert conversationalist and Maddie was so involved in their conversation she didn't realize they'd been circling the parking lot for nearly five minutes.

At last, they found an open space and parked.

"Tell me something, Maddie," Elliot said as he cut the engine. "During that entire conversation how many times did you think of Marcus?"

Maddie pressed a hand to her forehead as if she had a headache. Elliot's question made her think he was either a magician or a hypnotist. "Not once."

Elliot smiled another toothy grin. His teeth were almost too white to look natural.

"No, really," Maddie said incredulously. "I didn't think about him once, or my dad missing his promotion, or anything else I've been stressing about."

"Funny how you can take a few common things like weather and cars and spin it to make it sound interesting."

"I didn't do any of that, it was all you."

Elliot put an arm around the back of Maddie's chair, almost touching her shoulder. "What can I say, I'm a man that's good with words."

He had a satisfied look on his face that only he could pull off. She had the urge to kiss him. It was almost a need, like it was healthy for her to be around him. She leaned towards Elliot's face but gave herself enough distance to lean back nonchalantly if she changed her mind.

Wait!

But Elliot had leaned in too. His lips had not yet parted. Maddie leaned back to her original position.

This is too perfect, she thought. *A perfect guy walks into my life when I need him most, there has to be a catch.*

Then the words her father always said rang through her head like a catchy song, "If it seems too good to be true, it probably is."

"Well," Maddie said, as she angled her lips away from Elliot's face. "We should go inside, it's getting cold."

"I can turn up the heater." He reached for the temperature knob.

"No!" Maddie said, more loudly than she intended. "Let's just get in the mall before it gets too crowded.

"Oh." Elliot frowned. "I gotcha."

The mall was coming closer to closing time, although the parking lot was full, people were leaving, not coming.

"It's just a little cramped in here," Maddie said. "Might make it difficult for any sudden movements…. or strenuous exercise."

"And the mall wouldn't?"

"Well, not the mall per se, but maybe the after the mall." She smiled forebodingly. "But definitely not inside the mall," she added.

"I didn't mean to start in the car, it felt like one of those things that just sort of happen. Why don't you tell me what *you* want to do?"

"I told you already, go in the mall and talk in the food court."

When they stepped from the car several spaces around them had already cleared. They walked together to the giant mall, which seemed like a maze to Maddie no matter how many times she went there. There was always some sort of store relocating, or construction, or redecorating going on that threw off her sense of direction.

Maddie followed Elliot, hoping he was leading her to the food court. They walked around a corner, up an escalator, down the corridor, around another corner, and after ten minutes Maddie finally spoke.

"Do you know where the food court is?"

"No," Elliot replied. "I'm looking for a directory."

As they walked further, they ran into everything except a food court and a directory. Every time Elliot turned another corner he kept expecting to see one of the two and would get a little angrier each time he didn't.

They kept walking.

"Actually, I don't want to talk about Marcus right now," Maddie said, catching up to Elliot's frustrated speed walking. "I just want to relax, have some fun."

"Oh yeah," he replied, pointing to something ahead.

It was a mirror maze. It looked fairly new and also deserted. It was near closing time and everyone was either finishing their shopping or walking out of the mall.

There was a young man wearing a purple vest smiling as he waited at the booth to sell tickets.

"I remember when this place had a merry-go-round," Maddie said.

"Me too. When I was a kid my mom would usually take me when we went shopping here on weekends."

They approached the ticket salesman and his smile grew wider as he stared at his last customers of the night.

"Two tickets?" he asked.

"Yes please," Elliot said, as he took out his wallet.

"Ten dollars for two adults."

Elliot handed him the money and he stamped their hands. Maddie looked down at her stamp. It was a red dog with its tongue hanging out, and comical eyes that covered two thirds of its face.

"Enjoy," the salesman said. Then he raised the lift-up booth entrance and walked around them to unhook the velvet rope line divider. Then, after they walked past, he re-hooked the line divider, picked up a closed sign from his booth, and hung it over the rope.

Maddie started toward the entrance but Elliot blocked her path.

"I've got an idea," he said, facing her. "Why don't I go in first, you wait here for a few minutes, then go inside and try to find me, or I'll try to find you, or we'll try to find each other."

Maddie's face brightened, not quite a smile, more of an anxious smirk.

"What happens if you catch me first?" she asked.

"We'll just see what happens when it happens. What happens if you catch *me* first?"

"I'm not telling you until you tell me."

Elliot said nothing, smiled, then went inside.

Maddie stood by the entrance, tempted to peek inside. But that would ruin the game. She wanted to be surprised, by the layout of the maze, and by what Elliot would do to her when she found him. And she was *sure* she'd let him find her.

Two minutes went by, and Maddie went inside. The ticket salesman called in after her, "Don't take too long, *the-store-is-closing!*"

The maze looked endless, although she guessed any maze made up entirely of mirrors would look endless to anyone inside it. The normal lights flickered off and turned into party lights of varying colors. First red, then blue, then purple, then green, then yellow, then orange, then back to red.

Maddie walked around the corners and ended in a circular room of mirrors that seemed to have no way out but the way she entered it.

She waved and dozens of Maddie's waved back at her from every angle.

Elliot's eerie voice echoed throughout the maze. "Maddie…. where are you Maddie?"

She shivered, though she couldn't tell whether it was from fear or arousal.

"You better hope I don't find you first!" Maddie yelled.

"What are you going to do when you find me?"

"Your pants will be the first thing to go!"

No voice called back and she assumed he took it as a compliment. She pressed on, leaving the circular room and trying another path. The normal lights flickered back to life. It must've been set on a timer.

She turned a corner, a figure of a man appeared in the mirror. It had to be Elliot. No one else was there.

But it wasn't! After adjusting her eyes to what she was seeing, a clear image of Marcus stood inside the mirror's reflection.

A single worm squirmed halfway out of his skull. His eyes seemed to be sunken into his head and his skin was as white as the sheet they used to cover him in the hospital.

"Having fun forgetting me with your boyfriend?" he said. His voice sounded like he was in agonizing pain, yet trying desperately to manage it. His mouth was moving in the mirror but his voice didn't seem to come from any discernible location.

"I thought you were here to talk about me?" he said coldly. "I thought— "

Maddie screamed too loud to hear the rest. She dropped to her knees and wept into them. Footsteps echoed louder as they approached her sobbing.

"Maddie, what's wrong?" Elliot said, slightly out of breath.

She took a moment to catch her breath as well, although it didn't seem to help. "I saw Marcus.... in the mirror — I saw him!"

He kneeled down next to her.

He must think I'm crazy, she thought. *No guy wants a girl who gets psychotic visions of her dead brother.*

He put a hand on her back.

Poor girl, he thought. *She's lost so much and I'm all she has.*

"Well," Elliot said softly. "Everyone handles this kind of stuff differently. You *just* lost your brother. I can't say I wouldn't be seeing dead people if I lost my sister."

Tears ran down her cheeks and smeared her makeup.

"Thank you," she said. Her eyes were shiny from the tears that didn't fall. Her face looked strained and exhausted.

"It's all in your head," Elliot assured.

Maddie didn't want to hear this. Her face turned sour and she gave him an accusing frown.

"I mean, from all the stress, you know?" Elliot corrected himself.

The lights returned back to party mode, and the room suddenly turned red. Elliot couldn't tell from the lights what Maddie could be thinking.

"He told me I'd forgotten him. I haven't. I've thought about him more now than I ever have. I just wanted to think about something else for a change. Is that too much to ask?"

Elliot grasped Maddie's chin with his thumb and index finger, angling her face to look at him.

"You have a right to be happy," he said. "You went to his funeral, you've mourned over him, what more can you do?"

Maddie bowed her head and cried a bit more. Elliot rubbed her back while the water drained out of her eyes. When she finished, Elliot grabbed her hand and helped her up. She hugged him, his hand still in hers. It lasted a good ten seconds before they broke the apart.

"Let's find a way out of here," Elliot said. He might've enjoyed the maze if not for the little break down. In the end, it would work to his advantage.

But so what?

Elliot trusted himself not to leave her after having sex. He actually liked this girl, and everything that came with her.

Maddie sniffed. "Do you know where we're going?"

"No clue. I've never seen this place before, same as you."

They walked. After turning corner after corner, a bright light glowed at the end of a hallway. If Elliot weren't walking side by side with Maddie he'd swear he had died. A sense of relief cooled him as he picked up speed and ran with Maddie toward the exit. As they ran closer they saw their own reflections, but they were running too fast to avoid hitting the mirror. There was a loud crash, and they fell to the hard floor.

"Jerks!" Maddie cried, rubbing her forehead.

Elliot laughed, and when Maddie saw the bruise on Elliot's forehead she laughed too. They got up and found the correct exit, no reflection with it, and walked out of the maze. The ticket salesman was waiting near the exit to greet them.

"What took you so long?" he asked. "Most people finish in under ten minutes."

"We're tired, it took longer than we thought it would," Elliot said, as he and Maddie walked past him.

They stood together in an empty hallway. Six hours ago people would've been bumping into them while they rushed to return their sweaters.

They couldn't even find the way they came, but two corners away they found the food court, and a mall directory in front of it. At the far end of the food court were several glass doors leading to the outside.

"You've gotta be kidding me," Maddie said.

They walked across the food court and opened the heavy glass doors. There was a deck outlooking the lower level of the outside mall area. Only a few stores were outside, and most of their lights were off. A set of stairs ran down each side of the deck. At the bottom, between both of them, was a large marble fountain.

The lights that night reflected beautifully off every surface and Elliot almost thought Maddie would start crying again. He followed her down the right set of stairs and helped her search for his car.

"I think we're parked on the other side of the mall," Maddie said. She didn't look like she wanted to walk that far, but Elliot knew she didn't have a choice.

"I know tonight didn't go as planned," Elliot said. "But I think we deserve a second date."

Maddie inhaled deeply and did something Elliot suspected she wanted to do since they first met. She stood on her tip toes and kissed him. Her lips were dry, it'd been hours since she'd drank water, but she was too exhausted to care.

They took the long way, enjoying each other's company as they slowly walked around the mall.

By the time they made it to Elliot's car Maddie felt like she was being supported by two rubber sticks that were made to look like legs. When she sat down inside, the blood rushed back to her head and she could think.

She knew her mother was right. Usually she shouldn't talk to some guy she'd met by a mistakenly sent text, and almost always if something seems too good to be true, it probably is. But this time, in this one isolated incident, she was wrong. The cosmic planes were disrupted, reality blinked its eyes, and everything was all right.

Chapter 7

They were stopped in front of her house, the engine still running. It wasn't even close to midnight but they were too exhausted to keep going. Besides, Maddie had a feeling there would be many more dates to come.

She grabbed Elliot's defined cheek bones with both hands and brought his face closer to hers. Elliot resisted at first, purely out of surprise, but once their lips met he loosened up and let her finish. He grabbed her back with one hand and the nape of her neck with his other, helping her finish the show.

Maddie walked out and held the car door, ready to close it. "So I'll see you soon?"

"Definitely, I'll call you."

Maddie had heard that before, more times than she could count. Elliot's tone sounded different, it sounded genuine. He couldn't have used her because they hadn't had sex. It wasn't unheard of for Maddie to fuck her date on the first night out. As much as she wanted to see Elliot perform she wanted to look the best she could, tonight was not an example of that. Too many tears. Too much talking. What was important to Maddie was that Elliot was definitely *in*.

Maddie stopped at her front door and turned around. Elliot's car was gone. She didn't hear it drive away, it was just gone, like in a dream. She turned around and opened the door, slowly, so as not to wake her parents.

The first thing she noticed was her mom sitting on the family couch, the second thing she noticed was her dad stumbling to his room, a can of beer in his hand.

"You're home early," her mother said.

Maddie couldn't help but blush and smile at the same time. She was expecting her mom to say something about Elliot, that she liked him as much as she did.

"Well to be honest," Maddie said. "I kept thinking

about Marcus and I couldn't stop crying. I didn't think it was right to be hanging out when I was such a mess."

"Well I'd think Elliot wanted to be there for you."

"He did," Maddie said quickly. "But I didn't want him to see me like that. Don't worry though, I'll see him again."

Her mother crossed her legs and leaned back. "I bet you will."

The next morning Maddie prepared for school. The first thing she planned to do was tell her friends about Elliot. The night was so perfect she'd actually have to lie to make her story more believable. But there was nothing at school, nothing her jealous friends could say to change what happened.

She showered, brushed her teeth, grabbed her bag and went outside to wait for the school bus. No sense wasting gas. She didn't make it two steps out her front door, however, because a man a little older than her stood outside, waiting. He was holding a pen and clipboard. He reminded her of the people standing outside shopping malls asking for signatures to save the trees.

She didn't like him though. He didn't look like the usual door-to-door salesman. On his neck was a tattoo of a fire-breathing dragon, and dangling around his throat was a golden cross chain-necklace. For some reason it looked ironic on him.

"Whoa," he said. "Sorry to freak you out." He looked startled himself, yet he had a large, cocky smile plastered across his face.

Maddie couldn't shake the idea that the man was high as a kite and desperate for money.

"I don't have any money," she said. "And I'm on my way to school." She turned her gaze past him and tried to look for bystanders. To her dismay, there was no one outside but her and the man in front of her.

She thought about putting one leg back inside the house, but decided against it. What could he do? Even if he tried to grab her she could scream for help. Boy could she scream.

"That's cool," the man said. "Could I just get one moment to talk to you about— "

"I don't have any money!" she snapped.

Her voice was so loud he staggered back a few feet, almost dropping his clipboard.

"You bitch!" he yelled. "You don't even know what I want to talk about."

"Something to do with money, right? I don't have any money and you're going to make me miss the school bus."

His face regained its original cocky expression. "If you're late I can take you."

"I don't want you to take me, I'm taking the bus. Please get out of my way before I taser you."

Maddie, of course, didn't have a taser. The man stepped back and watched her hands cautiously, waiting for her to reach into her pockets. She did. But the man called her bluff and stood his ground.

"Seriously, I'll tase you." Maddie said shakily.

The man's smile turned sadistic. "Whatever you've got in your pockets I've got ten times worse in my car."

Maddie stood in her place, staring at the man. He didn't move, but he didn't break his gaze either. His smile stood on his face like a permanent fixture.

After a moment of silence, the man lunged forward and feinted. Maddie pushed him and, not expecting it, the man fell over. Maddie ran past him, screaming.

"Oh shit!" the man yelled.

He picked himself up and went to his car. He switched to reverse and backed up so quickly it made tire marks on the road. There were witnesses now, watching him as he drove off frantically. It was situations like these he was glad he had tinted windows. If only he had no license plates.

The man took his phone from his pocket and dialed Jasmine. He held the phone to his head as he sped away from the neighborhood, one hand on the steering wheel.

Jasmine answered on the second ring. "Hello?"

"Jasmine, you were wrong, the scam didn't work!"

"Why not?"

"I get to house number one, first fucking house, and she didn't even let me talk. She said she had a taser then she pushed me down and ran down the street screaming for help."

Jasmine was breathing heavily, like she was in the middle of an equally distressing situation. "What did you do then?"

"I ran back to my car and called you, the point of it is your scam doesn't work, no one wants to talk to people who look like me."

"Did you cover your tats? You're supposed to make them feel sorry for you."

"Well why don't you show me how it's done. Okay? Maybe it works for you but only cause you've got a pussy."

The man smiled to himself, expecting an angry retort — Jasmine took shit from no one.

"Yeah maybe you're right, I've got boobs on my side, first they get me out of a speeding ticket, then they help me scam dumb ass rich people."

The man knew she was right. He dug his nails deep into the leather steering wheel, leaving tiny indentations. He continued speeding until he reached the freeway, listening to Jasmine as she went on and on about how she'd scammed people. None of this information was useful to him, of course. He could never do what she did.

"—and that's where'd I'd start if I were you," Jasmine finished.

"Where are you right now? I'm picking you up."

"Corner of J and Oak Street, trying to get someone to buy me a pack of beer."

"All right, I can be there in twenty, you just sit your tight little ass right there and we'll pick up Jim and Michael."

"I don't like Michael, he never knows what to do."

"That's the point. He does whatever we want to do, no questions asked."

Jasmine knew exactly what kind of night he was referring to. She sighed heavily into the phone. "What *are* we going to do?"

"I'm not sure yet, just be ready for anything."

The man could hear Jasmine rifling through her handbag, looking for anything she might need for the night ahead.

"Okay," she said. "I'm waiting."

The man ended the call and proceeded to drive downtown.

When he came across shady alleyways and cut up cardboard boxes, that's when the man knew he was coming close to Jasmine. A stray dog limped onto the road and the man made no effort to avoid it. The dog didn't seem to react. It kept walking across the pavement, avoiding potholes with its limp legs. Its fur looked shaggy, even wet. The man felt sorry for anyone walking close enough to smell it. He was tempted to put it out of its misery but it had already crossed the road and disappeared into the bushes.

He was nearing a park. Large trees on the sides of the road casted their branches well over the streets. He drove under them, thinking that one day they'd fall and really cause some trouble.

When he came to the corner of J and Oak Street, Jasmine was waiting for him on the curb of the gas station behind it. She was sharing a cigarette with a rugged looking man wearing a beanie cap. The man pulled up next to her and rolled down his window, he made no eye contact with the man she was with.

"You ready?" he asked.

"I never got my six pack."

"I'll tell Jim to bring some beer, just get in the car."

"Then we'll have to share between four people."

"That's right, we will," he said, his ears turning hot. "You're not going to pay for it either way so what does it matter?"

"I wanted to get wasted."

He laughed. "That won't be a problem, I promise. By the end of the night you'll be so wasted you won't even remember drinking."

The man with the rugged beard got the hint he wasn't welcome and took off. Jasmine walked around the car and got in the passenger seat. The man started driving and merged with traffic.

"I know what you're thinking," he said. "Don't worry about your six pack, we'll have lots of that stuff tonight."

"Do you know where we're going?" Jasmine asked, crossing her arms defiantly.

"I told you, we're getting Jim and Michael, then we'll raise some hell."

Jasmine smiled. She liked the sound of that. She uncrossed her arms and rested her head on the window. Splattered remnants of the flies and gnats that somehow found a way to die on the side of the car, probably in a drifting incident.

"Do you know where they are?" she asked.

"Of course I do, I've been to their homes a thousand times."

"I mean from here. You know how to get there from here?"

"Downtown is like my home, I went to school around here."

The light in front of them turned yellow. The man accelerated, but it had already been yellow for a couple seconds.

"Connor slow down," Jasmine said mildly.

He kept accelerating and gave no answer to Jasmine.

"Connor slow down!"

The light was red as he cut through the intersection. Cars slowed down but didn't stop. He missed them by just a few feet. Three or four cars honked, he couldn't tell how many, they sounded too much alike, all honking at once.

A weak laugh escaped his throat and Jasmine slapped him across the face. For a moment the force made him drift into the next lane. He realigned the car and inhaled sharply.

"What the fuck!" he yelled.

Jasmine winced at his words. "Are you forgetting there's two people in this car!"

Connor didn't have a cogent response. He grunted and breathed heavily like he was trying to say something, maybe in a different language, and even struggling at that.

"You're just lucky there were no cameras," Jasmine said, her voice in a lower, stricter tone than before.

"You're just lucky I'm driving right now or I'd hit you back."

"What do you think would've happened if a cop would've seen you?" She didn't wait for him to answer. "You'd be screwed is what would've happened."

"Cops can't do shit. I can outdrive a cop. You ever seen their cars in a high-speed chase? They can barely break one-twenty, and that takes over half a minute."

"And this thing can do better?"

"It can go pretty fast from zero, and it drifts pretty good too."

Jasmine frantically bounced her knee up and down. She already wanted to leave. She'd risk a bus ride home rather than sit with Connor and listen to him talk about how cops aren't a real threat to him. She did like Jimmy though. Even with all the chaos and craziness the night would surely give, there was still Jimmy. He didn't belong in their group. He wasn't a run around robbing liquor stores type of person. Although someone had to talk to the cops, she supposed.

"Who's coming first?" she asked, trying to sound casual.

"Probably Jim. We're closer to him I think."

Jasmine smiled out the bug-stained window. Jimmy wouldn't yell at her. She'd be safe so long as he was with them. Michael was fine too, but he was mostly along for the ride, the thrill that tonight might go wrong and he'd be up shit creek without a paddle. He did anything Connor asked him to do, because Connor was as frightening as his tattoos said he was.

They pulled up to a run-down set of apartment buildings. At first glance they looked like the headquarters of an organized crime syndicate. Jasmine knew it was Michael's apartment complex because only someone like him could stand to live there.

Moss was growing from the cracks on the side of the buildings, and Jasmine would be damned if there weren't dozens of rats living inside the apartment's walls.... among other things.

Connor parked the car and called Michael. He answered almost immediately.

"What's up Connor?"

"You're coming out, I've got Jasmine with me and we're gonna pick Jim up next."

"What's the game plan?"

Connor paused for a moment. "We'll see what happens."

"Right on."

There was a dead silence in the car. The pressure was killing her, then she gave in. "I thought you said we were picking up Jimmy first?"

"I meant Michael."

Jasmine crossed her arms and stared out the window moodily. She gazed at Connor from the corner of her eyes to see if he was watching her, but he didn't seem to notice her mood, or care.

Michael walked out five minutes later. His hair was ruffled but he was wearing a striped collared shirt. He didn't look like one of the residents there. It was a miracle he'd never been mugged on the way inside of his own apartment building. He had a carefree smile as he ambled to the car.

"Get in the back," Connor said sternly to Jasmine.

"What?"

"Let Mikey sit in the front."

Jasmine shook her head, then her eyes drifted to the reddened knuckles on Connor's hand. They were no doubt a product of one of Connor's night fights.

She crawled over her leather seat and sat in the back middle seat. Michael opened the door.

"You didn't have to get in the back for me," he said.

Jasmine opened her mouth to talk but Connor was too quick.

"I told her to. I want you in the front seat tonight."

Michael looked bemused but excited. "Why? What's going on tonight?"

Connor laughed to himself, as if he was annoyed people kept asking him that question. "We'll just have to wait and see, won't we. But whatever it is, I want you in the front seat."

Jasmine felt an awkward tingling going down not just her own spine, but Michael's as well. An intuition of hers. Michael was as mentally as resistant to Connor's idea of a good night as she was, but he was willing to do anything he wanted, no questions asked. Jasmine, on the other hand, had questions to ask. Like —

"Are we doing anything that's going to get us arrested?" Michael asked, almost worriedly.

Connor laughed again, even harder this time. "You let me worry about us getting arrested."

Twenty minutes went by with mindless childlike banter between Michael and whatever Connor wanted to talk about.

At long last, they arrived at Jimmy's.

He still lived with his parents but he might as well be living alone. He wasn't sure when his parents were coming home or when they *were* home. They weren't drug addicts or child deserters, just the opposite. They were so busy working they hardly had time to check in.

When Jimmy stepped out of his house Jasmine opened the back door, her face warm and inviting.

"Michael, get in the back," Connor said.

"What?" Michael jerked his head to face Connor. His expression turned blank.

"I want Jim in the front."

Jimmy stopped halfway to the car, confused. He waited for them to figure it out.

Michael unbuckled and started to the back row. Jasmine pushed him back in a panic.

"What the hell is your problem?" Connor said to Jasmine.

"I wanna sit with Jimmy."

"*Jimmy*? Hell no, he's sitting up here with me."

"First you want me, then you want Michael, now Jimmy. I think you just want to control everything."

Connor unbuckled his seat belt and turned around completely. He looked at Jasmine warningly. He was in no mood to deal with her psychological evaluations. Jasmine's heart skipped a beat and her body felt like leaving itself.

"Let me…. tell you…." Connor said, his voice turning cold. "If I say Jim's sitting up front, next to me, then he is. If I say Michael's sitting with me…. he is. If I say you're sitting on the roof of the car — you are. Got it?"

Connor's deadly eyes made Jasmine feel naked, like she was getting a full body x-ray. She moved her neck just barely enough to create what couldn't be mistaken for anything but a nod of agreement. Connor turned back around and clicked in his seat belt.

After sensing the argument was over, Michael sat behind Conner. Jimmy replaced him, confused as to how he should act.

"Hey Connor," he said.

"Hey Jimmy?" Jasmine interjected.

Jimmy didn't move, almost like he didn't hear her.

Connor started the car and accelerated through the

residential streets, including their stop signs, and onto the freeway.

"I know you can't tell me about tonight," Jimmy said. "I understand that. But can you tell me what we're doing ten minutes from now?"

They were interrupted by the sound of a lighter. It was Michael, lighting a cigarette. Jasmine hadn't noticed it at first. Her attention was paid fully to the sight of Jimmy. Her eyes rolled sarcastically as she looked out the back passenger window, there were no fly guts back there.

Here we go again, she thought.

"You know the rules," Connor said. "If you're gonna light something up you've gotta hand one to me."

"Fine dammit," Michael said with the lit cigarette still in his mouth. He handed Connor the pack, regrettably, and Connor took out two, sneaking an extra one for later. Connor wrapped his lips around the cigarette and stowed the other in his pocket.

Then Connor put a raised a hand in the air. "Lighter."

Michael handed him the lighter and Connor lit the cigarette. A quick puff of smoke came from his mouth as he rolled down his window. Michael did not repeat his courtesy. The smoke from his mouth bounced off the back of Connor's headrest and drifted to Jasmine's nostrils. She coughed and waved a hand before her face, fanning the smoke away.

"Sorry," Michael said, rolling down his window. "Usually my friends don't cough when I smoke."

"Usually your friends smoke too," Jasmine said hoarsely.

Michael shrugged and blew out another cloud of smoke.

"Hey Jim, you want one?" Michael asked, his pack prepared on his lap.

"Ummmm...."

Just say no, Jasmine thought.

"Nah, I feel like we're going to be running tonight. Right Connor?"

Jasmine smiled to herself, as if Jimmy had somehow psychically picked up on what she was thinking.

"What makes you think that?" Connor said.

"Usually by the end of these things we end up running from someone. A cop, a security guard, a dog, a store owner."

"I resent that," Connor said, then nodded his head at Jasmine. "Jasmine, hit Jimmy for me."

She knew he was joking but the mere fact that Connor would ask such a thing, in front of Jimmy, made her want to give Connor a bloody nose. She sat idly, the wind from the open window took hold of her hair, only letting up when they stopped at occasional red lights.

Connor looked at Jasmine in the rear-view mirror. "No? Well, you hit me pretty bad a moment ago. Take it from me, the bitch can throw a punch."

"Come on Connor," whined Jimmy.

Jasmine's heart jumped in her chest. Something else happened. She couldn't tell because it happened so quickly but she swore her downstairs was tingling a little.

"I thought she's your friend," Jimmy continued, his voice was calm, yet at the same time defensive. "Is that how you talk to your friends."

"The bitch hit me while I was *driving*. Doesn't matter what I did, she hit me while I was behind the wheel. Bitch could've gotten us both killed. Now when I tell you that what word comes to mind?"

Jasmine knew Connor kept calling her a bitch not because he wanted to, but because he could test Jimmy's limits.

"Cunt," Jimmy said.

Everyone shared a laugh, even Jasmine. She knew his words were playful, unlike Connor's.

Jasmine's eyes switched between Connor and Jimmy, comparing them, sizing them up.

Who would win in a fight? she thought.

Connor had big arms, although Jasmine couldn't tell

how much of it was from fat or from muscle. Jimmy's arms were relatively small, but his shoulders were so broad they made an empty space on the sides of his shirt before his arms protruded. They were about the same size, but Jimmy looked like he might be half an inch taller, given that Connor was sporting an incredibly short military style haircut.

Then there was Michael. His scrawny arms, his frame a little on the short side. When he and Jasmine first met he wore glasses, though he'd since upgraded to contacts so he could better fit into the group. Without them, he was too blind to see clearly.

As they kept driving, Jasmine feared more and more what they might be doing. She filled her head with horrible scenarios of how the night would end, each worse than the last. Some of them involved her in a jail cell, others with her cold body lying in a ditch off the highway.

Stop it Jasmine, she thought. *Jimmy and Michael are with you, and if it gets to be too bad of a situation Jimmy'll put his foot down.*

"Something doesn't feel right," Connor said.

Jasmine and Michael looked at each other simultaneously. Neither one of them wanted to ask Connor a follow up question.

"This car's too empty," he continued. "I think we should get one more ass in this car."

"I'm not cramming myself," Michael said. "And if I am, I'm sure as hell not going to be the one siting in the middle."

"If it's a girl you're sitting in the middle," Connor replied.

They all knew who Connor was referring to. It was Amanda. She'd gotten a job about two weeks ago and didn't have time to screw around robbing liquor stores just for the hell of it. In fact, she was the only one of them to have a full-time job. She worked the drive thru at Steven's Vegan's, a vegetarian burger joint. Amanda herself wasn't vegan, but the pay was decent, and she got free food. Above all, it was far away from Connor and his type of people.

"Let's just leave her be," Jimmy suggested.

Connor accelerated, forcing a good scream from the engine before passing a car in the slow lane. He cut in front of them, slowing down to his original speed.

"Why's that?" Connor asked. A vein in his neck was bulging.

"Now Connor," Jimmy said calmly, placating him.

But his tone only made Connor's anger escalate to a point beyond reasoning.

"Yes, Jimmy."

Jasmine could feel the deranged softness of Connor's response, the quiet before the storm.

"There's a reason she hasn't seen us in a while," Jimmy continued. Then Jimmy moved his hands in a way that made it look like he was patting the air. "She's been stressed with her new job and I get the feeling she doesn't need tonight— "

"And I'm *not* stressed!" Connor howled. "She doesn't even know what stress is! *You* don't even know what stress is! We're picking up Amanda whether she wants it or not!"

What Jasmine feared most was that Amanda might actually want to see them. They'd all been longtime friends but she'd rather see Amanda do something useful with her life, rather than waste it with them.

They took the next off-ramp and turned right to travel the road for another ten miles.

Please run out of gas, Jasmine thought.

They didn't. And in half an hour they were pulling up to Steven's Vegans. Connor didn't need to guess if she was working. A full-time job is a full-time job.

Visible through the windows were all types of vegans, all the types of people Jasmine knew Connor hated. Perhaps the only out of place person there was an overweight man carrying a food tray with what Jasmine thought from her distance was a salad. He paid at the register and went to take a seat with only his own company. Jasmine half-expected Connor to drive the car through the glass doors and drag Amanda out by her ankles as she screamed and tried to hold onto the ground for dear life.

A big green sign greeted them as they approached the restaurant. It was the only vegan burger joint in town, no doubt, and Connor, or anyone of them for that matter, wouldn't be there for any other reason.

"You gonna ask when her shift ends?" Michael asked.

Connor didn't answer. He slowly drove to the curved line of the drive thru and stopped at the giant two-way intercom next to the giant green menu of vegan food. Most of the items on the list were vegan foods trying to disguise themselves as meat using some clever pun.

"Steven's Vegans, how can I get you?" said the lady voice on the intercom. They recognized it immediately as Amanda's.

Connor leaned out the window and cleared his throat. He spoke in an unrecognizable voice much deeper than his usual one. "Yeah, can I get a yamburger with curly fries?"

"Do you want to make that a large?" Amanda said back.

"No, the medium."

"That'll be six dollars and fifty-six cents, pull up to the second window."

They drove past the first vacant window and up to Amanda's. She stared at the computer register in front of her, already processing the next customer's order.

When Amanda saw them, she flinched anxiously, her microphone almost fell off her head.

"Connor?"

"Hello Amanda," he said playfully.

Her face went blank. It was obvious she knew he wasn't there to eat. "I'm not off work for another few hours."

"That's okay."

Connor unbuckled his seat belt, extended his body halfway out the window and lifted Amanda from under her armpits. Amanda screamed and giggled at the same time, while Connor struggled to bring her into the car.

She kicked, and soon stopped laughing, replacing her giggles with actual screams. Her blonde hair whipped erratically in every direction as she jerked her head in terror. Jasmine wanted to intervene, but she wanted more for Connor to leave her alone.

Before Connor dragged the rest of her into the car, Amanda hooked her feet around the open drive thru window, but Connor tugged her twice, and the grip of her feet gave in. One of the guys working in the back stared incredulously for a brief moment, trying to mentally evaluate the situation, then he threw his paper hat on the ground and ran over to try and start a tug-of-war with Connor.

Before he could make it to the window, Connor threw Amanda between Jimmy and himself, banging her head against the passenger door.

"Hey!" the employee yelled after them.

But Connor drove away, the tires screeching beneath them.

Jasmine was amazed that anyone could do such a thing.

Was he ever even a little bit normal? she wondered. *Maybe all this happened because his momma didn't hug him enough as a child.*

"Connor, what the fuck?" Amanda yelled.

Connor laughed and Amanda's face turned a deep red.

"Connor, if I don't get back there, *right now*, they're going to fire my ass!"

"Good," Connor chuckled. "Then you can get back to what's important."

"What's important?" Amanda's face turned even redder, if that was possible. "Robbing liquor stores?

Lighting dumpsters on fire? Is that what's important to you? If it is then I don't want any part of it!"

"We're a family," Connor said. "All of us." His words sounded broken, like the incipient of crying.

If Connor *did* cry it would be the first any of them had ever heard of it. Jasmine assumed his eyes were all dried up, no tear ducts at all. All his energy went to his angry outbursts and criminal lifestyle.

Every eye in the car was on Connor, including Amanda's from her uncomfortable lying down position. She stood up and started to the back row.

"You're sitting up here with me," Connor said.

"Fuck you," Amanda snapped, still climbing over the seats.

Connor grabbed Amanda by the loop in the back of her pants and flung her toward the front of the car. Her necklace rose into the air as she fell back and hit her head against the car radio. Jasmine cringed, and she looked at Michael, who was also cringing.

"Cool down Connor," Jimmy said. "You're going to really hurt her, then by the end of the day we'll be waiting together in an emergency room."

"She's fine," Connor said non-sympathetically. He checked Amanda, she hadn't yet opened her eyes. He nudged her shoulder. "Get up."

Amanda opened her eyes, but slowly, like a newborn baby.

"I'm not letting her sit up here with you," Jimmy said.

Connor sighed, finally admitting defeat.

Jasmine felt a slight sense of relief, of victory. She smiled at Amanda and made room as she took the middle seat.

"Is your head okay?" Jasmine asked.

Amanda rubbed it, checking the size of her lump. When her hand touched it her face tightened up a bit, and she quickly pulled her hand away.

"I'll be fine," she said timidly. She sat in between Jasmine and Michael and buckled herself in with her waist length seat belt.

"You want the window seat?" Jasmine asked. "You can lean your head on the window."

"I'll be fine. But how are you?"

How am I? she thought. *Not gonna lie, I'm doing pretty shitty but not half as bad as you.*

"I'm all right."

"I'm getting fired for sure," Amanda said weakly.

Jasmine's eyes turned to watch Connor, waiting for a reaction, but his attention was focused on the road, thank God.

"You're not getting fired," Jasmine said, then brought her voice to a whisper. "They got cameras there, right?"

"Yeah."

"Then they'll see this psycho kidnapping you, they'll have to give you a break."

The car came to a quick stop. Everyone jerked forward in their seats. Their seat belts were the only things keeping them from being thrown off their asses.

"Fuck!" Connor yelled.

Jasmine's heart skipped a beat. Did Connor hear her?

She turned her attention to a car almost stopped in front of them.

Connor struck the horn with his palm. The car made a deep, beeping honk. "Move it!"

Nothing.

Connor poked his head out the window and cupped his mouth with his non-steering hand. "Move your ass!"

Connor retracted his head back inside and swerved around the preceding car. As they passed they all got a look at the driver, who looked back at them. It was a man wearing suspenders and thick glasses that seemed to magnify his dead stare. Connor cut in front of him and decelerated to a crawling speed.

"You guys wanna fuck with this guy?" Connor said.

"Hell yea," Jimmy replied. Then silence. No one spoke with any objections. And so, Connor smiled.

The man tried to drive around them, but the road

merged into a single lane. Traffic was too heavy in the other direction to even think about trying to pass Connor. The man drove his car maybe five feet from the bumper of the car. It only made Connor laugh.

When the man honked the only thing he received was Connor's middle finger displayed out the open window.

After a while, the man turned to a different road and disappeared into a sea of cars. Connor's smile faded from his face.

They were doing fine though. If messing with other drivers and boxing them in was all Connor would be doing then Jasmine could live with that. But she doubted very much that he didn't have something else in mind.

They took two rights, then a left, and joined with Franklin Blvd, one of the main roads.

"Got anywhere in mind?" Michael asked, not expecting an answer.

Connor accelerated his car and crossed just barely in front of another car. The car behind them pulled to the right, barely dodging a streetlight, and crashed into a ditch.

Connor laughed in a sadistic manner and pulled into a large but vacant parking lot. Every face in the car turned pale except for Connor's, which was an engine red from his continued laughing.

No one else thought it was funny, but Michael's throat released a nervous, jolting laugh, which he couldn't seem to keep down. He closed his mouth but the nervous laughs kept rising from his throat.

Connor tried to stop laughing. However, Jimmy's serious gaze only made his laughter pick up again.

Tears were filling his eyes and streaming down his face when Jimmy started yelling.

"Fuck you Connor! What the hell's the matter with you?"

Connor threw his head back into his headrest and laughed even harder. He held his sides and rolled to face the open window so he couldn't look at Jimmy.

Good, Jasmine thought. *Let him choke on his own laughter. Wouldn't it be nice if suddenly he croaked over and we could all sleep well tonight?*

Connor swung his door open and fresh air rushed into his lungs. He nearly fell down, but held the steering wheel for support.

Jasmine considered opening her door and walking away. This was her best chance to leave.

No.

That would do more harm than good. He'd find her walking home and then there'd be hell to pay. She couldn't let that happen, she had to be smart.

"Why are we waiting here for someone to call us in?" she asked.

Connor sat up straight, regaining his composure. He waved a hand in Jasmine's direction.

"Shut—up," he breathed. His laughing had died down and his face was starting to turn to its usual color.

Jasmine slyly looked at Amanda's horrified face. She looked stunned, almost comatose. Michael had quit his nervous laughing and stuck a hand over his mouth to prevent it from returning.

Connor slammed his door and shifted the car back into drive. They took off around the parking lot and left at the far back exit. A small part of Jasmine hoped they'd get caught, even if it meant she was implicated, it might be best for everyone, especially Connor.

"Are you ever going to grow up?" Jimmy said. "Geez Connor you're like a child in a man's body, and that's a dangerous mix."

Like the driver Connor entangled with, Jimmy only received a finger in his face.

"Nice," Jimmy said. "That's a nice way to solve your problems. Is that what you're going to do to your future employer when he asks why you were late for work?"

"Oh, please," Connor said disdainfully. "If I ever get a job the only boss I'll have is myself."

"Oh really. What're you going to do? What skills do

you have? I'll make this easy by breaking it to you now, pissing off people is not a job, and robbing liquor stores is not a job."

"Jimmy, you're starting to sound like a rat."

Jimmy stared at him, completely unsure if what he was hearing was reality. Jasmine had never seen him look that way. As a matter of fact, none of them had. It seemed for a moment like Jimmy was about to grab Connor by the collar of his shirt and throw him out of his own moving car.

"Don't ever say that again you stupid fuck. Do you know how many times I've had to cover for you? Huh? Or has your insignificant two-dimensional mind blocked that out from all the drugs you do?"

"Whatever," he scoffed.

Jimmy's looked past Connor, his mouth dropped, and everyone turned their attention to the thing he was glaring at. It was a Ford Crown Victoria, the standard cop car. Everyone slowly sank into their seats and hid their faces. Jasmine caught a glimpse of the officer as he passed them. He had a radio in his hand, and was talking into it.

"Think they're looking for us?" Michael asked, to no one in particular.

"Nah," Connor said. "If they were they'd have pulled us over. I don't think the guy got a good look at us as he was crashing into that ditch." Connor didn't laugh again, but he was smiling crookedly.

"Connor," said Amanda's quiet voice from the back of the car. From the way she talked she sounded like she was further back than anyone else, like the trunk.

"Yeah," he replied.

"What would you have done if those cops were after us? Like they turned on their sirens and everything."

Without any thought Connor replied, "I'd have lost them in a back road or something."

"In a residential neighborhood you mean?" Jimmy said. "What about all the people walking around, getting their mail and stuff."

"That's their problem," he replied, with even less consideration than before.

Jasmine formed the word "wow" with her lips. Then she quickly checked to make sure Connor hadn't seen her.

They made more turns and ended up in a small neighborhood littered with stray dogs, dead ends, and barbed wire fences. They parked parallel to a park across the street, no one was there except for a stray dog lying under the shadow of a tree. It laid its chin on its front paws and its floppy ears folded on the ground.

The wind made the rusted swings shift back and forth, making squeaky noises they could hear from their car. They were years in need of maintenance.

"I got something fun for us to do," Connor said as he rolled down one of his sleeves, revealing something he had hidden. He pulled out a rolled-up joint then put it in his mouth.

"Lighter," he said, with his lips carefully holding the joint, his hand reaching out to Michael.

In seconds the lighter was in his hand and he lit the joint. A thick cloud of smoke came from his mouth.

Almost simultaneously, they rolled up the windows to keep the smoke from joining the outside air.

"Now were talking," Amanda said, reaching over Connor's headrest and pulling the joint from his hands. Connor made no move to resist her.

Amanda held the joint with her thumb and index finger, breathed a loud exhale then put the joint in her mouth and took a breath. Smoke came out her nose and mouth.

She passed the joint to Michael, who took a bigger breath than her, and he passed it Jasmine, who inhaled, then passed it to Jimmy. Jimmy took two small inhales and passed it back to Connor. By then the joint had been reduced to half of its former glory, and a faint glow protruded at the end of it.

"I know this place," Connor said.

"So what?" Jimmy retorted.

"I used to live here," Connor continued. "There's a kid who likes to play around this neighborhood, he's autistic. He's probably playing outside right now. I'll bet we could get him to come on a liquor store robbery with us. We could let him be our patsy." He took another draw from the joint.

Jasmine raised her voice with revulsion. "That's so messed up!"

"It'd be really easy," Connor pressed. "We could outrun him, no problem, we wouldn't even have to give him our real names."

Connor's face was almost hidden under the cloud of smoke.

"I'm in," Michael said.

Connor looked back. "Amanda?"

"Okay," she said flatly.

Jasmine opened her mouth, aghast. "If this is what we're doing then I'll have no part of it. I'd rather take my chances with the filthy city buses than sit here and be an accessory to your crimes."

Connor pointed to the door at Jasmine's side. "There's your exit. No one's stopping you. I'll even open the door if you want." His smiled occupied most of his face, it looked like the smile of someone who'd just been convicted of murder and was too desensitized to feel anything but sick satisfaction for the crimes they'd committed.

Jasmine opened the door, got out, and slammed it shut. Jimmy rolled down his window and called to Jasmine as she walked away.

"You don't want to walk alone out here. Just come back inside!"

Jasmine turned around. If it'd been anyone else calling her name she'd have kept walking.

She put a cautionary hand on his shoulder and looked importantly into his eyes. "Don't do this."

"I'll be fine," Jimmy said amiably.

Connor didn't waste time. He rolled up the tinted window and Jimmy's face turned to Jasmine's horrified reflection.

She watched them drive down the road, the car getting smaller until it escaped her vision completely.

Jimmy had an ominous feeling in the center of his stomach.

What if Jasmine had been right? he thought.

He looked over at Connor's reddened eyes. They made him look like devil. A small smile stuck to his face the entire drive.

They slowed down at a decrepit home that looked no different from the one's around it. Unfortunately, Jimmy knew that meant Connor had found his home.

The front door of the house suddenly opened and a surly faced boy walked out. His brown hair was unkempt and greasy, his face was round, and he had imperious eyes that looked like they belonged to someone much older than him. He left the door open behind him as he walked to their car and made no change in his expression when he noticed them, like he was expecting them to come.

Connor rolled down Jimmy's window, raised his eyebrows, and leaned to the open widow. "You looking for a ride, kid?"

"Anything to get me away from here," he replied angrily.

"Let the boy in," Connor said to Amanda.

She reached across Jasmine's formerly occupied seat and opened the door enough for the kid to grab it.

A haggard looking woman (who couldn't be mistaken for anything but the kid's mother) came rushing out in strides to accost her son. Her black hair was almost as dark as her eyes. Jimmy couldn't help sinking in his chair the same way he had when the police drove by.

"Jeremiah quit talking to strangers and get back

inside!" the woman yelled. And Jimmy's testicles retracted.

Jeremiah jumped into the car. He shut and locked the door an instant before his mother pulled on the door handle, futilely. She screamed and kicked the car door, causing a loud thud.

"Step on it!" Jeremiah yelled.

They took off just as the mother lifted her foot to try for another kick. When the car left her range, she kicked the air and fell onto her back.

"We did it!" Jeremiah yelled.

The mother stood back up and chased them to the corner of the road, then watched the car accelerate. Jimmy watched in the right-side mirror as she waved her arms balefully at them.

"Thanks guys," Jeremiah said as he buckled in. Jimmy didn't know why, but he was relieved for the kid.

"You looking to have some fun?" Connor said.

"I've only been in this car a minute and I'm already having more fun than I've ever had."

Jimmy already felt bad for what they were about to do to Jeremiah. He decided he couldn't let himself get too attached.

"What're your names?" Jeremiah asked.

"I'm Richie," Connor said. Then he pointed to Amanda with his thumb. "Back there's Katie, and next to her is Ted."

Jimmy checked to make sure Amanda had ditched her work name tag. She had.

"And up here is Jimmy," Connor continued.

Jimmy glared at Connor and flared his nostrils.

"Also," Jimmy said. "Sometimes we call Richie, Connor."

Connor visibly flexed his arms and tightened his grip on the steering wheel, but to Jimmy's surprise, said nothing.

"That's a weird nickname," Jeremiah said.

"Yeah," Jimmy replied. "We use it ironically because

we know it pisses him off. Reminds him of someone he doesn't want to be."

"Kid, do you want to make some money?" Connor asked abruptly.

"Of course I do. Doesn't everyone? Also, don't call me kid, I'm fourteen."

"Sorry, Jeremiah, is it?"

"Yeah."

"Jeremiah, me and my friends are picking up shipments of alcohol at a liquor store. We need you to keep an eye out for anyone who looks like they don't like that sort of thing. You dig?"

"I dig," he said fervently.

Jimmy suddenly turned around in his chair. Frightened, Jeremiah's eyes widened, and he inadvertently grasped Amanda's knee.

"Geez," Jimmy said. "Is life with your mom so bad you've got to get rides from strangers and follow them to liquor store robberies?"

Jeremiah, feeling abashed, loosened his hold of Amanda's knee.

Concerned that next time Jeremiah would grab something different of hers, Amanda crossed her arms and legs accordingly.

"He's not a kid," Connor said. "He's old enough to make his own decisions. If he wants to hang out with the big leagues, that's his own decision."

Jimmy raised his eyebrows. "Well?"

The kid sat silently for a moment, considering his answer. "I want to hang out with the big leagues."

Jimmy threw his hands halfway into the air, defeated. Connor, on the other hand, pumped his fist victoriously.

"That's my boy!" Connor yelled.

"Which liquor store?" Michael asked.

"We'll try the one off Fourth and Marconi."

"You want to do this downtown?" Amanda asked.

Connor didn't answer.

They parked on the side of the store.

"Who's driving the car away?" Michael asked.

"It's my car," Connor said. "So I'm driving."

"It's your heist though," Jimmy replied. "Don't you want to be upfront where the action is?"

Jeremiah looked at them both anxiously, unsure of what to do.

Connor turned the keys and pulled them from the starter. "Good point." He extended the keys to Amanda, she held an open hand to snatch them but he pulled his hand up and held them above her palm. "Can you drive stick?"

"Are you kidding? I've been driving stick before I was allowed to drive."

Connor dropped the keys into her hand, and she pocketed them. Then he turned to Jeremiah, who had the odd face of both nervousness and excitement.

"Do you know what your job is?" Connor asked.

"I'm lookout."

"You've just been promoted to supervising robber. It's a mix of burglar *and* lookout."

"Huh?"

"You're going to go in as our first line of defense, take as much liquor as you can and stuff it into your pants. No one will expect it 'cause you're a kid."

"It's a liquor store. Won't they be suspicious *because* I'm a kid."

Jimmy nodded in agreement, just outside Connor's peripheral vision. The kid's eyes fixed on him, then back to Connor.

"They sell other stuff too you know," Connor said. "Like lottery tickets."

"Oh."

The kid's eyes wandered back to Jimmy, hoping for some sort of advisement. It was obvious to Jimmy that he was a sort of lifeline. Before he could react Connor glared at him and his face turned flat.

"Does anyone have any weapons?" Michael asked. "In

case this goes south?"

"Nah," Connor answered. "We won't need them. By the time this guy knows what going on we'll be back here, starting to drive away."

Connor got out, followed by Michael, then Amanda. Jeremiah tried to leave but Jimmy reached back and closed his door from inside the car.

"What?" Jeremiah said.

"Don't trust Connor. He's planning on leaving you behind to take the fall."

"I can take care of myself," he said as he reopened his door.

Jimmy sighed. He didn't stop him from leaving again. Outside, they all congregated next to a nearby dumpster. Jimmy's sense of smell made him wish they'd chosen to meet someplace else, back inside the car, perhaps.

"Okay," Connor said. "Jeremiah, you go in first, act like you're looking around for stuff to buy." He considered his words, then continued. "Not alcohol though. Then me, Michael, and Jimmy will grab as much as we can before we run out. Only grab what you can when we start running. You got it?"

Jeremiah nodded.

"Good. When I yell run, that means…. you all run." He looked at Amanda. "You better be ready when we come out running."

Amanda walked to the car and got in the driver's seat.

Connor kneeled to Jeremiah's eye level and spoke to him condescendingly.

"Okay, Jeremiah. This is it. This is your chance to run with the big leagues. Don't fuck up, all right?"

Jeremiah smiled. "I got this."

Connor returned a smile. It almost looked genuine, like a real, human emotion. Jeremiah went inside and they followed him a minute later.

The cashier was already looking suspiciously at Jeremiah when they walked in. They all broke off in different directions. The cashier put one hand under the desk, possibly hovering a finger over the silent alarm.

Connor waved politely at the store camera. He knew very well that it had been out of commission for months. He'd gotten a tip about it when one of the store's former employees let him in on it. By now, the camera was just for show. Angry fired men are often the most informative.

Michael and Connor put their hands on the heavy liquor while Jimmy stuck with a twelve pack of the first beer he saw. Connor nodded at Michael, and Michael nodded back. Jimmy couldn't see what Jeremiah was doing, but whatever it was, it caught the cashier's attention. His eyes followed him throughout the aisles in whatever he was doing.

"Can I help you?" the cashier asked to Jeremiah.

"Just looking."

"How old are you?"

"Run!" Connor yelled.

Jimmy grabbed the twelve pack. It was heavier than he expected, and he had to swing it rather than carry it steadily. Jimmy was the closest to the door but somehow Connor ran past him. He was a fast runner, and had no doubt he could make it out the door before the cashier apprehended him.

But what about Michael? Or Jeremiah? He could hear the cashier scrambling wildly around the counter.

Oh God, what if he had a gun? That poor kid.

Amanda had the car started and waiting twenty feet from the store entrance. Connor had already opened the backseat door and was starting to open his own.

Jimmy ran and threw the twelve pack in the backseat. A moment later, he jumped in after it.

Michael dove into the car, leaving the door open behind him.

"Drive, dammit!" Connor screamed, his face turning red and his neck muscles pulsating.

Jimmy looked back at the store. Jeremiah had attempted to steal his own twelve pack but the cashier had him by the hair. He craned his neck and twisted around, swinging the twelve pack with him. He tried hitting the cashier with it but he kept a range far enough between him and the kid to dodge his swings.

Jeremiah dropped the pack on the cashier's toes, it was enough to make him recoil his feet, even yell a little. But he kept his grip.

"I said drive bitch!"

The car took off with enough force to make the back door close. A couple cars swerved to accommodate them joining with traffic.

"Slow down or they'll know we did something wrong!" Jimmy said.

"How much we get?" Amanda asked, looking at the backseats to answer her own question.

"We got enough, eyes on the road," Jimmy replied.

She looked back. The streets were the same as they ever were, except Jimmy felt differently about them. He was a part of them, no longer intertwined with the sweet suburban life he'd grown up in.

Two blocks down a police station stood at the corner. Time slowed down for Jimmy as Amanda drove more legally than she usually did.

Connor silently counted the alcohol, pointing a finger at each container. "That's one twelve pack, a forty of vodka, rum, and tequila."

"Was it worth it?" Jimmy asked sullenly.

"Hell yeah it was worth it!" Connor said, without hesitation.

"And the kid? Was it worth it for him?"

Connor's sardonic grin left his face, leaving only a small trace behind. "Hey, you heard him. He's a big kid, it's his fault for not being fast enough."

Jimmy gazed at the twelve pack he'd stolen. His mind faded back to the sight of Jeremiah swinging his own twelve pack, not quite keeping up with the rest of them. The cashier grabbing him by the tousled hair on his head, the satisfied yet enraged look on his face when he caught him.

Jimmy added his own visions to the memory. Jeremiah was screaming, "Come on guys, come back! I trusted youuuuuuu!"

Stupid kid, he thought. *All he had to do was say no, take his word, and get out.*

He shook himself from his train of thoughts.

"You guys know what goes good with liquor?" Connor asked.

"Drugs," Michael answered. "Lots of drugs."

"Sounds good," Jimmy agreed. He could use something to get his mind off Jeremiah, something other than the alcohol he'd stolen *with* him.

"Where am I driving to?" Amanda asked, her eyes still wisely on the road.

"The Castle," Connor suggested timidly. Everyone but Connor groaned simultaneously.

The Castle was the best place in town to buy drugs. It was also very sketchy, and even undercover cops didn't like to be there. Something in the air made it feel like you had a fifty-fifty chance of getting shot just for giving someone the wrong look.

"I don't even know how to get there," Amanda whined. "*And,* I heard the cops busted that place a month ago, so there's nothing left there anyway."

"It's not busted," Connor said. "If it were they'd have found a new one, and you'd better believe I'd hear something about it."

Jimmy shook his head at Connor's arrogance. He wasn't lying, though. He listened to the streets everyday as if they were his schoolteachers. Not like he ever listened to a word *they* said though.

The light in front of them turned yellow, then to red almost immediately. They were one car from the front of the line.

"Come on, you could've gone!" Connor screamed as he leaned over and honked the horn. He was, of course, the only one upset about the situation.

The driver rolled down his window and gave Connor a very animated middle finger, which he waved back and forth without worry.

Jimmy laughed. "Hey Connor, how does it feel to be on the receiving end?"

"He wouldn't be waving that finger if I cut it off of him. He'd be spending the rest of the night in an emergency room instead of making people wait behind him in traffic."

"You know you're going to die of a stroke before we even get to Castle," Amanda said.

"I thought you didn't know how to drive there?"

"I lied, but I really did think the police shut it down."

"Who has money anyways?" Michael asked.

Jimmy started for his wallet, but Connor quickly halted him.

"We don't need money," he said. "We could probably make a trade with all the stuff we got."

"We're keeping the rum," Amanda said. "If I'm getting fired, I might as well get drunk off my ass."

They parked by the Castle, three blocks down just to be safe. It certainly didn't look like a castle with its boarded-up windows, along with its scratched and faded paint. In fact, it looked like it might collapse from years' worth of dry rot and termite residency.

"Okay," Connor said, holding a bottle of tequila in one hand and a bottle of vodka in the other. "We'll try trading the booze, and if that's not enough we'll throw in whatever we have in our wallets."

"Fine," Jimmy said.

They left.

The sun was leaving their town and Jimmy had the feeling if he didn't get out by nightfall he'd be trapped forever in some drug dealer's basement.

There was a waist high gate guarding the front yard. It seemed to have no purpose, much like everything inside the house.

It opened to them with a slight push.

The derelict lawn was a vomit yellow color and even the trees looked sickly. In addition, each stone step leading up to the house had deep cracks in them.

If you look closely, you can see one of them leads to hell, Jimmy thought.

They stood face to face with the front door, waiting for something to happen. But they weren't sure what.

"Should we knock?" Michael asked.

Connor laughed. "Yeah, and say what, exactly? 'Oh hey, we're here to buy some drugs.'"

They waited for a moment. They could hear voices coming from inside the house, although they couldn't put a face to their voices. Druggies aged like dogs, they knew that. The people inside could either be a rough twenty-eight or a good forty-year-old — only one way to find out.

Jimmy opened the door and noise rushed onto their faces. People of all shapes and sizes were walking around the house. Only a few stopped what they were doing to notice them, and that was because they were close to the door.

The walls were covered in olive green wallpaper with little pink flowers littered throughout them. Every ten or so feet the wallpaper was torn, only surviving by hanging from an inch of itself left on the wall.

A man with a sallow complexion sat by the staircase, almost lying down completely. He turned his face and looked at them, bemused. Foam dripped from his mouth and onto his dark green shirt that almost matched the wallpaper. Jimmy didn't think he knew where he was. Gurgling noises escaped the man's mouth as foam continued to seep from it.

A man got up from a dusty couch lying in the corner of the living room (dying room?) and walked toward them. His stomach was so large it went beyond his arm's reach. Compared to Connor, this man was colossal. Suddenly, Jimmy found a new person to be afraid of.

"What do you want?" he said, not bending his fat neck to see them.

Connor cleared his throat. He spoke in a deeper, more intimidating tone than he normally did. "We're trying to score some stuff."

The man rubbed his nose and sniffed. "Stuff?"

"You know," Michael said. "Uppers, downers, all arounders — stuff."

The big man laughed, his shoulders bounced up and down. He looked like he was one big meal away from a heart attack. Still, Jimmy didn't want to be that last meal.

"We gotcha covered." He turned around, almost hitting a bystander with his enormous stomach. "Hey, Ricky!"

"Yeah!" replied an unseen voice somewhere in the back of the house.

"What uh…. stuff, we got left?"

A moment's silence, and then, "Lemme check!"

The man turned back around. "He's checkin'."

Jimmy nodded slightly. He looked back at the entrance. Someone had already closed the door behind them. He hadn't even realized how far they'd walked inside. This house plays tricks on you, he guessed.

The awkward waiting gave Jimmy time to observe his surroundings. The ground was scattered with used needles. Several people walking around were barefoot and didn't look like they were all too careful about their foot maneuvering.

The voice finally answered back. "We got coke, weed, acid, crank, speed, heroin, X, and some random pills — oxycontin, I think."

"How much for the oxycontin?" Connor asked, his voice small and barely audible.

The large man turned around and yelled back, "How much for the oxycontin?"

An older man holding a bottle of pills walked from around a corner and into the entrance room. He was, undoubtedly, the unseen voice from the back of the house. "Five a pill. It's high-grade stuff though, fucks you up."

Michael looked at Jimmy and raised his eyebrows, asking for approval.

Connor didn't wait for anyone to reply. "We'll take them. And we've got alcohol to trade for it."

Before the man could answer a freckled face girl cut past them and put a hand on the wall nearest the front door. She held her side like she was holding in her own intestines. Her face turned pale and her cheeks expanded. They all knew what she was about to do....

Vomit spewed from her mouth and onto the carpet, staining it a disgusting beige color. None of them could tell for sure just how many drugs were being spilled onto the carpet, they could only imagine.

The older man dropped the bottle of pills on the floor and wrapped his arms around the girl. Her, not expecting this, threw up once more, this time projecting it on the already dismal wallpaper.

Her head drooped and she let her legs dangle as the man carried her to the dark trenches of the house.

"We have a sink!" he yelled, as he carried away the half-conscious girl out of sight.

The large man coughed and rubbed his nose again.

"We have alcohol," Connor repeated, raising his two bottles.

"Shit, we don't need more of that. We got plenty of that stuff."

Connor timidly lowered the bottles. The older man came back, his face twisted like he'd just taken out a pungent bag of garbage.

"Shit. I swear man, these fucking tweaker chicks." He spun around in circles, searching the floor for the bottle of pills. "Did these kids take the pills?"

Jimmy's heart jolted. It was stupid of them to think they could barter with these lowlifes.

"Nah," the large man answered. "I've been watching them the whole time."

"Well then where's the fucking pills?" he asked. And when he said *fucking* his voice cracked like a teen going through puberty. Jimmy tried not to laugh.

Michael pointed to the lonely pill bottle sitting by a broken lamp on the floor. The older man looked at him, then picked up the pills and stashed them in his pocket.

"So you need any alcohol?" Connor asked, an inflection of hope in his voice.

"We could always use more alcohol," the older man replied. "You can never have enough of that stuff." His eyes gazed at the bottles. The labels were pointed away from him. "What you got there?"

"Some tequila and vodka," Michael answered impatiently.

"I told them we had enough of that," the large man said.

The older man turned to the large man in disbelief, turning his back on Connor and his friends. "Why the hell did you tell them that?"

"'Cause we do."

He grabbed the bottles from Connor's grasp. "These two I'll hide in my personal stash, keep them away from all these tweaker chicks. I'll trade you what's left in the bottle for your two bottles."

"How much is left?" Michael asked.

The old man put down the liquor and pulled out the pill bottle. He twisted the cap and opened it with a loud popping noise. A couple pills flew out but Connor caught them and handed them back.

"About half a bottle," the older man said, dropping the pills Connor caught into the bottle.

Jimmy raised his eyebrows and the older man caught a glimpse of it.

"But," he said. "It was a pretty full bottle when we got it, lots of pills."

"Uh, yeah, sounds good," Connor said. They made the trade. Jimmy peered over Connor's shoulder and into the bottle. There was a fair amount left, but not a good trade for two forty-ounce bottles, not even close. However, Jimmy got the impression they were lucky not to have been robbed.

Connor tapped the open bottle on his palm and three pills dropped onto it. He turned to Jimmy and Michael, offering them each a piece of their share. They took one each.

"Bottoms up," Connor said, throwing his head back and swallowing the pill dry. Jimmy and Michael followed in his action.

The older man had already walked off, carrying the two bottles by his sides.

Connor fist bumped the large man still standing close, and they walked off. Before the door closed behind them, they could hear glass shattering, followed by more yelling.

They fast-walked together and effortlessly pushed open the small gate guarding the front yard. Amanda was waiting for them with the engine running and the car parked with one tire on the sidewalk.

They couldn't seem to get inside fast enough.

"Let's get the fuck out of here," Connor said hurriedly, as he entered the car.

Amanda switched to reverse. "I knew you'd say that."

"Isn't there a better place to score some drugs?" Michael said.

"All right," Connor moaned. "We won't go back there you pussies." Connor made it sound more of a favor to Michael than an admission of his own fear of returning.

The night went on. They were somewhere downtown, searching for a place to pass out. Most of the streetlights were either broken or flickering, but they didn't care, they were the most dangerous things on the street.

"Are we picking up Jasmine again?" Jimmy asked, trying to sound casual.

"Hell no, she can go fuck herself," Connor said. "I'm not sharing my pills for a bitch that wouldn't even rob the liquor store with us."

"Can you blame her?"

"It's not my fault she thinks she's too good for us."

"Nothing's ever your fault, is it?"

"You got that right."

"Hang on," Amanda said bracingly. She hit the accelerator and passed a Ford Truck.

"Where are we going?" Michael asked. No one replied, he asked again. "Where—are—we—going?"

"To find a nice empty parking lot somewhere," Amanda replied.

Jimmy could barely keep his eyes open. The pills were taking effect. His body was numb from head to toe.

He felt about as tired as Michael looked, but he didn't want to retire, not with Connor in the car. If he fell asleep now, he might wake up somewhere on the side of the road. His head melted into the headrest as he leaned back into his seat.

He looked over at Connor, who seemed to be lost in thought, as helpless as he ever was, looking like a child. Jimmy could swear there was a half-smile on his face. He wondered what he thought about that made him look so exuberant. Beating up kids, probably.

And then he remembered Jeremiah.

He'll be fine, he thought. *They'll go easy on him. He's just a kid.*

"I think I found a spot," Amanda said. She slowed and turned into a large parking lot. There were cars still parked, but only a handful.

"Are we sleeping here?" Michael yawned. "I don't think I can make it."

Connor didn't answer. He was in a twilight state of consciousness, nodding off to sleep. Jimmy liked him this way, drugged to the point of harmlessness.

"You look like you could use a few more pills," Jimmy said to Connor.

"I—uh, wha?" he said.

Jimmy laughed. He could tell Connor wanted to hit

him, but he couldn't gather the strength to do it.

"Can I get one of those pills?" Amanda asked, parking the car.

Connor closed his eyes and breathed heavily. Amanda searched Connor with her eyes, but found no pills.

"Fuck this, I'm going out smoking," she said, as she opened the door, removing the keys and taking them with her.

Jimmy wished he'd told her to leave the heater on. Then he imagined Connor taking the wheel and trying to drive. There was no reality where that wouldn't end in disaster.

Jimmy stepped out to join her. A cigarette might keep him awake, if nothing else. His footsteps were a disarray of hopeless stumbling. Stepping on the pavement felt like being barefoot on an ice rink. Then he remembered the miserable bastards he'd seen at the Castle.

To make things worse, the cold night air shook him even more. He tapped Amanda on the shoulder.

Startled, she flinched and screamed, like she'd seen a dangerous wild animal. Her cigarette fell from her mouth and her lighter flew into the darkness of the air. She put a hand over her chest, checking her heart rate.

"You scared the hell out of me!" she said.

"I—I sorry, I jus wanted a cigarette."

She laughed at his incoherent babble. "Here," she said, handing him one from her pocket.

He looked better to her. Maybe it was the shadows hiding his worst features. Maybe it was the way he was acting lately, she couldn't tell. At that moment she felt the urge to kiss him. But her mind told her to get him to do it, make him think it was what *he* wanted.

She bowed her head slightly and simpered. Then she crossed her arms behind her back and swayed back and forth in a girlish sort of way.

"So," she said. "Just you and me."

Jimmy gazed in both directions to confirm this was true. Connor and Michael were lying back in their seats, their eyes shut. He turned back to face her. Then suddenly, Jimmy's face brightened a little. A soft glow was showing from behind the U-Mart.

"Come on," Amanda said, picking up her lighter and walking toward the source of the light. A voice in her head told her it might be trouble. Then another voice told her Jimmy could fight off whatever it might be.

They reached the source of light. Three homeless men were huddled around a trashcan fire, their palms facing the flames. The one in the middle looked at them, his sullen eyes shining from the fire. The other two looked when they saw him gazing at the newly arrived trespassers.

"You kid's got some change?" the middle one asked.

"Uh, sure," Amanda said. She didn't want to lie. She didn't believe she *could* lie.

She pulled out her wallet and counted three dollars, one for each of them. They took it without thanks.

"Mind if we warm up with you?" Jimmy asked.

"You mean you don't have a warm place to go?" The left one asked.

"We do," Amanda said. "We don't like the people there, we'd rather be with you."

The middle one smiled, it was visible, even through his thick beard.

"Sure," he said. "Get closer, we don't bite."

As Jimmy and Amanda drew closer, the facial features of the homeless became more apparent. All three of them had beards of some level. The middle one's was by far the thickest. He had a bulbous nose and cracks along his face, mid-sixties at least. The man on the right was wearing a camouflage military uniform, though Amanda doubted he served any time, just like Connor never served despite his military haircut. His hair was long, brown, maybe black. It was too difficult to tell in the darkness. The man on the left was the skinniest, his nose was long and pointy. It was easy to tell him apart from his friends since his arms had sleeves of tattoos.

"You guys have smokes?" the middle one asked.

"What?" Jimmy said.

"I smell cigarettes on ya."

"Oh, yeah, but they're not mine."

The middle one frowned. He held his palms out before him, facing the fire. The left one rubbed his hands together, hoping to get enough friction to warm them.

"They're mine," Amanda said, digging into her pocket. "And you can have one."

She took out a cigarette from the pack and handed him one. He held it close to the flames in front of him and it lit.

"I have a lighter," Amanda said. "I'd have let you borrow it too."

"I have the biggest lighter in the whole world right here," he replied, pointing to the fire. He smiled at Amanda. She smiled back, embarrassed by the fact that a homeless man was making her blush.

"How'd you guys end up here on this fine evening?" Jimmy asked.

Amanda's stomach growled in pain. It was churning in anticipation of having to listen to one of their sob stories.

"We don't live here," the middle one said. "I sleep in a shelter and when they tell me my free time is up I'll move to the next one."

"No, I mean how'd you end up homeless?" Jimmy said.

None of them spoke. Amanda thought Jimmy had gone too far. What if they had PTSD? What if one of them had a war flashback and threw them into the fire? What if—

"I was a veteran," said the one in camouflage.

Amanda finished her cigarette and flicked it into the open fire. The flames enlarged, swallowing the cigarette, then shrunk down to its original size.

"After I quit," he continued. "On account of my arthritis, there was nowhere left for me to go. It was all I knew. My unemployment dried up and I was out on the street, begging for money."

"You didn't get another job?" Jimmy asked.

The man stared into the flames. The glow reflected the sadness from his eyes. "It was all I knew."

Jimmy looked at the middle one. "And what about you?" he said scathingly. "How come you're on the street?"

"I don't have to tell you anything," he growled.

"We gave you money. The least you could do is humor us with a quick story. Nothing too personal, just a brief explanation."

"*You* didn't give us anything," he said, then pointed to Amanda with his still lit cigarette. "She did."

"Where do you think she gets her money?" Jimmy lied.

The middle one sighed. "My wife divorced me, took half my shit…. I got depressed…. started drinking…. lost my job…. wound up here."

Jimmy's smiled, apparently satisfied. His eyes turned to the last man. His legs were shaking uncontrollably, possibly from the cold, or possibly of the fear that Jimmy would ask him.

"And you?"

In addition to shaking legs, his tattooed arms started shaking. "I can't remember a time when I wasn't living on the street. I've been going from city to city doing odd jobs, begging on the street. I ran away when I was just a kid…." He took a moment to regain his composure, then continued. "My daddy hit me and my momma when I was young, so I ran from home and I've been moving on ever since. I never stay in one place for too long."

There was an eerie silence after that. Amanda bet Jimmy regretted his question.

She looked at him. He had a weirdly satisfied look on his face.

"Thanks," he said.

"For what?" the last man asked.

Jimmy stood in silence, as if he was considering his next words thoughtfully. "For giving me perspective."

Amanda knew Jimmy better than to think he did it just to get perspective. She figured he did it to make himself feel better about his own life. And she was fine with that. Despite the tension being high between them, her mood was strangely better.

After a long silence Amanda knew there wasn't much left to talk about. She said goodbye and the middle one walked around the trash fire to offer her a greasy handshake. She took it, reluctantly, then walked off and disappeared into the darkness with Jimmy.

Chapter 8

The middle one watched the girl and her presumable boyfriend as they walked out of sight. Off they were, to a dark silhouette of what looked like a nice warm car. He walked back to the fire to join his "friends". If he fell asleep next to them and didn't wake up with what few belongings he owned stolen from him *then* he'd know they were his friends.

He pulled down his beanie cap to better cover his ears and addressed his camouflage wearing "friend".

"About how long do you think the fire will last?"

The man wearing camouflage blew an uncertain exhaled and shook his head. "Don't know, maybe another hour, hour and a half, tops."

His hand burned intensely, he waved it around to cool it off, then looked down and saw the withered remains of his cigarette. He'd completely forgotten he had it.

Wait!

What if it caught fire to his beanie when he adjusted it?

He felt frantically around his beanie cap. There was no heat coming from it, only the cold night air left on it.

"Geez," said the tattooed one. "I thought that kid was gonna ask me if I'd ever sucked dick for money."

They all laughed. The middle one laughed so hard he coughed, and his throat burned worse than when he smoked the cigarette.

"You—guys know—where there's a liquor store— around here?" asked the middle one, his words stuck in between his coughs.

"If you look on K Street," said the one in camouflage. "I think there's one down there someplace."

"Oh," he bowed his head in disappointment, then raised it again. "Do any of you got liquor?"

"No," said the tattooed one. "I don't even have

enough money to feed my goddamn dog, wherever he is." He looked around tentatively, as if the dog could be right behind him.

The middle one coughed into his hand and bent over from the pain it caused him.

The night was quiet, more so than usual. Normally there'd be at least a car go by, and in Los Angeles, that was not uncommon, even in the later hours. Hell, there could be a traffic jam at three in the morning and he wouldn't think twice about it.

The middle one walked along a sidewalk, talking to himself with his head so far down he could see only his own footsteps.

"Gonna get me some liquor," he muttered.

He looked up. Four dark figures approached him.

"Hey man," one of them said in a fake upbeat tone. "We're selling magazine subscriptions for my kid's baseball team. You wanna buy one?"

They were kids. Well, teenagers technically.

"Is this a joke? I'm fucking homeless. I don't give a damn about no baseball team." He tried moving past them, but they moved together in a diamond military formation.

"Yeah, it's a joke. Ha-ha." He wasn't smiling.

A pain grew in the homeless man's stomach. He wished he were back at the fire, safe from teenaged druggies.

He took a step back and tripped over something. It was a kid with his leg was extended in a tripping position. He couldn't see his face, only his spiked hair towering over him.

The next thing he saw was the bottom of his shoe. It struck him repeatedly in the forehead and he could feel the gang of teens crowd around him to steal what little he had.

He twisted and turned on the ground, trying to protect his face and privates. They searched through the many pockets of his coat, then his jeans. He made no attempt to resist. It would only make it worse, he was sure of that. He'd been in this situation not too long ago.

Not the beanie, please don't take the beanie, he thought. *You can take anything else, just leave the beanie. It's so damn cold.*

He rolled onto his stomach and wrapped his hands around his ears, squeezing his beanie tight around his head. The kicking stopped; the kid's footsteps trailed off into the night. One of them tugged on his beanie, trying to pull it off, but he was resilient. The kid gave him one more kick to the back of the head then ran off to join the others.

"I got his watch," said one of them. It was the spike haired kid. He was dangling it before his face, observing it from the brightness of the streetlights.

"You think the pawn shop will think it's stolen?" asked the leader of them.

"Doesn't matter," answered spiked hair. "These bums never report when stuff goes missing."

"I almost got his beanie. The poor bastard held on tight, I let him keep it."

"That doesn't sound like you," replied spiked hair.

The leader shrugged. He thought about taking out his shades and putting them on, they'd cover his battle wounds nicely. On the other hand, they'd be too conspicuous. He thought better of it and walked ahead of his pack — lone wolf style.

"Hey Butch?" yelled a heavily tattooed kid to the leader of the group.

"Hey Casey," he yelled back.

"Whatchu get from him?"

"Jack shit. A better question is, what did *you* get from him?"

"I got his wallet," he yelled back, feeling for the lump of the wallet in his pants. "There wasn't much in it though, I already checked."

They walked on, shouting to one another, completely disregarded the time of night. No one was dumb enough to call the cops on them.

It was common knowledge that gangs ran loose around their neighborhood. The way they saw it, if you were out past midnight, and you got mugged, it was your own damn fault.

Butch dragged his feet across the pavement, trying to scrape the blood off his shoes. He turned around, walking backwards, still ahead of the group. "Speaking of dumb, beaten-up bitches, how's Megan doing?"

"Better now since she dropped your sorry ass," laughed the spiked hair kid.

Butch led them to a poorly maintained building that looked like a halfway house. When they walked inside, the guard dog (a well-built Doberman Pinscher who'd been lying patiently on the hardwood floor) lifted its head in alert, peered at them, then lowered its head back to the floor.

They each walked past him. Casey momentarily brushed its head as he walked by. Then he put his new belongings onto the kitchen table with the rest of his gang. From the homeless man they'd acquired a watch, a wallet with no more than twenty dollars (twenty-five if you count coupons), a broken tooth brush that sort of looked like a shank, and a half-empty pack of gum.

"What do you think this it all worth?" Casey asked to the group at large.

"Jack shit is what it's worth," Butch answered, banging his fists onto the table, making the objects jump slightly into the air.

"That's it?" said spiked hair. "I thought there would be more."

"The guy's fucking homeless. What'd you expect?" Butch snarled, removing his bruised fists from the table and rubbing them. "Still, better than nothing. The homeless do make the best victims — no one cares about them, and they rarely file police reports."

Footsteps thumped down the staircase. They made hollow thuds as they touched the floor. Everyone in the room froze. It was their "dad", Mr. Fox, or as they called him, Fox, on account of his red hair. They knew he was expecting a much bigger haul tonight.

"What do we have today gentlemen?" Fox asked, rubbing his hands together and sounding relatively more pleased than usual.

No one wanted to speak. Fox looked at Butch, expecting the leader to say something, then finally, Fox's stare broke through him.

"What you see is what you get," Butch replied. "It was a tough night, only one bum."

Fox peered at the items before him, frowning. The only thing he seemed interested in was the wallet. He picked it up and rifled through it, then threw it back on the table.

"Trash! This is all trash!"

Everyone tensed up, Casey and Martin (the spiked haired kid next to him) raised their shoulders in terror. Then Fox took a deep breath and closed his eyes. When he opened them again, they were all still afraid.

"Is the wallet real leather?" he asked calmly.

"I think so," Butch said. "But that's really something the pawn shop owner would know. He had coupons in there too."

Fox looked at Butch like he was as insignificant as an ant under his shoe, a look Butch had never seen before.

"Coupons? Fucking coupons? Have you ever seen me, even once, use a *fucking* coupon?"

Butch looked down.

Red and blue lights pierced through the window shutters. Everyone rushed to the window and separated the individual shutters an inch to see the outside. A siren turned on but the sound was traveling away from them.

Butch exhaled, the tension in his muscles softened. He stepped back and fell onto a couch. Casey joined him.

"That'll be for us one day," Fox said sullenly, walking out of the room.

I'll be long gone before then, Butch thought.

The siren and flashing lights died down completely. Butch closed his eyes. He could still see their colors glowing in the night. However, that might've been a memory from his childhood, he couldn't tell.

Butch retired for the night. He planned a full day tomorrow, and when you're the semi-leader of a street gang, that means a lot.

He walked into his bedroom. Stains had been left on the walls and floor from whoever last lived there. His bed was less than a foot off the ground and had metal posts that looked better suited in a military base. It didn't look like a bed at all actually. He always slept with a pillow under his head and a pillow over his head to drown out the inevitable noises made at four in the morning.

He was in an open street. No cars, no noise, just him. He looked around for his "brothers", none of them were there.

A foul smell emerged from around the street corner. He fell to his knees and held his nostrils closed. The smell was so awful it made his eyes fill with water, and he had to squint them to see properly.

Around the corner came the source of the smell. It appeared to be an army of homeless men, and they were closing in. They held no weapons but outnumbered him two hundred to one.

He rose from his knees and started to run away, but the same image came from the other direction. He ran towards the park next to him, then halted abruptly. It was overrun by homeless as well.

He balled his fists and shouted, "What do you want?"

"We want our stuff back, all of us," answered someone from deep within the crowd. A cheering roared throughout the mass of people.

"You'll have to go to the pawn shops then. That's where we sold it to."

They came even closer, marching to him with the organization of army ants. Their ragged faces and bushy beards became clearer as they approached him. They stopped looking like blurry figures and more like people.

"We don't have healthcare," one of them said. "Real hard to go to a hospital with a broken ankle when you can't even afford a place to sleep."

Some of the faces he recognized. He'd robbed them. Only now he didn't have his "family" to back him up.

"What do you want from me?" he said again. "I don't have much either. The only reason I don't sleep on the streets is because I do something about it."

"I used to have a place to sleep before I lost my mind in Vietnam!" one of them shouted. He was wearing his old military uniform, minus the hat. He had a cardboard begging sign he tricked to hang around his neck with string.

They collectively stepped closer toward him. Butch fell to the ground, his hands clasped over his face like they'd once done to protect themselves.

"Don't touch me you filthy animals!"

They grabbed his shoes and started pulling them off. Butch scream uselessly and kicked at their faces, he could feel he hit a couple, but they overtook him. Before he knew what was happening next, he was looking at the inside of his shirt as they pulled it off. His socks came off next, then his pants. He lied on the street, naked, with dozens of feet flying at his face.

People from the outer edges of the crowd were budging their way through to get their share of the beat-down. A coolness ran down Butch's temple and his lungs closed up. He felt suffocated. He *was* suffocated.

He woke up, gasping for air and covered in sweat that stuck his body to the bed sheets.

The next morning Butch felt groggy and weighed

down. The sun poured through the shutters of the window and caused a sharp pain in the back of his head. If only their windows were tinted, or at least boarded up a bit.

He opened the door. Casey stepped from his own room at the same time. He was rubbing his eyes.

"Did you sleep in last night's clothes?" he asked.

"Yeah, I was too tired to care." Then Butch remembered his nightmare. His headache returned at the mere thought of it. "I had a pretty twisted dream too."

"Who cares," he snarled. Butch learned not to care about Casey's snide remarks. It only meant he loved him like a true brother.

They walked together down the stairs. Martin stood in front of kitchen stove, half-mindedly making eggs. He flipped the flat, cooked egg in the air and tried to catch it with his skillet. He missed though, and the cooked egg fell onto the stove and into the fire. It burned with the yolk liquefying instantly, and the whites turned to a burnt black color.

"Shit," he said to himself. He turned around and jerked at the sight of them. "You didn't see that."

"Me and Casey are heading out," Butch said.

"We are?" Casey asked, turning to him.

"Yeah, get your shit and let's go."

Casey grabbed a coat off the rack, and they left.

"Where are we going?" Casey asked, closing the door behind them.

"We're going to see Donald, buy some weed."

"Why don't we just go to Castle?"

"When was the last time you had a good experience at Castle?" Before Casey could answer, Butch answered for him. "Never. We're going to a public place, outside, in the daytime."

Casey didn't say anything. They kept walking and Butch kept glancing at his phone to text Donald.

Butch led Casey to a U-Mart near where they mugged the bum. They passed an empty, rotten smelling trashcan lying in the alley before reaching behind the store.

Donald was already standing there, looking around for people who might be cops.

He wore black shades. The kind of shades Butch refused to wear when he wanted to be inconspicuous. His arms were as thin as the clients he sold meth and heroin to.

He was white, too white, and looked sickly, even dying. He'd always looked that way, even on a good day. It was when he had color on his skin when something was wrong. Butch knew him from childhood, and he knew he didn't play games. A true businessman he was.

Donald smiled and waved at them, folding his shades and hanging them from his collar. Butch waved back in a half-assed sort of way.

"All right," Butch muttered to Casey. "To talk to this guy you've got to either say fuck, shit, or damn."

Casey nodded.

When they finally reached talking distance Butch turned to Casey, letting him speak to Donald.

"Uh, we need some damn fucking high grade shit. You know?"

"What?" Donald said.

Butch laughed with a closed mouth, his face turned red. Casey turned red too, but for a different reason.

Butch gathered himself. "He means pot, herb, weed, grass, tree— "

"All right," Donald groaned, holding up a hand to halt him. "I got it. You know when you text that you need to talk you need to be more specific on what you're asking for. Lucky for you I have what you want."

"I wouldn't be surprised if the cops were looking at my phone texts," Butch explained. "Things have been pretty hot, you know?"

He shook his head. "I don't think the cops worry about that stuff. Not unless you're a mad dealer."

"You mean like you?" Casey said sarcastically.

Donald ignored him. Normally he'd find that type of

remark amusing, but he looked too weary to pick up on his sarcasm. Then he spoke to Butch. "No, I'm talking way up there, drug lords and stuff…. kilos."

"Gotcha," Butch said curtly.

Donald took the hint and headed to the pickup truck parked behind him. He closed the door behind him as if he didn't want them to see his hidden compartments. The windows were as tinted as could be while still technically being legal, or maybe they weren't legal. All they could see was a silhouette Donald hunched over the inner console. And they waited….

When he emerged from the truck, he didn't seem to be holding anything.

Butch narrowed his eyebrows as he approached them. "You forget something?"

"Nope." When he drew closer, he glanced in every direction then pulled a see-through bag of pot from his jacket sleeves. He handed it over quickly and Butch snatched it from his hand, shoving it into his front pocket.

"You got something for *me*?" Donald said.

"How much?"

"Oh yeah, right. Um, I forgot to weigh it but it's some pretty high-quality stuff. You'll be listening to The Doors and sitting in beanie bags within the hour."

Casey laughed.

Donald smiled at him, satisfied, then continued. "We'll say…. fifty dollars."

It sounded steep, but Butch didn't argue. He'd known Donald better than to think he would shorthand him. If Donald said it was worth fifty dollars, then it was worth fifty dollars.

He took out his wallet.

"What the hell are you doing? Get that out of here," Donald said, looking around frantically.

Butch turned away, his back to Donald, and counted the money. He counted twenty-seven dollars. Then he poked Casey with his elbow.

"Help me pay for this," he said.

Casey blinked disbelievingly. "What? I didn't even know what we were going to do before we left the house."

"You've got money, find some."

He took out his wallet. There was more than fifty dollars, but he didn't care to let Butch know that.

"Here's thirty dollars and that's all I'm giving you," he said, handing Butch the money.

Butch smiled. "Cool."

He grabbed it and added twenty of his own to the handful of bills then gave it to Donald. He quickly counted it.

"Enjoy," he said to the both of them.

Butch shook his hand, then Casey.

"Nice to meet you," he said to Casey.

"Likewise."

Donald nodded to Butch, went back to his pickup, and left them to their day.

He was headed home on the freeway, going seventy. Donald still lived with his parents. So what? Lots of kids lived with their parents at twenty.

He took the off ramp to take an emergency piss at the nearest gas station.

He pulled into a gas station, barely paying enough attention to even know it was a gas station (it was a place to piss, that's good enough) and made way to the bathroom on the outside wall.

Damn, it's locked.

He ran inside.

"Can I get a key!" he yelled to the cashier, who was in the middle of dealing with a customer.

"You have to pay for something first," he said to Donald, then diverted his attention to the customer first in line. Three people were ahead of him. A tall man, an old man, and a fat man holding so many snacks that Donald thought he might lose balance.

The tall man left, and the old man stepped forward.

"Hello there, how are you doing today?" the cashier said.

"Oh." The old man was apparently not expecting to be questioned. "I'm doing very well, how are you?"

"I'm doing great, what can I help you with?"

Donald rolled his eyes. *Come on!* he thought.

"Well let's see, I need twenty on pump two, and I'll take a pack of cigarettes."

"What kind?"

"Reds."

The cashier turned around and grabbed Marlborough Reds off the rack of countless other varieties of cigarettes.

"I'll need to see your ID," the cashier said, as he put the pack of cigarettes on the glass counter.

You've got to be kidding me! The old man's ancient! You're only doing this to fuck with me!

With trembling hands, the old man took out his ID and handed it to the cashier. He scanned it, then took the old man's money and handed him the change.

"Receipt?"

"No thanks."

Now onto the fat guy. He dumped his chocolate bars, gummies, bags of chips, and two sodas onto the counter, paid for it, then left.

"How can I help you?" the cashier said, smiling as he apparently enjoyed the agony of watching Donald's bladder expand, threatening to explode in the store with each passing moment.

Donald grabbed a pack of gum off the mini rack and threw it on the counter. "I'd like a pack of gum and a key to the bathroom."

Donald thought he was going to piss right there in front of the cashier. He put a hand on his lower stomach, realized the ridiculousness of it, then took his hand away. The cashier turned to the wall behind him and grabbed a key hanging on a rusted nail. The key was connected to a tiny plastic ladder, probably so it couldn't get lost.

Donald didn't wait for the cashier to calculate the cost of a pack of gum. He tossed a five onto the counter and snatched the key from his hands.

He ran out of the store, almost running through a couple of incoming customers who dodged out of the way just as they opened the doors.

The clock was ticking. Donald stuffed the key into the lock and wiggled it around.

It wouldn't turn!

He almost thought the key the cashier had given him wouldn't work, like some sort of practical joke. After a few more yanks and turns the lock clicked open, and Donald ran inside.

The lights were barely working as they casted a sick green glow across the room. It was a cramped space, which made the smell of piss more intense. There was dried piss on the floor too, which stuck to the bottom of his shoes as he walked to the urinal.

Someone fired the janitor, he thought.

He unbuttoned, zipped down, and went. Sweet relief. He actually sighed as he let it out. This gave him enough time to look around. The cracked mirror over the sink, the graffiti on the tile walls, the doors missing from the two stalls, the piss on the floor. He'd been here before. It looked like a place where he'd sold someone Crack about a year ago.

Then it hit him. It *was* just that bathroom. Of course he didn't actually sell the Crack in the bathroom, but behind the gas station. He only remembered it because he'd used it afterwards. And he needed it in an emergency then, too.

It wasn't a place people walked into unless they absolutely had to. The smell was revolting, worse than any other bathroom he'd seen. He'd almost take his chances pissing on the outside wall of the building.

He zipped up and washed his hands (they were out of soap), then went to give the cashier back his key.

The cashier smiled again. It was not the normal paid

employee hospitality smile. Donald now knew for sure
he was glad to have made him wait.

He got back in his pickup and drove back home. On
the way back he tried to seek out any other place he
could remember selling drugs.

He counted two of them.

The first, a public park, which at this hour was
occupied by school children, few older than thirteen.
They were throwing a basketball around, and a fat kid
was vehemently trying to keep up. There it was where he
sold cocaine.

The second was a motel parking lot. He thought about
all the STD's that were almost acquired from within the
walls of that wonderful establishment, saved only by the
trusty rubber condom. And there he sold some tabs of
ecstasy, or so he told them it was ecstasy.

He pressed on.

His house, which he feared his dad was already home,
knowing full well what he had done…. what he was
about to do.

When he opened the front door, he didn't see his dad,
or anyone else. He knew his dad was home because his
coat was spread over his recliner chair, as if some flat
invisible man might be wearing it as he watched TV.

He went into his bedroom. His dad was waiting for
him with crossed arms, giving him the same face he'd
expected. What he was looking at, clenched tightly in his
dad's hands, he did not expect.

It was a see-through bag that held yellowish-whitish
rocks, which his dad didn't need to second-guess what
he thought they were. It was his bag of crystallized
cocaine, Crack.

Donald's dad held the bag of Crack to his son's face.
"What is this gonna do for you!" he yelled, his face red,
the veins in his throat pulsating. It was the veins Donald
hated the most, even more than the yelling.

He threw the bag onto Donald's chest but Donald
caught it before it hit the ground.

"Dad I — "

"I don't want to hear it," his dad said, waving a dismissive hand in the air.

And Donald was glad he cut him off, because he didn't have the words to finish his sentence.

"You used to be a good kid Donny, you know that?"

Again, Donald was at a loss for words.

"You had a bright future ahead of you, what about college? Did you forget about that?"

Donald spoke only with his sorry eyes, hoping his dad would keep talking so he wouldn't have to.

"I'm gonna get a phone call one of these days telling me my son is in jail! And you know what I'm gonna do Donny? You know what I'm gonna do? I'm not bailing your sorry ass out of there. Not until you've proved to me that you've wised up. Not until you agree to go to college!"

"I'm going to a party," Donald muttered, before leaving the room.

"A what? Not with that bag of crap!"

Donald threw the bag into the air behind him. He could hear it fall to the ground.

"You don't need to go to a party!" His dad yelled, but made no effort to stop him. "You need to get some help!"

Donald left the house, slamming the door behind him.

He hadn't planned on going to a party but seeing his dad like that gave him plenty reason to leave. It shouldn't be too hard to find a party, though.

There was Dean, he hadn't talked to him in months but he always knew where a party was. And if Dean could get over the fact that he hadn't returned his calls for a while, Donald would be in business.

He couldn't blame his dad for saying what he said. Yet still, whenever a dad and son walked by, he didn't refrain from scowling at them. The same thing went for best friends, moms and daughters, and any other social pairing he could think of. It wasn't the fact that people were together that bothered him. It was the way certain people acted so mushy around each other, it seemed artificial to him, almost forced.

He texted Dean asking how he was in order to not sound too focused on his own needs of finding a party.

He texted back within a minute, probably already on his phone.

"I'm doing fine, haven't seen you in a while. You want to go to a party tonight? Some of our high school friends will be there."

Good ol' Dean, straight to the point, not treading around the edges.

"Yeah, sounds like fun. Give me the time and address and we'll hang out."

Dean did, and Donald looked down at the address, reconciling.

"Who's hosting the party?" he asked.

"Sarah Bernheart. She went to high school with us."

Donald remembered her instantly. *Burn-heart* was a better name for her — typical prom queen type. She was pretty, preppy, fake and smiley. Donald didn't want anything to do with her, despite having asked her to senior prom and getting shot down just as quickly. Everyone in the hallway was watching, too. He wasn't holding flowers or anything, but you could always tell when someone was about to ask someone to a dance. It was like a sixth sense every high schooler had. It was even more obvious when the asker was nervous, which Donald definitely was.

So what? That seemed like an eternity ago to him. Ancient history. Besides, who else would even remember that? Dean didn't remember, why would anyone else?

"I'll be there," he said, then drove off.

It was nine. The party had just begun, and Donald wasn't going to waste a single minute. These were the type of people his dad was talking about. An under aged drinker was sprawled across the front lawn, curled in a fetal position and holding his side.

Some familiar people looked at Donald and waved as he parked just a little down the road. The street was already jam packed with parked cars and he knew that surely he'd be sandwiched within an hour.

He opened the door and hopped from his truck onto his pavement. The feeling in his stomach was the same as it always was before a party. A tingly feeling that endless possibilities could happen.

He walked inside. The bass from the music was almost deafening. He was surprised to see groups of people having conversations over the music, though they did have to yell pretty loud to hear each other. Anyone walking by could easily eavesdrop.

There were lots of people he already knew, but no one he actually *liked*. People stumbled around, tripping over each other and then apologizing. Maybe Dean gave him the wrong time. Perhaps the party had started earlier. Or maybe these people had already loaded on alcohol before even showing up. Preloading, he thought they called it.

He made his way to the kitchen (the epicenter of alcohol) and poured himself a plastic cup of beer from the mini-keg. He sipped it and sifted back into the family room. Sipping from his drink again he looked down into his cup. The pool of brownish liquid showed a vague, distorted picture of his reflection. He conjured up an image of his dad's face, scolding him every time he sipped his alcohol.

"Donald?" said a voice from somewhere in the mob of party animals. Donald flinched thinking it was somehow his dad. "Donald? Is that you?"

Donald looked around wildly. He worked hard not to bump anyone. He searched all the heads in the room but couldn't see who had called his name.

"Donald," he heard again. This time the voice was closer, clearer. He found the face it belonged to.

It was Justin. He was swimming through a sea of people to get closer to him. It made Donald feel threatened for some reason, and he backed up, falling backwards onto a couch. Amazingly, he did not spill his drink and he set it on the ground beside the couch. Then he looked up at his impending pursuer.

"It's me, Justin," he said, pushing aside the last of the people separating him from Donald.

Donald sighed just subtly enough for Justin not to notice. Justin smiled and waved frantically at Donald, who held up a hand in return.

Justin wasn't entirely disliked. In fact, most people thought highly of him. But something about him rubbed Donald the wrong way. Maybe it was the way he pretended to be interested in everything and everyone he ran into. Or maybe it was the way he seemed to have everything together even though everyone around him was falling apart.

Justin made his way to Donald, standing over him at the couch. "So how've you been? I haven't seen you since high school. You look great!"

Donald knew this was impossible. His skin had become even paler since high school. He'd lost pigment from being inside most of his days.

"Thanks, you too."

"Are you still with— "

"Lauren, no."

He frowned. "I'm…. sorry to hear that. I always thought you made a great couple."

"You'd be the only one," Donald said. "Everyone else thought she was too good for me."

"Well everyone else is a dick," he said sincerely.

Donald smiled inwardly. He felt better, but he didn't want Justin to know that.

"Who are you seeing right now?" Donald knew Justin had to be in a relationship, he always was.

"Her name's Amy, she's somewhere around here I think." He looked around anxiously, then gave up. "I'll introduce you later."

"Okay, Justin."

"Actually," he said importantly. "I think Amy's got

some single friends. She might've invited them here, too." A smile slowly spread across Justin's face.

"I see where you're going, but it's not necessary. I'm perfectly capable of finding my own date."

Justin frowned again.

Donald noticed and met the frown with one of his own. "It's okay, really."

"Whatever. That's fine."

Donald didn't believe him. Then Justin quickly disappeared back into the sea of people.

The crowd thickened. There wasn't a single hand not holding either a joint, or a cup, bottle, or can of alcohol. He should've brought a breathalyzer. That way, he could check which girls were the most drunk.

A heavily intoxicated girl tripped nearby and fell flat on her face. The liquid in her drink flew from her cup and landed on a girl's silver dress. The yellow alcohol stain was painfully apparent on its light color.

A woman standing closely gasped and used a hand to cover her gaping mouth.

Donald stood for a clearer view. For a moment the girl didn't want to move, and Donald thought she might be dead, or at least unconscious. When she did stand up, he felt stupid. Several people walked over to help her regain balance. Donald was one of them. He grabbed her elbow and could feel her weight as she almost fell again.

She rubbed a bump on her forehead, her eyes glazed and unfocused. "What happened?"

"You fell over and hit your head," replied another guy holding onto her.

"I think I need some fresh air," she said, panting heavily, like the onset of a panic attack.

"Okay."

People cleared a path as they led her to the backyard. They sat her on a small stone wall close to the backyard fence.

"I'm okay, really," she said. "I'm not as drunk as I

look."

Donald focused his eyes. She did look pretty drunk. Now he *really* wished he'd brought a breathalyzer.

He took one more look around the backyard. There were plenty of witnesses to help in case of another tip over, no pool to drown in either. He said his goodbye and walked off to join the party.

The girl sat, thinking that if she stood too suddenly, she might vomit. But that would be good, vomiting might sober her a bit. A party was never fun when she got *too* drunk. She'd made more than a few mistakes that she didn't care to mention in polite conversation.

Everyone around her looked like they were having a good time. People were smiling and laughing at things that weren't really funny, just a side effect of the alcohol, really. No one was looking at her though. She couldn't have that, no attention.

Her muscles wouldn't move. Her eyes began to sink and her head fell toward the hard surface of the short concrete wall she sat on. She didn't fall off, but she was too exhausted for her own good.

When she woke there were still people outside. The party didn't seem to be coming down, if anything there were more people than before. Or maybe she only thought so because she'd been drunk when she saw them. Like double vision.

She had sobered up considerably. She doubted that her stomach would give in if she stood up this time. Still, better to try it slowly. She did, and no vomit came from her mouth.

There was a ping pong table set up by the lawn with cups of alcohol sitting across it. She looked around for someone to talk to. She didn't know anyone. The girl who invited her ended up not showing, but she was having too much fun to resent her.

A curly haired boy sat by himself on a lounge chair.

His back was not in decline, but hunched over, elbows on knees, as he held his face with his hands. He was staring at the ground, apparently lost in thought. The perfect target.

She walked to him, a little wobbly (thank goodness she made the last-minute decision not to wear heels). As she approached him closely his face came into focus.

He was cute. She couldn't see why he'd be alone at a party. And at a Sarah Bernheart party, no less.

"Hi," she said in a shrill, girlish tone, as she walked up to him.

He barely lifted his head to see her. "Hi."

"Whatcha doing?"

"Trying to enjoy myself…. on the last day of earth."

It all made sense to her now.

"What makes you say that?"

"A meteor the size of Wisconsin is headed for the West coast. The media didn't report it to avoid widespread panic. NASA tried to avoid it from hitting us but they couldn't do it. Now we're all fucked."

His words sounded crazy, but certain, nonetheless.

"How do you know about it then?"

"I have a friend in NASA," he said casually.

For a brief moment she almost believed him. Then she thought he'd have better things to do than sit around by himself at some party, waiting to die, if there was any truth to what he was saying.

And if it was true, that he had a friend working for NASA, it would be pretty difficult for him to trust some kid not to go spreading around his secret.

The girl brought her face closer to his and aimed her words into his ears. "Well then, maybe you and I should enjoy these last precious moments."

He smiled. "I'm not afraid of dying. But I am afraid to die…. *alone.*"

They kissed vehemently, as if angry at the world for not bringing them together sooner.

The boy liked the way their lips created a quiet suction

noise every time they kissed. He got an uncontrollable erection that made its way down his jeans, pressing tightly against them.

The girl didn't notice it as she took hold of his neck and brought his face even closer to hers.

Both of them had at least a few drinks prior (her more than him), and the boy wondered if his alcoholic breath was bothering her.

He felt like a teenager again, sneaking into college parties and drinking their beer, hoping he could pass for a college student. Sometimes it worked, sometimes it didn't, and sometimes they were too drunk to care.

He didn't need to lie anymore. Although his paychecks suddenly got bigger when he explained their numbers to some woman he wanted to sleep with. They'd buy it every time. No matter how high he set the numbers they always believed him.

By the time they were done making-out they were both panting. She was breathing the same way she had during her panic attack.

When they stood back up together, the girl dropped down instantly, then picked herself up.

"I'm Walt," he said.

"I'm," she hiccupped. "Naomi."

"Naomi, would you like to go inside with me. Maybe find a place more quiet."

She smiled, then covered her mouth to hide it. "Ummm, okay," she said timidly, more as a question than an answer.

Walt could sense the hesitation in her voice. When she said *okay*, it cut through his stomach.

"Or we could just go back inside and drink?" he offered.

"A true gentleman. Unfortunately, it's getting late and I think my ride is leaving."

"It's probably for the best. Tonight's not the night I want to start having to take care of crabs anyway."

Her eyes widened and her mouth gaped open. She

stood motionless, staring incredulously at him, waiting for him to act sarcastic, to tell her he was joking. But his face remained impassive. The look on her face made him laugh a little, though, it gave new meaning to the word *dumbfounded*.

Walt could see in her eyes she wanted to slap him. He wasn't sure what he'd do if that happened. If she *did* slap him, some guy watching would rush in to comfort her and tell her he was a jerk, not even knowing the nature of the situation. Then he'd proceed to take her someplace quiet, the way Walt had intended to. She would let him do it too, but only because Walt was watching them.

None of these things happened. Instead, she twitched an arm as if she was going to slap him. Walt flinched a little, and Naomi, feeling satisfied, gave him the middle finger and walked off into the house.

Walt was losing his game. Normally by now he'd already be leading her into someone's bedroom. The condom sitting snugly in his wallet would have to be used on someone else. He could find a nice sorority girl, whatever it took, because he wasn't going home dry on potentially the last day of his life.

A girl passed by, glancing at him. He caught her in the act and retuned her gaze, only more fervidly than she had. Her hair was almost to her hips, which, along with her hair, seemed to move side to side like a pendulum as she walked.

She stopped in front of a group of people and turned around halfway to see if he was still watching her. He was, and he walked to her.

"So how were you invited?" he asked. "Do you know the host or did you just tag along?"

At first, she didn't look at him. He wondered if she ignored him or if she simply didn't hear.

"Hello?" he said uncertainly.

She turned to face him. "Hello?"

"I said, do you know the host or did you tag along with some of your friends?"

She shrugged and shrunk her head into her neck. "Some of my friends said they were going to a party and I guess I just came with them."

"So you tagged along." He corrected.

"Uh, yeah, I guess I did." She turned pink.

"I'm Walt." He offered his hand. She didn't take it or seem to notice.

"I'm Jackie."

"Jackie?"

She nodded.

He thought of the name, it sounded like a stripper's. A fake one someone might use to keep creepy guys from searching them on the Internet.

"Well *Jackie*, how would you like to go find someplace quiet where we could talk?"

She didn't nod or shake her head, she only turned back to her group of friends. He didn't pursue her further. What was wrong with him? It wasn't his looks, it couldn't be. If ever he needed to get laid it was on his last night on earth.

Is it possible to die of blue balls? he thought.

He walked around, exploring the house, looking for women. At the end of a hallway, cramped tightly with people, was someone's bedroom. It looked to him like it belonged to some girl. The room was lit by a black light projected from somewhere he couldn't see. People's already bright neon clothes were glowing even brighter, almost like they dressed knowing the lighting would be there.

Sitting on the nightstand was a framed photo of a group of female friends jumping into the air wearing graduation gowns.

On the floor was a circle of teenagers passing around weed and booze. He walked to one of the boys sitting down. A boy next to him handed him a joint, as of proper etiquette. He took one hit, coughed, then raised it in the air, offering it to Walt. He waved it away with a dismissive hand.

Walt sat next to him, grunting heavily. The boy peered at him, Walt caught his gaze, and when the boy turned away, Walt decided it was too late to ignore him.

"I'm Walt," he said. He held a hand out to shake, but it was too low and too dark in the room for Walt to see it.

"Donald," he replied, smiling. Walt put his hanging hand back down.

"Do you know whose house this is?" Walt asked.

"Sarah Bernheart. I went to high school with her."

"So you know her pretty well?"

"She's a cunt."

Two girls stopped talking to scowl at Donald from across the circle. Walt noticed, and suppressed a laugh.

"Why is that?"

"She just is. Have you never met a cunt before?"

The same two girls looked at him again, stood up together, and walked out of the room. Donald waved goodbye as they left.

"Good riddance," he said.

"They must've been friends with Sarah."

"Or they didn't like the way I was talking. But fuck them anyway."

The joint made it back to Donald and he took a large inhale but didn't cough. He raised the joint to Walt's face. It was so close that the fumes were practically rising into his nostrils. He took it.

Walt shrugged. "What the hell? Might as well try it on my last day on earth."

Donald narrowed his eyes. "What do you mean?"

"Well," Walt said, leaning toward Donald and lowering his voice. "I have a friend in NASA who told me that a meteor the size of Wisconsin is headed for the West Coast." Walt took another inhale, then passed the joint along.

"Sounds like your friend is bullshitting you."

Walt shook his head. "It's not like him to lie. I've known this guy for years and I've never once heard him lie."

"I think you've just never caught him."

Walt felt a little annoyed. Why couldn't Donald at least accept the fact that there might be some probability, however unlikely, that a meteor was going to put them in a hole in the ground?

"Why would he lie about that? Why would *anyone* lie about that?"

"So that you'd go around and tell people, then when it didn't happen he'd say ha-ha it was all a joke. I bet he's laughing right now just thinking about it."

Walt straightened his spine, as if to gain a height advantage over Donald. Then he leaned in closely as he did before.

"He *wouldn't* do that," Walt said, enunciating every word perfectly.

Donald leaned back, almost falling onto the person to his other side. "All right, geez don't take it so personally. But you have to know how it sounds to other people."

Walt leaned back and loosened his gaze on Donald.

"So it's the end of the world," Donald said, humoring him. "What are you going to do?"

Walt smiled as he had earlier, before they started to argue. "Hopefully get laid one more time before we all die."

Donald smiled too. "Well maybe one of these chicks will buy your story and want to get laid with you."

Walt snickered, then his smile faltered.

Donald changed the subject. "So it's your first time trying weed?"

"Yeah," he said, "I guess now's as good a time as any."

"Well you don't want to start with *that* stuff," Donald said, pointing at the joint now being held by someone halfway in the circle. "That's some pretty strong stuff to try your first time, fucks you up. I should know. I grew it myself."

"Or," said the guy on the other side of Donald. "You wanna try this shit for your first time, so you know what the best stuff is." He laughed, much harder than he would have sober. Each time he laughed a puff of smoke came from his mouth.

Donald's eyes were whiter than they should've been, courtesy of the black light. Parts of his eyes looked ghostly compared to the contrasting red the marijuana gave them. It made Walt uneasy, it looked unnatural to him.

"So about this chick," Walt continued. "You know any of them here? Any suggestions?"

"Why don't you try going for Sarah, the one throwing the party."

Walt straightened his spine again, as if to was warm up his self-esteem. "Okay, where is she?" He sounded ready to stand.

"I haven't seen her yet, but I'll point her out when I do."

"Where's her room?"

"We're in it."

Walt's eyes darted around the room, studying it, looking for anything she liked that he could use to his advantage. Then he remembered the picture. Without another word, Walt stood and walked to the nightstand, retrieved the framed graduation photo, and brought it back to Donald.

"Which one is she?" Walt asked, standing over him. Every girl in the picture looked pretty, it was clear as day, even under the black light. He couldn't go wrong with any of them.

Donald raised a finger to point her out. "Ummmm," he said, studying the photo carefully. "It's kind of hard to tell in here, but I think that's her." He pointed to the most centered girl in the photo.

Her face was white with a few freckles around the nose area. She was blonde haired with an athletic build. Her tits were a little small for what Walt normally preferred, but he was willing to let that slide.

"Not bad," he said, keeping his cool. "I wouldn't mind

giving it to her, but of course, I'm gonna need everyone to clear the room."

Donald grinned. "We'll cross that road when we get to it."

"You want to make a bet on that?" Walt asked indignantly, almost standing up, then sitting back down. People from across the room glanced at him, not sure of what he'd do next. A few people took out their cellphones, ready to record something exciting.

"Sure, twenty bucks says you can't give it to her by the end of the night."

"Deal."

The person next to Donald was offering the joint to Donald's back but he was too busy dealing with Walt to notice, so he passed it to the next person after Walt.

Walt walked off into the still cramped hallway. He was one of those people you looked at once, then looked away when you realized he was crazy. What Walt didn't notice about himself is that, apart from being good looking, he also carried with him a huge, constant smile wherever he went. He didn't know it was there, the nerves in his face refused to tell him it was happening. Maybe it was a byproduct of his good looks. Even though he thought the world was going to end he couldn't help but smile.

Walt started looking in the most obvious place a host goes when her party becomes overcrowded, upstairs.

It was barricaded by a pile of chairs and a sign taped to one of them reading: **Upper level off limits**.

Walt disregarded it and stepped over the chairs.

"You can't go up there!" A girl behind him yelled.

He continued walking. "Piss off."

The upstairs had several rooms, only one had its light on. When Walt got closer he could hear talking from inside.

Walt knocked, then opened the door, not waiting for an answer.

A lithe body blocked his path. He was face to face with

the pretty blonde he'd seen only in a picture. She was older now, obviously, and had accumulated a few more freckles since the picture was taken. Walt thought they were kind of cute.

"Didn't you read the sign?" she said. "No one's allowed up here."

"I'm here to see you." He smiled, more widely than he normally did.

"Who's that?" called a voice from behind Sarah. Walt opened the door just enough to see the person. It was a guy about his age, shirtless, and sitting lazily in the bed. Bed sheets covered the lower half of his body.

"Well?" said pressed.

Walt stuttered, in his head and out loud. "Um. I — uh."

Sarah squinted at him like he was stupid. And he felt pretty stupid.

"I —uh, never mind."

He staggered back and trudged down the stairs. No sign of Donald. He didn't intend on paying him. What twenty dollars? He didn't have it. Except of course for his spare gas money. To be fair, Donald probably didn't intend on paying him either. He looked around to see if he had a clear path to the front door. He did.

If Donald asked what happened, he hadn't seen her.

He made for the door, only a few people were standing near it, and none of them were Donald. As he crept silently over the chairs guarding the bottom of the staircase, a figure walked from around the corner. Of all the people it could've been, it was Donald.

"Hey there, Walt."

Walt stopped with one foot stuck on the staircase and one foot on the flat ground.

He cleared his throat. "I didn't see her."

Donald grinned. "You know what, I've been looking for her too. I haven't seen her anywhere else. You should check upstairs again."

"I just *did*, she wasn't there." He started to bring his

other foot off the staircase, but Donald stopped him.

"There's a room, two doors down. Try that one."

Donald smiled. He was sure of himself, as if he knew Walt was lying.

"All right," Walt sighed. "But you're making me do this for nothing."

He trotted back up the stairs. This time he'd pretend to go inside and talk to her, maybe wait there for half an hour then come down looking tired, yet victorious. Maybe he'd do some pushups to appear sweaty and out of breath.

No.

Donald would surely check to see if he was lying, he might even approach Sarah herself about it. His best bet was to actually do it.

Walt knocked on the door, which weirdly seemed bigger and more menacing than before. Sarah answered again, wearing only her bra and panties.

"Yes," she said mildly.

"Actually," Walt said. "There *is* something you can help me with."

"Oh?" she said, looking neither confused nor excited.

"I'd like to take you and fuck you so hard you won't walk straight for at least three days."

Sarah opened the door wider, revealing the shirtless man once again. "Join the club."

"Huh?"

"Why don't you come in and join us?"

Walt's mouth opened slightly, his pupils dilated. He'd never considered a three way before, certainly not with another man. Walt looked down at Sarah's almost bare breasts. They were a D cup at least. Then he realized it'd been too long since he last spoke.

"What the hell?" he said, starting into the room.

"Wait a minute." She slightly closed the door on him. "It can't be 'what the hell', you're either all in or you're all out."

Walt considered it…. "I'm all in."

Life's too short not to take risks, he thought.

Sarah opened the door entirely and Walt followed her in. The other man's arms were crossed behind his head, proudly looking like he'd already slept with Sarah.

"Hey," said the other guy.

Walt didn't answer him. He took off his shirt and threw it onto the floor. Sarah was already unhooking her bra. Walt came behind her, fell to his knees, and pulled her panties down with one hard yank. She turned around and looked down at him, her vagina in his face.

"Thanks," she said, unexpectedly.

"Anytime."

Walt looked back at the half-naked gentlemen lying in bed. He didn't dare venture to the bed, not yet, not until she was there with him.

Sarah started walking toward the bed. Walt stood to his feet. The other man leaned forward and sat on his ankles, the covers fell down. He was wrong. It wasn't a half-naked man — it was a naked man. He didn't know what to expect, only that he was going to be taking as much of Sarah as he possibly could, but even that couldn't cloud the thought of having another man less than two feet away.

The man shifted his knees, revealing his privates. Walt grabbed his clothes off the ground and threw them on, starting with his boxers. He finished dressing as he ran away.

"Where are you going?" he heard the girl ask as he ran from the room. The guy she was with just laughed.

He put his shirt on backwards walking out of the hallway, the tag was sticking out of his collar. At the bottom of the stairs Donald smiled, waiting for him. He took out his wallet and quickly handed him the only twenty he had. With Walt's fumbling hands Donald was barely able to grab it before it slipped through his grasp.

Walt walked out of the house, passed the losers who thought it was a good idea to stand *outside* the party, then climbed into his yellow H2 Hummer. He sat for a moment, his key lodged in the ignition, gazing down from his lifted vehicle at the unsuspecting guests who didn't know their lives could come to an end that night. Some of them would have a cup in their hand when it happened. Alcohol would go flying around the room, and Walt would smile again…. one last time.

He was on the freeway, going eighty-five in a sixty-five zone. It wasn't until the last minute that Walt realized he'd almost missed his exit. From the third lane over he cut to the far right without using his turn signal. A car honked as it slowed down behind him, but he didn't care, he made his exit.

What would he do on his last day on earth? Parties weren't what they were made out to be. They were only hyped so that more people would come, but the people who came were full of themselves. He needed to go to someplace that felt like home.

He could go to the outdoor skate park after hours and watch the sunrise, if it would. If he killed himself there, he could take control of his situation rather than having it done for him by a giant meteor.

The road turned residential. He recognized his middle school as he drove past it. His first blowjob was there, in the gym locker room. The coach gave him the keys and asked him to lock up after he picked up the last remaining towels. The coach was new and didn't have enough time to learn that Walt was a "trouble kid". After the students drifted off to their next classes Walt coaxed Gwen, a pretty, shorthaired blonde, to suck him off in the shower room.

He was nearing the skate park. There was a closed and locked metal fence, but Walt could climb it, no problem. There were no barbed wires but there were cameras near the entrance. But Walt knew where they could see, and where they couldn't. He came by often and made friends with the security. They only really got involved when two kids crashed into each other and got into an argument over who bumped into who.

One day in the security room (it was more of a shack really) Walt could see the cameras all had blind spots. He tested his theory and proved himself right again and again by hopping the fence after hours, never once being caught.

It was there that he met his first girlfriend. He even once won a skating competition there, and a small sum of money to go with it. The only successful, worthwhile thing he'd ever done. No one could blame his skating skills on his parents' money. Nope, his skills were all his own.

The skate park was within eyesight, about to be behind him. He turned his car into the parking lot and got out. He stared at a long-chained fence guarding the perimeter. He could remember everything that happened on his first day there. The way he acted depended greatly on the people he'd met at this park. The things they did together. It was fun for a while, then they sort of drifted apart. Their group of skater friends were struck with college, unplanned pregnancies, shotgun weddings, jail time, and worst of all, forgetting.

What started off as a group of seven (sometimes eight) dwindled down to five, then three, then two, and now just him, standing by himself, wondering where they all were.

He decided not to sneak inside. No sense risking jail time over an end of the world conspiracy that might not even be true.

But not even a security cart was in sight. He opened the door of his H2 Hummer and looked every which way for signs of life. Strangely, he almost hoped a security guard would catch him, but he didn't know why. He walked to the lonely skate park and clenched the fence, his fingers hooked around through the openings, and he sighed. The once great skate park of his childhood beamed with ghostly faces of his past. If he thought hard enough, the night turned to day, and kids rolled up and down the wooden ramps performing flips and other respectable skateboarding tricks.

Walt leaned forward on the fence and closed his eyes. He wished the fence would suddenly disappear. His body weight would plunge him to the other side and he'd wake up flat on the ground. He opened his eyes. Standing before him was what used to be the best thing in his life, visible to him through the pattern of a honeycomb pattern fence.

He climbed back into his Hummer. Walt took out his cell phone and texted his friend from NASA. "Any sign of that meteor yet?"

Then silence. His stomach grumbled. A last meal. Right! Every convict on death row got one, why shouldn't he?

He started up his car and travelled down the road. He knew it well, but there were too many choices to choose from. Most of the picking he had was fast-food restaurant chains. Anything tastes good on death row, he guessed.

As his car rested in the drive thru, trapped between two cars, his phone buzzed as he was ordering. "And I'll take two medium— hold on."

He looked down at the phone. What could be more important than a last day text? It was his friend from NASA.

"It was a false alarm. The meteor didn't make a course for earth. We'll live to see another day."

"Fuck," Walt said out loud.

"What was that?" the drive thru attendant asked.

Walt thought he spoke more quietly than he had. "Nothing. Uh, I'll take two medium fries and a double cheese burger."

The digital screen showed his order and the prices that conveniently added up to his total cost.

"Pull up to the second window, please."

He did. The drive thru attendant was a typical teenaged, minimum wage worker. His hair was as greasy as the meals he served, his eyes tired and overworked. He handed Walt his food, Walt handed him the money.

"Thank you, have a great day."

He drove off and parked in a nearby space.

"Fuck," he repeated.

He wished the meteor was going to hit earth. He'd counted on it. Now he was forced to continue living in the real world, face himself in the mirror each day, take shit from his boss.

Walking outside was a woman holding an empty can of gasoline. She looked timid, desperate. Walt seemed to be the only one sitting in a parked car. He pushed the automatic chair adjust button and lowered his seat as far as it could go.

Before his eyes drifted below the line dividing the window from the door, the woman spotted him.

Shit.

Walt rolled down his window before she could accost him.

"I don't have any money," he said defensively.

Still, she walked towards him, swinging her gas can. "I swear I'm not using it for drugs, I just need a little bit, change even."

She certainly didn't look like the sort of woman to use drugs. She looked like a mother. He didn't doubt that she might have a kid or two waiting in her car with the windows cracked.

Her eyes twinkled at Walt, begging. He sighed a surrendering breath. She smiled. Walt reached into the inner console. He really didn't think he'd find much. When he was finished searching, however, he found six dollars and fifty cents, much more than he expected.

She was still smiling as he opened the door and stepped onto the parking lot surface. She held out her hand and thanked him. He placed the money gently onto her hands, making sure not one cent dropped. He touched the soft skin of her hands.

"Thank you," she said, and truly meant it.

"So, where's your car?"

"It's a few blocks away. I'm completely out of gas, no one bothered to give me money like you did though. No, not tonight. They've all got places to be, no time for a poor woman who— "

"I don't need your life story," he interrupted. The woman blinked, looking affronted. He continued. "I'm not going to pretend I've never been in a situation like yours, but why didn't you start asking for money before you *completely ran out of gas?*"

"I lost track of how much I had. I noticed the gas light and pulled over when I could. I saw your nice Hummer and figured you might have a couple of bucks. I guess I'm not *completely* out of gas. I could make it another five miles or so."

"How far is your house?"

"Twenty miles."

He sighed. "Of course it is."

"What do you mean?"

"Look, if you've got to get home I can give you a lift, otherwise that money is the best I can do."

"No," she said looking at the money he'd handed her. "This should be enough. Thank you."

He looked offended at what she said. She tried to keep a gracious face.

"No problem," he said unconvincingly, then climbed into his Hummer.

She walked back to her car a few blocks away, just like she said. Two boys waited patiently as their mother walked closer. One of them, sitting in a child safety car seat, swung a rattle she could hear from outside the car, the window being cracked open.

She walked up to the car door but didn't open it.

"Mommy will be right back," she told them. "She just needs to fill up this gas can and she'll be done."

"Kay," replied her other kid waiting in the back seat.

She set off, crossed three roads, and filled her gas can at the station. Some people looked as she bent over, as if

she was doing something wrong. Although some of them
she thought might've been checking out her ass.

Back in the car her kids started fighting, while she was
busy focusing on the traffic ahead. It was almost stand
still, one car moved forward, so did she, then they'd stop,
then repeat.

"Mom! He's poking me!" the one in the safety seat
whined.

"Am not!"

She used to freak out when her kids yelled in the car,
it'd make her flinch. She'd grown used to it now and she
learned to ignore their childish complaining.

"Mom!" other one yelled. There was a sudden rapid
kicking on the back of her chair, making her head bob
forward each time. Every mother has a line, and her kid
had crossed it.

She pulled into the bike lane and stopped dead in
front of a **No Stopping Anytime** sign. Her face
scrunched up and her jaw clenched. Her children
widened their eyes and what little hair they had on their
arms stood in full salute.

"You kids listen. I haven't had decent sleep in weeks.
And I need you two, just for a moment, to sit down and
shut up."

The kids were stunned in their seats, exchanging looks
of horror. She turned around and accepted their silence
as submission. And she drove again.

The kids didn't say a word the entire drive back. It
was the best sound a hard-working mother could hear,
silence.

In nearly half an hour they arrived home. Daddy was
undoubtedly there, and would ask how their trip to
grandma's went. They were separated but not divorced.
All the love in their marriage had worn out years ago,
right about the time they had their second child. There
had been disagreements on how their money should be
spent, Thomas, her husband, thought it would be better

used on casinos and cigarettes. The neighbors called the police on more than one occasion. They had their suspicions on who could've called them in.

The mother went inside with her kids. She would've held their hands if not for her Thomas's jealousy of her kids' favorable affection.

The house was the same as it always was, plates not put away, juice boxes turned over. It was a nice house otherwise, but the people who lived there never allowed it to look its full potential. They'd stopped hosting parties months ago, partly because the house turned to hell, partly because of the separation.

The mother walked to the television and turned it to a child appropriate channel. The kids both walked into the room, the bigger one holding the hand of the smaller one. They gazed at the TV for a moment, then went to another room.

"Don't go upstairs!" The mother yelled. "If you do, you'll need me to carry your brother!"

They gave no response. The mother sat on an armchair, exhausted, and watched the children's show by herself.

"Honey?" called a voice from upstairs.

"Yes," she said weakly.

Footsteps thumped down the stairs, and from the entrance of the room Thomas stopped and stared at her.

"It took you longer than usual to get back. I was getting worried, you almost made me call you."

"We ran out of gas." Her words were void of any sense of happiness. "I had to ask a stranger for money."

Thomas looked at her with doleful eyes. He lowered his voice to a sympathetic tone. "Why didn't you call me?"

"You know I can't do that."

"Do what?"

"Ask you for something."

He shook his head and walked away. The TV suddenly turned louder from the commercials. Her attention turned back to it and nothing else mattered.

Half an hour later Thomas returned with a sorry look on his face. At first she thought he was going to apologize, then he spoke.

"Jacob called. He says he's coming home tonight. Frankly I'm surprised he didn't call from a police station."

Jacob was their first born and most troubled child. Their second youngest, Richard, was diagnosed with ventricular tachycardia, a heart condition that has prevented him from running, watching certain shows, even laughing. Jacob sometimes lurched from around corners of the house and scared Richard almost literally to death. They put him on procainamide but decided the side effects were much too severe for a nine-year-old to handle. They planned on giving him a surgical procedure for an implantable cardioverter-defibrillator, which was scheduled in two weeks.

Then there was Gregory, who looked up to Richard as a sort of role model, being that it was the only brother he was able to speak with on a daily basis.

They didn't plan on telling Richard about their separation, not before the surgery at the very least. Having Jacob come back into their lives was the last thing he needed right now. They sent him to live with his uncle for a reason. Not that his uncle had any wisdom to bestow upon him, hell no. They'd do anything to get him away from Richard.

"No, no. Tell him he can't do that," the mother said.

"That's what I said, but he just kept saying he was coming."

"Then we'll just leave him outside. Not let him in."

Thomas narrowed his eyes and looked at her disbelievingly. "We can't do that, he'd scream and wake the neighbors. Besides…. he *is* our son."

She took her hands and clasped them over her ears. She didn't want to hear it. That kid? *Her* offspring? It was like a bad dream she could never seem to shake off.

He sighed. "What do you want me to do?"

"If he comes in this house he's got to stay away from Richard. I don't even want him in the same room, and Richard sleeps with his door locked."

Thomas gave her a thumbs up. "Got it."

"And what did your brother say about him leaving?"

"Jacob said he ran away from him, said he couldn't take any more of it. Hard to blame him, my brother treated me as badly as Jacob treated Richard."

"The apple doesn't fall far from the tree, does it?"

"Don't give me that shit! You know you're becoming more like your mother every day."

She stood up and pointed a finger out of the room.

"I guess I'd better call my brother and tell him the situation," he said before leaving.

The mother sat back in her chair, wanting to cry.

Later that night the doorbell rang. The mother crawled out of her bed (she'd recently slept on a separate bed from her soon to be ex-husband) and ran to get the door before Richard could. Richard put up a fuss that night about locking his door before going to bed. She explained to him that Jacob was coming back and there was nothing he could do to stop it.

Richard didn't think Jacob would be a problem, he believed he had to have changed. He always looked for the good in people. It was a quality his mother admired and worried about at the same time.

She opened the door. Jacob stood in front of her, arms spread open, waiting for a motherly hug. She looked surprised, but gave him one. Trapped in her son's arms she noticed his hair was well kempt and his shirt had no stains she could see from the porch light. This was not like the Jacob she'd once known.

The hug broke. He smiled at her with wishful eyes. Truly he had more intentions than just coming back to live with them. Perhaps he needed money.

"Well come inside, it's getting cold."

He dragged his feet on the welcome mat and proceeded inside.

"Your room is the same way we left it, down to the last bundle of dust."

"Home sweet home," he replied.

"I'd like to talk but we've all got things to do tomorrow."

"I understand."

They hugged one more time then parted ways. He strolled to his room, the mother to hers, and they didn't speak again that night.

The following morning the mother woke with an empty bed next to hers. Thomas often went to work early, he didn't like to, but it was an excuse to avoid talking to her. On this morning, with Jacob back in the house, he had plenty reason to leave early.

She walked down the stairs half-awake. At the bottom of the staircase she saw something that shocked her into full awakening. Jacob had made himself breakfast (a simple bowl of cereal) and prepared places for everyone else to sit, even Thomas, who he didn't know had gone to work.

He was sitting down helping himself to his bowl of cereal, completely unaware of his mother's presence.

"What're you doing?" she asked.

"Just making some breakfast," he replied, in between mouthfuls of cereal.

"Are you getting ready for school?"

Jacob stared deeply into his glass of milk and continued shoveling spoon fulls of cereal into his mouth. The mother knew the answer, yet she decided to press him further.

"You are still going to school, aren't you?"

"I stopped going months ago."

The mother blinked hard and shook her head. Months? She'd imagined his attendance had probably been spotty, skipping classes, leaving school early. But not going at all? And for months?

"Do you think you don't need school?"

"I think school is right for other people, just not me. Plenty of successful people dropped out of college."

"*College*. Not high school."

"High school is just what happens before college. I'm saving extra time, getting done with dropping out early."

The mother's mouth twitched into half a smile. She wanted to laugh, but she couldn't encourage him. "That might be fine for today, you just got back. Tomorrow on the other hand, you're going back to school. No excuses."

Jacob's cereal was only milk now. He lifted the bowl to his lips and drank what was left, then stowed it away in the sink.

"And you're going to start helping out around the house," the mother added.

"Okay."

"I'm going to get your brothers ready for school. I don't want you even talking to Richard. Understand?"

"My own little brother? Who I haven't seen in months? Okay."

"Don't give me that! You know very well why you can't talk to him!"

"All right," he said coldly.

As if fate itself was tempting him, little Richard came from around the corner, aghast at the sight of his brother. Jacob looked at him, blinked, then walked to the sink to hand wash the dishes. Richard sat down, knowing he shouldn't and *couldn't* talk to his older brother.

The table was too high for him to see well, but his brother walked over and poured him a bowl of cereal from the box and milk gallon still sitting on the kitchen table. Richard could barely reach the bowl as he took hold of it and slid it closer to his face. The spoon he was holding looked ridiculous in his tiny hands. Richard was a well-fed boy, but he didn't look it. It wasn't out of the realm of reality that he might have something other than a heart condition to worry about.

The mother poured a bowl of her own raisin bran cereal and joined Richard at the table. Jacob joined them soon after.

"You wanna hear a joke, Richard?" Jacob asked. Richard lifted his head but said nothing. "Two priests walk into a— "

"Stop!" The mother yelled. She reached across the table and clasped a hand over Jacob's mouth. Jacob twisted his head, avoiding her grip.

"What's wrong mom? He can't hear jokes now too? You might as well just shoot him!"

The mother stood from her chair to get better leverage. Jacob struggled and wrestled with his mother. She tried to get an advantage and accidentally pushed Jacob to the floor, his chair falling on top of him.

"Get off!" he yelled, while putting his palm over his mother's face. Her neck jerked and twisted around. They wrestled on the ground for another moment, Richard hopped off his chair and moved for a better view. After a moment the mother ceased and pulled herself up, panting.

Jacob lied on his back for a moment. His mother casted a shadow over him with the kitchen light above. He pulled his knees closer to his chest, ready to kick if he needed to.

The mother, hunched over, pointed a finger to outside the kitchen. "Go — to your room," she panted.

Jacob picked up his chair and tucked it under the table. He circled widely around the table so that he kept distance from his mother. Then, when he neared the kitchen exit, he walked off to his room.

"We're getting you that surgery soon," the mother said to Richard. She was still panting, now hunched over the kitchen table, grabbing it for support. She looked at her knees, they were bruised. It could have been from when she fell over and not from Jacob. Still, if Thomas asked, it was from Jacob.

He hadn't changed, it only looked like he had. Jacob was a deceptive son, always had been. His eyes cried only crocodile tears.

She finished making her kids breakfast, then their school lunches. Richard went off to the bus stop and she dropped off Gregory, her youngest, at kindergarten.

When she arrived home the kitchen was spotless from the mess she'd made preparing the food, even the living room was tidied up. She hadn't had the time for that since her separation had started.

Probably Jacob trying to make up for this morning, she thought. *When Thomas hears about it he might send him to a boarding school, or better, a reformatory.*

Yeah, picturing Jacob fending off kids bigger than him. It brought her a small wave of pleasure, then it dissipated.

She didn't know why Jacob was the way he was. Certainly there was no one on her side of the family as sadistic as he was. And as far as she knew, no one from Thomas's side was either. Of course, in no way did they raise him to act the way he did. They raised him no differently from their other kids, and they turned out much different.

The mother walked and sat down at the end of dining table, which they saved for special occasions.

"Jacob!" she yelled across the house. She heard a door open, and then….

"What?"

"Come here."

Jacob did, looking confused when he walked into the room.

"Sit down," the mother said, pointing to a chair. Jacob grabbed the chair opposite hers and pulled it out.

"Closer," the mother said.

Jacob sighed, walked around, and sat on the chair closest to hers. "What?"

"I want you to tell me everything you've been up to since you left. I know you won't tell me *everything*, but tell me what you will."

Jacob looked at her, thinking carefully about what he'd give her.

"It hasn't been a joy ride," he said. "I'll tell you that. Dad's brother wasn't always easy to live with. Sometimes he gets home late. Sometimes I sneak out because I know I'll be back before him. If you're wondering why I do the things I do, I don't know." He looked at her intensely. "I'm really trying to change, mom. I didn't know Richard couldn't hear any jokes. It's been so long that—" Jacob paused for dramatic effect, it didn't work on his mother, she knew his tricks. "It's been so long that I've forgotten what you looked like."

The mother smiled inwardly. "Oh for Pete sakes, it hasn't been that long. You're acting like we abandoned you as an infant. I happen to know, very well, that Uncle George has a few framed photos of us throughout the house."

"You might wanna double check."

The mother closed her eyes and pursed her lips, as if she took back what she'd said. Her eyes opened. "Keep going."

"There's not much to tell. I stopped going to school, the teachers were riding me and I couldn't keep up."

The mother lifted a single finger to her face. "One thing," she said. "All you needed to do was keep up in school, just one thing. We're not asking for A's, we've accepted that that's not realistic. All you needed to do was pass high school. I'm sure you'll get held back now, too much time has passed."

"Mom, this is a good thing, I can focus on bigger stuff now."

"Like tormenting your little brother, who has a heart condition?"

Jacob sat still, watching his mother closely. "Tell me what I need to do."

She sat up, the chair almost tipping behind her. "You need to get out. I don't care where you go, you can go back to your uncle's for all I care, just get out."

He looked at his mom, his eyes pleading her. "What does dad think?"

"When your dad hears what you did to your brother this morning he'll be right on board."

"What did I do exactly? Try to tell him a joke? Mom." He looked at her gravely, making his next words sound important. "He *needs* to laugh."

"He has ventricular tachycardia. You know he can't get excited. You'd know what it was if you ever paid attention when we talked to you, just like you never paid attention when your teachers were talking. I can see you're beyond schooling now, you were right, I agree with you. The best thing you can do is join the workforce, the military perhaps, they'd straighten you out. In fact, that's the best idea I've had all day. I'll go and look into a military school. I'll even let you pick it out."

When the mother started out of the room Jacob rose from his chair and followed her.

"You can't."

She didn't answer. He followed her down the hallway.

"I'll do whatever you want, I promise. I'll go back to school with those terrible teachers, I'll face all those mean kids who used to beat me up."

"What was that?" She stopped walking and faced him. For a second she thought it might be a lie, then she remembered he had come home with bruises on several occasions, although he might've been picking the fights himself.

"Yeah, I — there was this kid, Jeremiah, I think his name was. Anyways, he has autism and these guys were punking on him when they should've been in class. I don't know why Jeremiah was there but I assumed they kept him there. They were laughing at him, calling him, well…. I'm sure you can guess what they called him. Then I remembered Richard, I thought about his disability. So I stood up for the kid, they didn't have any problem with me until I talked back to them. I'll admit I threw the first punch knowing I couldn't fight off all three of them. I sort of hoped the guy was man enough that he didn't need his friends to jump in, but they did. After that, those same kids punked on me all the time." By the time he finished talking his throat had become thick and his words sounded hoarse.

"What happened to the autistic boy?" the mother asked, sounding intrigued.

"Huh?" he sniffed, as if on the verge of tears. "Oh, I don't know. I think he moved or stopped going there, I don't know."

"Why didn't you tell me?"

"I knew you'd go to the principal or make me go to one of those stupid counseling sessions. That'd only make things worse. Besides, you know dad always says it's those endearing moments that makes the man."

"Jacob," the mother said, her voice equally as hoarse. She thought she might be on the verge of tears herself, then she closed her eyes, opened them, and continued. "We're your parents. You can talk to us about anything."

She hugged him tightly, and Jacob smiled.

It worked, he thought. *She bought the story.*

Jacob *had* stood up for Jeremiah, eventually. Only he neglected to tell her that he was one of the people that bullied him in the first place. The bruises he had were from a different story, which he wasn't prepared to tell. He wasn't as heroic as his explanation made him out to be. His conscience would, however, allow him to tell half-lies and still rest easy enough to sleep at night.

He pushed away from his mother.

"Sorry," she said, as she wiped her eyes with her shirt sleeve. "It's just I had no idea."

"It's okay mom, I don't blame you for hating me."

She swallowed. "I don't hate you."

"Then why did you send me away?"

"Because you didn't know how to get along with Richard. He's very fragile, and he's about to have surgery. He's going to have some time to rest after but then I think he can laugh again, and you can tell him your jokes. What was that one again? Something about two priests and a bar?"

"What? Oh, I can't remember."

"I'm not going to send you to military school. You do need to go back to school though, just not today. And in a couple weeks, when Richard's had his surgery, you can talk to your little brother again."

He smiled. "Okay mom."

"Don't make us have him wear ear plugs, okay?" she laughed. Jacob laughed too. "Tonight your father and I will discuss what we're going to do. In the meantime, please don't give us a reason to send you to military school, got it?"

"Got it."

It was seven when Thomas got home, then a half hour later when they approached Jacob with their plan. They were gathered in the family room, Jacob sat in a chair as his parents towered over him.

"Jacob," the mother said. "We talked it through. We called Mrs. Harrison and she agreed to take you in for a while—" She stopped herself mid-sentence. "Until your brother's had his surgery," she corrected.

Mrs. Harrison was an old family friend and neighbor. The only thing Jacob liked about her house was their dog Roofus and Rover. It was a two headed dog. Jacob could vividly remember both heads chewing on a rope toy, both struggling, jerking their heads back and forth in a never-ending tug-of-war.

Mrs. Harrison herself was a mother, though she looked very well like she could be a grandmother too. He didn't care much for her kids. They were too perfect for his taste.

The father? He had long since passed away. He left her well off without him, years later she had no job except being a mother.

"Is their dog still there?" Jacob asked.

"Yes, Roofus and Rover are still alive," Thomas interjected, in a tone as if it might make Jacob feel better.

"You ready for a little R & R?" the mother said in a childlike manner. R & R of course, meaning Roofus and Rover. It was a joke she'd used for years, and to Jacob, it'd gone stale the first four or five times she said it.

"You can stay tonight," Thomas said. "Then tomorrow, after Mrs. Harrison picks up her kids from school, your mother is driving you right over there."

"Can't wait," Jacob replied, forcing a smile.

"You'll live," Thomas said mildly.

"I don't want you bothering her kids," the mother added. "If I hear that you do—"

"It's straight to military school," Jacob interrupted.

The next day, Jacob went without a fight. He wanted to say goodbye to his little brothers but his mom would only allow him to speak with Gregory.

When he walked with his mother into the Harrison's home everyone's eyes followed him around the room. The three Harrison kids looked at him like the bubonic plague had returned. Mrs. Harrison, however, had glowing, hopeful eyes.

"We'll make sure he's taken care of," she assured. Her youngest daughter took shelter from behind her mother's leg, adding insult to Jacob's character.

"We really appreciate it," the mother said. "We just need a place for Jacob until little Richard gets his surgery."

"Take all the time you need," Mrs. Harrison said. "Carolin, get off of mommy's leg, you don't need to hold me like that."

Carolin looked at Jacob cautiously and slowly let go of her mother's leg. Jacob smiled at her, but she didn't change her expression.

The mother turned to Jacob and looked at him gravely. "Don't you do anything mean to Mrs. Harrison or her daughters."

"Aye aye, captain." Jacob gave her a mock salute.

The mother was less than amused. "I mean it. If you don't treat them well...."

Jacob knew what she meant but was obviously too afraid to say out loud in front of the Harrisons.

You'll send me to military school, I know.

Mrs. Harrison smiled at them reassuringly. The mother said her goodbyes then left with the sound of her car's engine pounding away in the distance.

Jacob took one more look through the window as his mother's car sped off excitedly, as if she was happy to be leaving. Jacob turned around to the room full of Harrisons, who'd been pretending not to stare at him worriedly.

"So," he said, clapping his hands. "What do you like to do for fun?"

"Well," Mrs. Harrison said, bracing herself for one of Jacob's rude teenaged remarks. "You're in luck, tonight's game night. We're letting Carolin pick the game tonight. Carolin?"

She was the youngest girl, and the same one who'd held her mother's leg previously.

She put a hand to her chin. "Ummm.... I want.... checkers."

As Mrs. Harrison walked to the cabinet where she kept the families' board games, Jacob took an assessment of the house. It was small, and not as nice or as big as his house. Yet somehow it seemed more like a home, more complete.

The family room looked like the cover of some home furnishing magazine. Everything looked as if it was made within five years ago, and if it wasn't, it was kept in pristine condition. Bravo Mrs. Harrison.

After removing several board games, Mrs. Harrison reached into the dark corners of the cabinet and pulled out a box of checkers. She held it before her with both hands, and with one big huff she blew off a full coat of dust off stuck to the lid.

"Been a while since we played this one," she said. "Jacob, you know the rules of the game?"

He'd known checkers since he was five, back in the good ol' days, before his authority issues. "Sure."

She smiled. "Good."

Mrs. Harrison carried the game and set it on the carpet while her own kids sat in a perfectly formed circle. A perfect circle, except for the space they left for Jacob. Jacob sat. He was the tallest amongst them. It made him smile a little.

"Since there's five people and two boards. Why don't we take turns?" Mrs. Harrison said. She looked at Carolin, then at Jacob, like she knew they needed to establish a sense of trust. "Carolin, why don't you go with Jacob. Abby, you can go with me. Justine, I'm afraid you'll have to wait a turn."

"What about Robyn?" Justine asked solicitously.

"Who's Robyn?" Jacob asked, just as curious.

Mrs. Harrison looked at him worriedly, as if he'd crossed some sort of social boundary. "Robyn is my oldest daughter, she went out with friends and won't be back till tonight. We can certainly start and finish a game before she gets back."

Jacob didn't remember Mrs. Harrison having another daughter, although it'd been years since he'd last seen her.

He played his game. Mrs. Harrison obviously let her daughters win, even when she had clear opportunities to best them. Jacob, on the other hand, wasn't quite as generous. He beat Carolin first, she didn't score a single point, then Abbie, then Justine. It felt like dominos, one falling down after the other.

Last was Mrs. Harrison. She wasn't too keen on having to watch all three of her daughters being bested by some outside child. Her intentions were set on beating him, it was clear in her eyes.

Justine and Abbie were going against each other but

they were much more interested in the mom versus Jacob match. They played their game half-mindedly as they watched them, only making a move from time to time in order to continue the match.

Mrs. Harrison made her move, crowned her kings, Jacob did the same, in the end, it was Mrs. Harrison who won the match. Her daughters cheered and hugged as they sat next to their mother. Jacob couldn't help but clap sportily during her exultant triumph in an insignificant board game.

The door opened in the distant front of the house. Jacob found it so unexpected that he jumped a little. It was Robyn, presumably. Her hair was black with a streak of reddish orange, resembling a robin bird she most likely set to portray. Her eyes were dark and uninviting. For some reason, Jacob was turned on like a switch. She seemed to be, much like he was, the outcast of the family.

"Hi," said Mrs. Harrison, waving to her.

Robyn barely looked in her direction as she swung her backpack off her shoulder and dropped it carelessly next to the coat rack.

"Hey," she replied without intonation.

"We have a guest, Jacob. He's Madelyn's son, he'll be staying with us for a while."

"Hey," she said, in the exact same way she'd spoken to her mother.

Jacob laughed quietly to himself from Robyn's lack of enthusiasm. With any luck to Jacob, Robyn must've just been dumped or blown off from a date. Sad desperate girls were Jacob's specialty. Then Jacob realized Mrs. Harrison probably had a doors—open—when—boys— are—home policy. She couldn't watch them forever though. Sooner or later, she'd need to divert attention to other matters.

He realized Mrs. Harrison had unspokenly forbidden him from flirting with her daughter, and that's what enticed him. Forbidden fruit, Romeo & Juliet, which was coincidentally, the only book Jacob ever read with pleasure.

The kids, all except Abbie, dispersed, sensing that game night was over.

"What's wrong with Robyn?" Abbie asked her mother.

"Who knows? Could be a number of things. I'll talk to her, but I don't know how much good it'll do."

"Why doesn't *he* talk to her," Abbie said innocently, pointing to Jacob. Jacob smiled but hid it once Mrs. Harrison looked at him. "He's a teenager," Abbie continued. "So won't Robyn relate to him or something?"

Mrs. Harrison tried to keep her cool. "I—uh, he's a boy. I think I'd relate better to Robyn, being a woman *and* her mother."

Mrs. Harrison left the room hurriedly before further uncomfortable conversations occurred. Jacob and Abbie were left to each other with the checkers still laid across the carpet.

Abbie looked at him. "How about a rematch?"

It was late that night when Jacob woke from a jerking leg. The first thought that came to him was that Robyn was probably alone now, no Mrs. Harrison to intrude.

She could have to share a room with her sisters though, that would make things difficult.

No. A girl like that would probably get sick of her little sisters, and in a house with so many rooms, she'd have to have her own.

Jacob had little opportunity to get a layout of the house. Most of his day was spent in the family room, or helping in the kitchen. All places Mrs. Harrison could keep an eye on him. When the day was done, she hastily led Jacob to the room reserved for visiting relatives. It was a small room, no bedspread, only blankets, but thick ones. His small suitcase was packed tightly into the corner. It was too small to keep him there for more than a few days without washing clothes.

The moonlight beamed perfectly through the window shutters. His eyes adjusted to the darkness surrounding him and could see well enough without the aid of his cancelled cellphone.

What if Robyn didn't like him? He'd be thrown out for sure. A picture flashed in his head of Mrs. Harrison throwing his clothes onto the damp lawn, the sprinklers spraying them before he could pick them off the ground.

Then, a second scenario: one of him attempting to knock on Robyn's door just as she opened it to get a glass of water. She screams and wakes the entire house. He'd tell her he was sleepwalking. She'd say she believed him, but wouldn't, and would later ask his mother if he had a history of sleepwalking the next day.

Why would he want to flirt with her now anyway? She'd be asleep for sure. She wouldn't even listen to what he had to say. He decided to wait for morning, after she got home from school if he had to.

He doubted he could sleep again. Yet, after planning out carefully what he'd say to Robyn he exhausted his conscious and drifted off to dream of Robyn.

The next day Robyn hadn't joined family breakfast. Mrs. Harrison tried knocking on her door, then pulled on the doorknob when she didn't open. She'd locked it, apparently too upset to even want to see someone.

The other daughters remained silent. They were too wise to bring up their older sister's strange behavior. Their breakfast was much more nurturing than what Jacob's mother usually made for him. He'd get cereal, a power bar, sometimes waffles, if he was lucky.

The Harrison's received waffles (or pancakes, depending on their preference), orange juice, eggs, bacon, and a little bowl of fruit on the side. Jacob almost felt like leaving a tip. Thinking this reminded him he didn't have any money *to* give, even if he wanted to. He frowned, then picked at his eggs, cutting them into fractions with his fork.

Mrs. Harrison looked at Jacob, opened her mouth, then closed it after reading his facial expression.

Breakfast was silent. Jacob was amazed at how much work the Harrisons could do without talking to each other. Cleaning dishes, getting ready for school. He hadn't expected children to be so well behaved. This was cut short by Robyn escaping her room and walking out the front door. There was a hum of her car engine that faded as she drove down the street.

Mrs. Harrison had finished helping Abbie pack her lunch when she turned to Jacob. "I'm going to drop the girls off at school. Would you like to come along?"

This sounded more of a request than an offer. Jacob agreed. He could tell Mrs. Harrison didn't trust him alone in her house.

The girls were already holding their bag lunches and carrying backpacks over their shoulders. Both of them were dressed in rain coats, just in case.

Jacob smiled. He couldn't remember the last time he was that prepared for anything, a future ahead of him.

They dropped Justine off first. Mrs. Harrison offered to drop Jacob to his last high school, but he refused. Next was Abbie and Carolin. Jacob saw the ride home as an opportunity to confront Mrs. Harrison about Robyn.

"Why is she in such a bad mood?" Jacob said, then realized he hadn't specified who he meant. "Robyn, I mean."

Mrs. Harrison spoke as if she'd known he would ask. "As I told my kids before, I have no idea. It seems like there's always something."

Jacob had an intense temptation to say "women", but thought better of it. Then the temptation subsided completely. "So I take it she got that red streak in her hair to make herself look like a robin?"

Mrs. Harrison laughed. It was a genuine hearty laugh Jacob had never heard her make, until now he'd only heard her motherly pity laugh.

"That could be it," she said, then brought her voice to a more serious tone. "Out of all my kids, I'd say Robyn talks to me the least."

"I think she's just getting older. That's what happened to me, teenagers, you know?"

"She's pretty, isn't she?"

Jacob was so startled by Mrs. Harrison's sudden change of attitude that he couldn't tell if he was stammering in his mind or out loud. He took a moment to regain his mental composure, then spoke.

"She is." He swallowed. "Do you think…. we have things in common? Me and her I mean."

"I got a little bit of that vibe from you."

Jacob smiled. "So what kind of guys does she like?"

"She's gone out with a lot of losers and other guys I don't approve of. It got so bad she had to switch schools."

Jacob didn't need to press her further. He decided Mrs. Harrison approved of him, but he didn't know why. He was probably just as bad as any of those other guys. He was a high school dropout.

They drove in silence for another twenty minutes. They were nearing the Harrison's home. Jacob wondered what they'd be doing for the rest of the day. Thank God his mother hadn't requested he'd be dropped off at school. Or maybe she had requested it in private, knowing he'd put up a fight if she did it in front of him. Maybe Mrs. Harrison decided against it and didn't want to cause a conflict.

They stopped at a stop sign two blocks from the Harrison's house. A group of kids about Jacob's age walked across the road. They looked like they should've been in school, and Jacob looked like he should've been in their group. He was actually glad to be in a heavy metal vehicle to separate him from them, like an animal in a cage.

They parked outside and walked into the house. It seemed empty with only the two of them. He half-expected kids to laugh and chase each other in circles around the family room, knocking over chairs as they avoided being tagged. Then there was Robyn, avoiding all of them, barricaded in her room.

Jacob did exactly what he thought he would do. He helped around the house, cleaned things, went with Mrs. Harrison to get groceries. It wasn't as bad as he thought.

Halfway through cleaning the dishes side by side with Mrs. Harrison, Jacob asked, "Where's your dog?"

"Outside, in the doggie house," she said, as she stacked another washed plate into the clean plate pile. "You miss them, don't you? Hard to blame you, it seems to be the main attraction of our house, like a circus show."

"I always thought they were fun to look at."

"I'll bring them in when we finish cleaning."

When she did, Jacob was surprised to see them now, wobbling and growing gray whiskers. He didn't know why he was startled. It'd been years since he'd last seen them.

"Do they still have a rope toy?"

Mrs. Harrison smiled. "Oh, that thing got torn up years ago, and it didn't help for them to bang their heads against the wall when they played with it. Jacob looked back at the dogs. They'd somehow lost the allure they'd carried when he was a child.

Things were different that evening. Instead of Robyn locking herself away from the world, she sat down with everyone, more specifically, next to Jacob. She had a look on her face that Jacob knew meant she'd sleep with the next guy to offer. He figured she was mad at someone and maybe wanted revenge.

"So Robyn, how was your day?" Mrs. Harrison asked.

"Well, I stayed away from you know who and all of his friends." Then Robyn unobtrusively laid a hand on Jacob's knee. No one noticed but Jacob. "I got into a girl huddle with my friends and they talked me through the day." She stumbled over her next words. "I know I made a bit of a scene earlier, but I'm better now."

"That's good."

Robyn dragged her hand closer to Jacob's groin. There was something wrong with this situation. For some reason Jacob couldn't get hard with Robyn's entire family watching them. It'd be embarrassing if Robyn made it all the way up there only to discover that his junior had gone soft.

He put a hand on hers and she discontinued further exploration. Robyn tried to look at him, then looked away. Jacob made gave no reaction.

The clinks and clanks of the silverware mixed with everyone talking about their day drove Jacob crazy knowing he had an attractive girl's hand not four inches from his junior. He was afraid he'd start sweating and everyone would notice. He took a sip of water and wiped his forehead.

Dinner was over. Jacob miraculously finished dinner without slipping up or needing a change of underwear. He helped clean the dishes.

Later that night, Jacob sat in his room waiting for everyone to fall asleep, all of course but Robyn, who, being a teenager, wouldn't sleep before midnight anyways.

It was nearly eleven. The outside air was still. Jacob was tired, if only he hadn't mentally exhausted himself by imagining Robyn in bed with him all day. Ironic.

He opened his door and an inopportune creaking sound amplified through the hallway. He winced, then waited silently. When no one came he opened the door completely and walked to Robyn's room. Around the corner came a set of footsteps, it was too late to turn back, he was already touching the doorknob and leaving now would make too much noise.

The lights flickered on, his heart jumped. It was Mrs. Harrison. She must've fallen asleep watching television, then gotten up when he opened the door.

His face was like a stone, all the blood had drained

from it and he imagined he looked like a ghost in the dark hallway.

She approached him with a smirk that made him too uncomfortable to even move. She slipped her hand in her pocket and took something out.

Stuck in between two of her fingers was a condom. "If you're going to have sex with my daughter it might as well be protected sex."

Jacob took it. He was afraid it was a trick then disregarded the theory. She wouldn't have gone through the trouble only to trick him.

"When did you grab this?"

"After dinner," she said, still smiling. "I wanted to give it to you before you made your move."

"I had no idea you'd be so…." Jacob couldn't find the word he wanted, then he settled with, "Cool."

"I'm no prude," she said.

Jacob stared at her, waiting for something else to happen. She winked at him, then walked down the hall, turning off the lights before leaving to her room.

I might never want to leave this place, he thought.

Sweet Mrs. Harrison he'd known years ago when his mother dropped him and his brother off to be babysat. The mental image would be replaced with a much older Mrs. Harrison handing him a condom. People could change, he guessed. *He* could change.

He had an unquenchable sexual thirst. The image of a naked Robyn shot into his head like an emergency broadcast.

He knocked.

"Come in," came an excited voice, not sounding the least bit tired. He opened and stepped into the room.

Robyn was laying spread across the bed in nothing but a bra and panties.

"Sorry, I sleep in my underwear. Hope you don't mind."

"Don't apologize," he said. "I do too. I noticed you were feeling a little down, so I brought you a present."

She knew what it was, yet she still seemed surprised. She got to her knees and flipped her hair behind her. "You did?"

Jacob held the condom Mrs. Harrison had given him.

"No, need, I'm on the pill," Robyn said.

Jacob wanted to use the condom for more than just pregnancy prevention. "It's lubricated, his and her pleasure," he lied.

"Oh, well in that case, slip that bad boy on."

He did.

Jacob lost track of the time. The first time he did Robyn he lasted maybe five minutes. It'd been a while since his last release. But Jacob was among a small minority of people that could continue without a break, acting as if he hadn't just came.

He actually thought he might have to turn the condom inside out. He laughed at the idea, but only in his head.

By the time they were finished Jacob knew he had to walk back to his room so that the other children wouldn't know he'd slept with her. His legs felt weak, and tired, so did Robyn's. She was so tired that she didn't even remind Jacob to leave. She slept on her back, the way Jacob had left her. He rolled onto his side and slept naked in her bed.

It was morning. They woke simultaneously by a gentle knocking on the door. It was followed by no voice but they both knew exactly who it was. Good ol' Mrs. Harrison trying to keep them from embarrassing themselves.

"Oh, shit!" Jacob said, throwing the bed covers off of him and rushing to pick up his clothes. "I forgot to leave last night."

"Hurry up," Robyn said in a hushed tone. "Abbie sets an alarm to wake her up."

Jacob dressed himself as best he could in under ten seconds and ran out of Robyn's room and into his own. Robyn redressed herself.

A condom dangled halfway out of the mini trashcan. Jacob must've missed his throw sometime last night.

She walked into her private bathroom and performed her morning routine, eliminating any trace of having slept with someone the night before. Hair combed, teeth brushed, makeup applied, Robyn left her room and set out to the kitchen where Jacob and her family were waiting silently.

Oh God! What if they know? she thought. *No. No they can't all know, Carolin and Abbie are too young to know that stuff anyway.*

She came in quietly, sitting next to Jacob where he'd already set a place for her, forks, knives, and everything.

"Mom, can we get oat flakes next time?" Abbie asked.

"I'll look for them next time we're shopping." She avoided eye contact with anyone. Robyn got the feeling that something was wrong, like somehow her mother knew.

They finished breakfast with nothing out of the usual happening, except of course for her mother's lack of attention. The lunches she'd packed were only half-full and Jacob had to remind her of the snacks she'd missed.

Robyn said goodbye and left for the front door. Jacob hurried and blocked her just as she reached it.

"Can I ask you something?" he said.

You've already had sex with me, why do you need to say anything? she thought.

"Shoot."

"Did you put that streak in your hair to make you look like a robin? Robyn."

She blinked absentmindedly, almost as if she didn't quite hear what he'd said. "A what?"

Jacob laughed. "A robin bird."

"There's a bird called robin?"

Jacob laughed even harder.

"Can I ask *you* a question?" Robyn said.

"Ask away."

She leaned closely to Jacob, so that she could see every

detail on his face. "Do you think my mom knows about last night?"

Jacob stared at her incredulously. "She's the one who gave me the condom."

"*My* mom?"

Jacob shushed her and looked to see if anyone was watching them. "Yes, I was surprised too, but she seems to be A-Okay with it. You can relax."

Robyn unknowingly lowered her shoulders, relaxing as Jacob told her to. "I have to go, I'll see you later."

She opened the door and walked to her car, she could hear Jacob blowing her a kiss, but she didn't turn around to return one, or accept his.

Chapter 9

She was standing in the hallway of her indoor high school, taking books from her locker, putting books back. When she closed the locker door a face appeared close to hers. She was startled, but had expected it sometime that day.

"Can we talk?" said the man. He was a good-looking kid, white collared shirt, long brown hair, eyes that shimmered without the need of light.

"There's nothing to talk about, Evan."

She slammed the locker door, it echoed through the hallway. Some people glared at them as they strolled by. She bolted down the hallway, her arms crossed over her books and pressed tightly to her chest. Evan followed her down the hall, almost walking sideways so that he could look at her face.

"If we could just talk about things. I think we owe each other that much."

Robyn laughed sardonically. "I don't owe *you* anything." She looked for one of her friends to come to her aide. There was no one. Her class was down the hall, anyways. But the hall was becoming deserted, and it made Robyn uneasy.

"Do it for us," Evan continued. "For our relationship."

"There is no relationship," Robyn said curtly.

She made it to her class at the end of the hall, turning around before stepping in. "By the way, last night I fucked some guy, and he was *way* better than you."

She stepped in, and the heavy steel classroom door closed behind her. She didn't hear any cursing or shouting, not even footsteps, as if he was still standing outside. Robyn peered out the tiny door window. No one was there.

By now, every seat in the class was taken, except for the one's in the front row. Robyn ambled to one of them and put her books on the desk. When class ended she planned to tell her friends about how she slept with some strange new guy that was living with her for a while. She'd tell a few people, they'd tell a few people, then the entire school would know she was over Evan.

She waited through another pointless English class (English would never be her major anyway), and walked out the door before anyone else could. Evan stood directly in front of the doorway. She almost ran into him, but missed by a narrow distance.

Did he stand outside her entire class? Or did he leave his class early to wait for her? Both were plausible conclusions.

"Robyn," he said. "I'm not leaving you alone until we talk about it."

"No."

"Who was it? Was it Vincent?"

"No. It was no one you know."

He grabbed her by the shoulder and spun her around. She was shocked, too shocked to slap him.

He lowered his voice to an aggressive whisper. "Look, can you just tell me who the fuck it was. You already know who I did. It was a mistake, I admit it. Can you just tell me who your mistake was and own up to it? Two wrongs don't make a right, Robyn."

By the sound of Evan's voice Robyn could tell she'd won the emotional battle between them. Evan hadn't put this much effort and focus into anything before, especially not her.

"His name's Jacob. And he's not a mistake, he's living with me for a while and I'm seeing him again tonight."

Robyn smiled in a way that was just for show. It was working. Evan wanted to yell at her until she cried in front of the whole goddamn school. He knew, however, that would make him look worse than her. No one walking by would see a girl who'd wronged him and gotten just what she'd deserved. All they would see is some guy verbally assaulting a poor defenseless woman.

Realizing he'd lost, Evan walked away before Robyn's squad of girl friends could arrive.

He finished the day avoiding his usual group of friends. By now they'd hear what'd happen and would want to talk about it. Knowing them they wouldn't shut up until he explained to them every last painstaking detail.

When he arrived home that day he swung his backpack from his shoulders and threw it on the ground. He guessed this was probably how Robyn acted when she'd heard about him and Adrianna. He could feel his ears turn red, only his ears. His muscles tensed so tight he had to hit something. It was more of a reflex, really. He swung his fists at the wall so loud the noise could be heard four rooms down. And it was.

"What the hell are you doing?" called a voice from an open room. The man stepped out and fast-walked toward him. "Are you trying to ruin these walls?"

Evan said nothing.

His father walked to where he was and stared at the place Evan had hit.

He wasn't considerably bigger than Evan, despite him being a six-foot-two high school quarter back in his own high school years.

Evan peered around his father's shoulder to make sure the mark he'd made wasn't as bad as he thought it was. His imagination had a funny way of doing things to him when he was angry.

It wasn't bad, just a scratch on the paint. But that small scratch, no matter how insignificant, would be a long-lasting reminder of Evan's outrage.

His dad turned toward him. "You know you'll be repainting this."

"I'm sorry, Robyn and I— "

"Oh, you and Robyn broke up? Big fucking deal! You're a teenager, you're doing what teenagers do. If you

took out one of your high school breakups on my wall
every time, I'd—." He shook his head. "Just fix this
soon."

"I will dad. I'm sorry."

His dad walked back to the room he came from with a
newly given angry slumped posture.

It was a scratch, Evan thought. *Just a scratch.*

A small hanging picture could cover it with room to
spare. White-out could fix it and no one would notice. If
only he'd released his tension when his dad wasn't
home.

This is Robyn's fault, he thought. *I only slept with
Adrianna because I thought she'd slept with Vincent.*

It didn't make sense for Vincent to have slept with
Robyn, though. He was his best friend and fellow
football star, and he'd heard somewhere that he had a
tiny pecker. It couldn't be him. He'd have noticed if he
was acting funny or sneaking around. However, if Robyn
was mad at him, Vincent was who she'd find first. It'd
make him the angriest.

Evan wanted to make sure he was screwing around
too, even out the playing field. That way, people
wouldn't look at him like, "Poor Evan, he couldn't keep
his girlfriend interested so she slept around with other
guys."

He had a gut feeling she'd done it with someone. He
couldn't shake the feeling. He always trusted his gut.

His brother entered the house wearing the bike helmet
he usually wore riding home.

Evan's head was already pounding knowing his
brother would want to talk to him, and now of all times,
when he needed a punching bag more than ever.

His little brother took off his helmet, revealing his
ruffled curly hair. He shook his head like a dog to get a
normal feeling back in his head. Then he ran his fingers
through his hair to straighten it.

"Hi," his brother said, half-smiling at him.

"Hey," Evan replied, not returning a smile. He started

toward the hallway.

"So I was thinking," the little brother said, running in front of him. "You know there's a county fair coming up and I— "

Evan walked through his little brother, and he fell to the ground. His helmet hit the tile, and spun in little circles, the buckles fluttering. Evan didn't mean to trip him, but it worked, he stopped talking to him.

"Not now!" Evan snapped as he walked down the hall in angry strides.

The brother stood weakly to his feet, using the wall to balance himself. His hips were sore but he managed to bend and retrieve his helmet. The second time he straightened his back a sharp pain shot down his lumbar. He pressed a hand on it and let out a pathetic moan.

He turned to look at his room. It was past Evan's and he didn't care to risk bumping into him again as he walked to it.

He fast-walked into the kitchen and grabbed the well underused home phone — long made inferior by the cellphone. The thing is, he had a cellphone. He just couldn't pay his dad the monthly payment on time to use it.

He searched through his contacts and copied his friend Ollie's number from his cell to his home phone. He dialed.

"What's up Kenneth?" squeaked Ollie. He was a late bloomer and hadn't gone through puberty like the rest of his class. Kenneth was his only friend.

"You wanna hang out?"

"Sure, go to a movie?" Ollie said, almost immediately.

"My dad told me this morning it's a good day to be outside."

"And do what?"

"Throw the ball around?"

Silence, and then, "Okay."

Kenneth knew he had nothing better to do. How could he? He had no friends.

"Sounds good."

"I'll be there in ten."

"Cool."

He hung up, then he remembered the baseball his dad gave him a few months ago, said it was one he'd used as a kid, back in the "good ol' days".

He walked soundlessly to his room, first making sure Evan wasn't roaming around the hallways. Kenneth lied on his stomach and reached under his bed, feeling around for anything that might feel like a baseball. Hiding under his bed was years of abandoned magazines and childhood toys. He reached deeper, and then he felt something round roll away from his hand. He snatched it and pulled it from under the bed. It was the baseball, torn and discolored.

He tossed it into the air a few times to get a feel for its weight. Ollie might not think a game of catch was as exciting as he did, but if he wasn't doing something with him, he'd most likely be studying.

Kenneth imagined his friend alone in his dark room, sitting at his desk, reading his homework with only the light of a library desk lamp. He was sweating profusely over the strain of his homework and wearing glasses with lenses too thick for his own good. His glasses fogged up and he had to take them off to blow on them.

Kenneth stood in the doorway of his father's office. The door was left open, but Kenneth knew that was by no means an invitation to disturb him. His father was staring intensely at his computer screen, typing something.

"Hey dad."

His father grunted and kept typing.

"I invited Ollie over to play outside."

Another grunt.

"Me and him are going to play catch with the baseball you gave me."

Clearly these were the only words his father heard

because he swiveled around in his chair. If Kenneth could guess, the key words that caught his father's attention were, "catch", "baseball", "you", "gave", and "me".

"Now, you be careful with that," his dad said importantly. "I don't want to have to fish that out of a tree or something."

"I'll be careful."

His dad swiveled around and continued typing. His fingers hit the keys so loud Kenneth wondered if he was trying to drown out any further conversation Kenneth might initiate. He frowned, then walked out of the room.

The doorbell rang. Kenneth was already sitting close by in the family room, watching TV. He stood up and strolled to the door. The doorbell rang again impatiently.

"I'm coming," he said, approaching him.

He unlocked the door and opened it. It was Ollie, and just as he'd predicted, was wearing his glasses with lenses too thick for his own good. His eyes were slightly magnified from them.

"Hi, Ollie."

"Is that a baseball?" Ollie asked, pointing to Kenneth's hand.

Kenneth looked down at it. He hadn't realized he'd picked it up when he answered the door. It was unconsciously more important to him than he thought.

"Yeah, we should go to the back, toss it around."

"Uh." He pushed his glasses from the bridge of his nose closer to his eyes. "Okay." He wiped his shoes on the welcome mat and stepped inside.

Kenneth led him to the back. It was a vast, lush green yard with a play structure his dad assembled when he was a kid. There was even a tree house, but he couldn't remember it being built.

Kenneth stood opposite Ollie about fifteen feet and threw him the baseball underhand. Ollie barely caught it, then threw it back the same way.

"Can I ask you something, Kenneth?"

Kenneth swallowed. There could be a million different things Ollie could ask him, he might not like it. "Sure."

He threw the ball back. Ollie caught it.

"Why do you think no one likes me?"

Kenneth continued passing the ball back and forth, debating whether to tell Ollie the cold hard truth, or to gently set it down for him, or both.

"I think you need to have more confidence."

"Confidence?" Ollie said, as if he'd never heard the word before.

"Yeah." Kenneth threw the ball back. "And maybe switch to contact lenses," he added, with a little sarcasm.

"I need these to read."

"Contacts work for that too."

"Well I heard those things could roll into the back of your eyes. Some girl got it stuck there for three days I think. She had to go to the doctors to have it removed."

"Ollie, do you believe everything you hear?"

"Shut up."

They laughed together a little.

"You know what?" Ollie said.

"What?"

When Ollie caught Kenneth's next throw, he held the ball. He looked on the ground for something. Kenneth walked toward him.

"What is it?"

Ollie picked up a stick that looked like it'd fallen from the tree behind him. "We should hit the ball around."

"What? Ollie, no!"

"Oh, come on. I won't even hit it that hard." He held the ball in front of him and readied the stick at his side.

Kenneth didn't know what to say to stop him, so he picked the first shocking thing to enter his head. "Ollie, more people would like you if wouldn't do dumb shit like this."

Kenneth considered "shit" to be a shocking thing to say at his age. Ollie, on the other hand, heard it all the time at home. He tossed the ball lightly into the air before him and struck it with his stick. He must've hit it harder than he wanted, harder than Kenneth even thought he could. The ball rose and flew over the triangular heads of the fence. It landed, undoubtedly, in Mr. Peterson's backyard.

Kenneth flinched, expecting to hear the noise of a shattering window. But there was none. He lowered his shoulders and loosened a bit.

"You idiot!" he yelled. "That was really important to my dad! He's gonna kill me now! He'll probably never give me anything again!"

"Relax," Ollie shrugged. "We'll just climb the fence and get it back."

"You couldn't climb that fence to save your life! You're too short!"

Ollie looked at him and blinked. Kenneth wanted to punch him right in his stupid face and break the thick-lensed glasses covering his stupid beady eyes.

"Then I'll climb the tree," Ollie said mildly.

"No!" Kenneth yelled as Ollie walked to the tree. He jumped and extended his arm for one of its branches.

Kenneth would've found his failure to climb pretty funny under different circumstances.

After watching Ollie fail for half a minute, Kenneth decided to take over.

"For fuck's sake, I'll do it."

Kenneth jumped into the air and grabbed a branch on his first attempt. He hung for a moment to look at Ollie's face. He was satisfied doing it right his first time after watching Ollie fail repeatedly.

Kenneth pulled himself up and climbed two more branches, then climbed over the fence.

He fell to his knees. The shock from the fall hurt his feet and he cursed under his breath.

He couldn't find the ball at first. There was a field of various rocks in Mr. Peterson's yard. It would be easy for a ball to get stuck between them. He could hear no dog

barking, that was a good sign. Although he guessed he'd
have heard a dog barking before today if there was one.

Behind him was the rustling of leaves. Branches bents
and fluttered. Then Ollie dropped down next to him. He
was amazed Ollie even made it up the tree.

"I took a running start that time," Ollie explained as
he picked his glasses off the ground and wiped them on
his shirt.

They heard more rustling, this time from ahead of
them. Near the side yard was a small white ball lined
with red stitches.

"There it is!" Ollie said, pointing to it.

The rustling got louder, and around the corner came
Mr. Peterson holding a garbage bag of what sounded like
aluminum cans. He dropped the bag next to him and
waddled over towards them. Without his cane Mr.
Peterson looked ridiculous and animated.

Kenneth and Ollie turned around and clawed at the
fence, trying to get ahold of it.

"How are we supposed to get back?" Ollie yelled.

"I don't know, I've never done this before!"

Kenneth looked behind his shoulder. Mr. Peterson's
legs wobbled over the bed of rocks separating them. He
was struggling, but getting closer.

"If I break my leg, I'll sue the both of you!" he yelled.

"Leave us alone!" Ollie yelled back.

Kenneth kicked the fence with as much strength as he
had in his scrawny legs, trying to break a hole in the
fence big enough to escape. The wooden boards barely
even bent.

They both turned around and searched for another
escape route. Too late!

Mr. Peterson grabbed the two boys by their collars and
pulled them close enough to him that they could smell
his breath. His teeth were a stained yellow and they
almost glowed in the daylight.

"You'll get your ball back this time, but you'll never
jump that fence again. Understand?"

The boys nodded in fearful agreement.

"Good," Mr. Peterson continued. "Because if anything happens to you on *my* property that makes it *my* problem. You two can take your ball and go out the side fence. But if I catch you back here again — "

"We know," said the one with glasses.

He let them go, they picked up the baseball and hurried off.

When the Mr. Peterson entered the house his wife said, "Congratulations Bert, you've managed to scare off another one of our neighbor's kids."

"We don't need them, Janice! We don't need any of them! These kids have no respect for adults!"

His wife held out a placating hand and patted the air. "That may be true, but can you honestly say you weren't a little rebellious at their age?"

"I was working at my father's construction company, I didn't have *time* to be rebellious."

"Times have changed, Bert."

"Well they shouldn't have," he scoffed. His voice was becoming hoarse. He decided to save his breath, grabbed his cane leaning on the fireplace, and walked off to his car.

He struggled with trembling hands to jam the key into the ignition. Damn arthritis.

He pulled the key back and lined it up with the ignition. His glasses helped, but only a little. He stabbed the key into the ignition and turned it. The car made a rapid rumbling noise like it had something stuck in its throat, if it had a throat.

He grabbed his remote garage opener from the glove compartment and clicked opened the garage. It moved as slowly as he did, ascending and folding parallel to the ceiling. He coughed, then pulled his car out before clicking the garage opener one more time. Then he pulled out onto the hot blacktop and drove.

Mr. Peterson had a bumper sticker that said, "Catch me if you can".

Ironically, he was the slowest driver in the neighborhood. Kids sometimes chased his car to see if they were faster. They'd yell at him too. He knew people called him names beside Mr. Peterson. There was the classic grumpy old man (one of his favorites), Bad Bert, Mr. P, wrinkles, or simply, bastard.

Take your pick.

Mr. Peterson looked briefly at the sky from the seat of his blue 1959 Cadillac convertible and marveled at the fact that there were no clouds to be seen.

He drove on and merged cautiously onto the freeway. He drove in the slow lane. He *always* drove in the slow lane. Any other lane was just too much. Too much honking and too much passing. Eventually, he got tired of honking back and returning middle fingers.

Ten minutes later he pulled into a bank parking lot and parked in a shaded space, far from the other cars. As he reached into the glove compartment his back made a loud crack, and he pulled out an envelope.

He stepped onto the pavement and walked up the ramp leading to the bank, his hand hovering closely above the dirty handrail.

People often called him a grumpy old man but he enjoyed many little things. Things like how his bank had automatic doors so he wouldn't have to show counterfeit gratitude to some young couple holding the door open.

The bank was crowded as usual. No surprises there. Tellers were writing in their perfect handwriting. Forms were being filled out, and the line kept moving.

Mr. Peterson held his envelope tightly, almost like he expected someone to take it. There wasn't much of course, there never was. In his envelope was just some debts finally paid back to him from long ago. It was a rare occasion when he was repaid, and so was going to the bank.

There was a bowl of candy on a nearby counter. He'd never seen an adult take from it. It was mostly there to keep impatient children from pouting while their parents took care of business.

Mr. Peterson listened to the mindless chatter of the people in front of him.

"Can you believe gas prices?" One person said.

"I know, I only came here because it was on the way back home."

Mr. Peterson thought about pushing the line along. The beautiful day was burning sunlight and he was missing it by standing inside with a bunch of youthful degenerates.

These people don't know the meaning of hard work, he thought. *They probably didn't earn their paychecks.*

He thought further. It hurt his head to think so hard, but he couldn't help it. What could he do?

Only at that moment, standing motionless in a train of busy people did he realize he'd married the wrong woman. He should've married Sheila. She ended up being as saggy as Janice, in places that used to be perky. Age comes to us all, and it sneaks up quietly.

However, Sheila was dead now, her husband got lucky. He doesn't have to listen to any of her incessant whining. He remembered meeting Sheila with his Naval buddy, who ended up marrying her. He was stuck with Janice. Mr. Peterson and his buddy decided to pick their girl, back off from the other one, and let nature do the rest. But now he had the overwhelming sensation he'd picked the wrong one. How was he supposed to know Janice would live this long?

The line moved up a space and the people moved forward, systematically, like robots.

It was funny to Mr. Peterson how suddenly his new epiphany came to him, just standing in line, with too much time to think. And the line moved again.

He was near the front of the booth. Two people were ahead of him now, an Asian girl in front. She was pretty, with her perfectly straight long black hair down almost to her butt. She was wearing very short jeans that showed her long athletic legs. Mr. Peterson guessed she probably ran a lot. He looked at them closely, his eyes adjusting. She *definitely* ran a lot.

The girl finished her business and walked off, her hair barely moved when she did. As she passed, she paid no attention to him.

The next man talked with an accent, probably something European. Mr. Peterson figured his country could've fought a war against his at some point.

His conversation lasted maybe five minutes, then he was gone.

Mr. Peterson walked warily to the teller's desk. He was a young kid, most likely paying his way through college. He had short, well combed jet-black hair that was slightly spiked at the front. A gray suit wore tightly to his torso. It had no wrinkles that Mr. Peterson could see (although with his eyesight that would be difficult to spot anyway).

"Hello," he said with a forced smile. "How can I help you?" His voice sounded robotic, and well trained.

Mr. Peterson raised his envelope with his thin, bony fingers, and pulled out a single check.

"I'd like to cash this," he said as he slowly handed it to the teller.

"Of course. I should tell you though that there are ATMs for that, much faster."

Mr. Peterson twisted his face to make it look as angry as it possibly could be. "I don't like dealing with all that technology."

"Okay, that's perfectly fine, I just thought I'd mention it."

Mr. Peterson pointed a shaky, bony finger in the teller's direction. For a moment the teller was glad to have a desk separating them.

"Every time," Mr. Peterson continued, his voice sounding as elderly as ever. "That I come here, you people always try to get me to sign up for something or give out my personal information, all I want to do is deposit one simple check." Mr. Peterson couldn't find the strength to louden his voice.

"Do you have your ID with you?"

"Of course I do," Mr. Peterson replied, finally lowering his shaky finger. "What kind of a moron goes to the bank without an ID?"

The teller considered his question rhetorical and ignored it. "I'll need you to show me your ID and fill this out."

The teller handed him a slip of paper and Mr. Peterson grudgingly took it, then his face turned white and he handed it back.

"I remembered I already did." He unzipped his coat pockets and ruffled through them, putting things out on the counter as he dug deeper. Finally, he pulled out the deposit slip and handed it to the teller.

"Will that be checking or savings?"

"Savings."

The teller took the check and punched something into his computer.

"Will that be all for today?"

"Yes," Mr. Peterson said, already moving away. When he turned around, he bumped into something that felt like concrete to him. He fell back, his hands flailing in the air. A hand grabbed to reach him but only grazed his chest. When he hit the ground, someone gasped, and it gave him a slight comfort to know someone was concerned about him.

A muscle-bound man towered over him. His head was block shaped and looked disproportionate to the rest of his body. The bright light above made him almost look frightening.

Am I dead, he thought. *Has it finally happened? Did I pick the wrong day to leave my cane in the car?*

"I'm so sorry," the man said, grabbing his elbow.

The old man writhed on the hard floor and moaned.

"Don't touch me!" he screamed. People looked at him from their places in line.

"I didn't mean to," the man said. "I looked away for

one second and you were there."

The man kneeled down to help, but the old man struggled and screamed even louder.

"Watch where you're going! You kids never think about the consequences of your actions!"

The man gave up, the more he tried to help, the more the old man screamed, and more people looked. He looked around, unsure of what to do, then resolved to just walk away. He was embarrassed that somewhere in the bank's security database there was footage of the old man screaming at him.

He walked out of the bank, his business unfinished. He'd just wasted his gas money, and his time. Before leaving the bank the man turned around at the automatic doors, several people were helping the old man to his feet.

Stupid, he thought. *Is one person helping not enough?*

Rain drizzled down on his head almost immediately after stepping outside. There were little dark dots on the pavement from the rain.

A moment ago the sky was clear. Not one cloud.

He shrugged to himself, to nature, to his luck, then stepped into his car.

He decided to pick up a twelve pack at the super mart. Maybe, *hopefully*, if he downed the pack soon enough he'd forget about the old man incident. He'd fall asleep in a drunken stupor and wake up with a lovely hangover.

He took off into the road. The man made sure to rev the V8 engine extra loud as he passed several people walking by.

The supermarket stood before him, stretching across the parking lot like the Great Wall of China. It was very popular in his neighborhood, and he thought surely he'd bump into someone he knew there. Hopefully, someone he wanted to see.

He got out and walked inside, ignoring the door

greeter as he welcomed him. Then he grabbed a cart and headed straight to the alcohol section.

Something strong, he thought. *Something extra strong.*

"Daniel? Daniel is that you?"

Whose voice was it? He'd heard it before, but he couldn't match a face with it. He looked around, but found no one looking at him.

Must be another Daniel, he thought. *Common name.*

"Daniel?" the voice said unsurely.

"Yes," he answered. Was the voice coming from his own head?

It was a short girl with a ponytail. Her body was as athletic as his, only she was slim. She smiled at him, but he couldn't return the gesture not knowing who she was.

But there was something about her. Something familiar….

Julia, he thought. *My one-night stand.*

"You look so…. different," she said.

Different? He played that word in his head. *You mean to say muscular…. taller…. happier.*

She was right though. He did look different. She knew him in high school as the shy, scrawny, weird kid. He even had braces until his senior year. After a well-structured workout routine, on top of a natural growth spurt no one expected at his age, he changed. Their one-night stand of course, was one of her drunken mistakes. But now, as Daniel saw in her face, it wasn't so much as a mistake anymore.

He smiled, satisfied that his newfound looks had far surpassed what Julia looked like now.

"Aaron's with me too. You want to see him?"

Daniel opened his mouth but she didn't wait for his response. She turned around. Aaron stood in a different aisle across from them, observing a phone charger.

"Hey, Aaron! Aaron, look who it is!" She gestured Aaron to join them. He put back the charger on its shelf and walked to them in no real hurry.

Daniel didn't care to see him, or Julia for that matter.

He knew this was out of courtesy and nothing more. He'd most likely never see her again, not unless they accidentally ran into each other like they had now.

"Hey," Aaron said listlessly, approaching them.

"You remember Aaron, right? From high school."

"Sure I do," Daniel said, then pointed a finger at Aaron. "I think you beat me up once."

Aaron rubbed the back of his neck. "Uhhh, could have."

Daniel straightened his back, giving himself even more height over Aaron. *Who's the big guy now?*

"So what're you doing here?" Julia asked.

"Getting beer."

"Having a party, are you?"

"No, just having a rough day. I bumped into this old guy at the bank. I tried to help him up but he just kept screaming, right there, in front of everyone."

"Why'd you knock down an old guy?" Aaron asked contemptuously.

Daniel frowned and peered directly into Aaron's eyes, ignoring Julia completely. "Well I didn't do it on purpose."

Daniel could tell by the look on Aaron's face that he was yielding. He recognized that look as the same when Aaron had hit him and Daniel just gave up. He could remember every scrape and bruise on his body brought to him by Aaron. He had to lie to anyone asking about them, sometimes he'd act as though he'd accidentally hurt himself. It felt silly, but it was less embarrassing than what'd actually happened.

"I've gotta go," Daniel said abruptly.

"Oh, uh—okay," Julia said tentatively. "See you around?"

"Maybe."

Daniel picked a twelve pack at random and added it to his cart. He thought that would be enough but decided to grab a condom as well, extra-large, which he thought might've been a little bit of an overkill. He'd grown all right, but not *everywhere*. Still, on the off chance someone else he knew was watching, he'd want to look his best.

He ambled across the oversized supermarket, his rolling cart leading the way, and stopped at the smallest line at the cash registers. He'd been lucky enough to get one with a pretty cashier around his age.

The line cleared and he unloaded the booze and condoms onto the small conveyor belt. He had his wallet already in hand as she scanned his items. She gazed at him from across the register and before she could speak, he knew what she'd ask.

He handed her the ID. She frowned uncertainly at it.

"It's my birthday," he said, smiling at the pretty minimum wage cashier.

At least she isn't whoring herself, he thought.

She stared intently at the ID, the dates matched up, he was twenty-one.

She handed it back to him with a smile. "Happy birthday."

"Thanks."

"You doing anything fun?"

Daniel stretched his arms over the register, and she, not knowing what he was doing, stepped back. He grabbed his condoms and held it at eye level, answering her question.

She laughed, but still made it sound quiet and professional. "Hope you have fun."

He paid using a debit card, a receipt spit out from the machine, she bagged his condoms and beer and threw the receipt with them.

He took the bag and gave her one more gaze. Another customer stepped to the register but she still locked eyes with Daniel, ignoring the customer briefly, who cleared his throat. She blinked hard, as if coming back to reality, and tended to the customer.

"Sorry. You find everything okay?"

"I'm going back there this time tomorrow," Daniel

said to himself as he loaded his beer and condoms into the car.

Maybe I'll tell her that funny story about the bank, he thought.

Daniel stepped inside the car and made it home in time to see his brother preparing to leave.

He wasn't his real brother, not really. It was his cousin. Daniel still liked him more than his actually brothers, who'd moved out long ago, never to be heard from again, except on holidays.

His cousin even looked like he did when he was younger, before the rapid growth spurt. It seemed he was turning into him too, and that was the way Daniel wanted it.

"Where you headed Lucas?" Daniel said, rolling down his window and pulling into the driveway as Lucas was leaving.

"Going to Emma's house." He said it in a certain amiable tone that told Daniel exactly what he meant. He didn't know if he should offer his condoms or not. He decided against it. He'd bought an extra-large and couldn't be sure.

"You have fun," he replied.

"Thanks. Oh, and happy birthday."

Daniel offered Lucas a fist bump through the open car window.

Lucas met his fist bump. He waved goodbye as he got into his car. Okay, it was a scratched-up rust bucket, but it was still a car, dammit. He could afford it on a monthly basis and the gas mileage was reasonable.

He was sixteen and had only gotten his driver's license a few months ago. Lucas was nervous about driving anyone else, including Emma. Still, there was nothing stopping him from going to her house by himself.

Emma's place was a twenty-minute drive from where Lucas lived. It was too far if you asked him. It wasn't even her parents' house, it was her grandparents'.

There was a saying, summer girlfriend. Well, this was his winter girlfriend. She had been for several years. She'd come from Tennessee every Christmas break, and much to his dismay, not once did they have sex. No. Santa never put any condoms in his Christmas stocking. No sir.

It wasn't Christmas break though, she'd gone there to take care of her grandparents, keep an eye on them and make sure grandpa didn't wander off and forget where he was. She went to school that year somewhere near Lucas, he forgot the name of it. Thankfully, he'd seen her more this year. Too much though and his parents might get suspicious.

She'd invited him over. This was it. It *had* to be it. A few of his friends had already lost their virginity, and of course, they'd exaggerated a lot of what they did. Judging by the way it sounded, some of them had to be Greek gods. Surely *some* of them lied about it, at least some of them. Not everyone lost their virginity as early as he would.

Lucas didn't need to lie. He knew that those who talked of it the most never actually did it. Like most high school kids, he knew that it would spread like a wild fire the minute he told one person. But would Emma care about that? His entire school knowing of her sexual encounter, and the day after she had it? How would the other kids look at him once they knew? He decided he was thinking too hard and turned on the radio.

Careful Lucas, he thought. *Let's not think too much unless we want to think ourselves into a soft dick.*

He adjusted his chair, and he relaxed a little. The music was smooth coming out his speakers. He turned up the volume, and he felt powerful. The loud music made it tempting to start speeding. He wanted to get there as fast as possible, but he didn't need a ticket. He eased off the gas pedal and remained very conscious of his speed the rest of the way.

He stood in front of the house, nervous as ever, with two condoms in his wallet.

Was that enough? Should I have brought more? I'll probably be okay.

He rang the doorbell, the door opened.

"Lucas!" sang Emma.

Lucas had never seen a more beautiful girl, no need to convince him of that. She'd matured much faster than other girls her age. Her breasts showed well through her white t-shirt, and her hair was draped over them, making them look rounder. Lucas couldn't tell if she was wearing a bra or not. He could tell, however, that she was wearing more makeup than usual, as if she was getting ready for some sort of an occasion.

He liked to think she wasn't wearing panties either — unlikely, but one can dream.

She wrapped her arms around him, almost knocking Lucas back. Her breasts were so big she couldn't touch her stomach to his while they were hugging, there was too much in the way.

The hug lasted about half a minute. No one wanted to say anything because neither of them wanted it to end.

Her house was a little run down, that wasn't saying much in her neighborhood though. If it wasn't a little run down it would look out of place. Her grandparents couldn't afford much.

"Come inside," she said. "Grandpa and grandma are out at a family reunion. They wanted me to go with them, but I told them I was sick."

"They didn't want to stay here and take care of you?"

"Nah, they don't really get out much. It's like a vacation for them."

Lucas stared at her for a second and blinked absentmindedly. He liked small talk, but there would be plenty of time for it later.

She broke the silence. "Would you like to come in?"

Of course he would, she thought. *That's why he's here.*

He smiled. "Sure."

She led him inside and into the family room. It was the biggest room in the house by far. She'd cleaned before Lucas arrived but wished she'd cleaned up further. She probably wouldn't be satisfied with that either. She was too much of a neat freak.

There were lit candles on the counters, on dressers, the floors even. They were vanilla scented. One of her friends told her the scent of vanilla was an aphrodisiac. She wasn't sure if she believed her, but it couldn't hurt.

It was almost too strong. Emma didn't notice it at first because her senses had become adapted to the smell. Only from the contrasting fresh air when she opened the door did she notice it being so overpowering. She put two fingers in her mouth, wetting them with her saliva, then unlit a few candles on the counter.

Emma hadn't thought to put on music or a sappy romance film. It would be better to let Lucas decide that stuff. She knew her grandparents didn't have much to choose from anyways.

Lucas sat down on the couch and waited.

She spun her neck and her hair whipped fully behind her. She started to sit on the couch, then Lucas stopped her.

"Sit on the floor, between my legs. Your back looks a little tense, I think you need a back rub."

She smiled, and the candles flickered a little. She was glad to have the darkness conceal her body, especially during her first time. She sat between Lucas's legs, as requested, and laid back against the foot of the couch.

He unhooked her necklace and put it on the seat cushion next to him. When he started rubbing, he became suddenly aware of how soft her skin felt. He enjoyed the sensation.

Then, a thought occurred to him. Hair pulling?

If I fuck this up the whole night will be ruined and — too late!

He gently tugged on the hair closest to her scalp. She moaned, but did not flinch.

He'd seen it so many times before in pornography that he figured she might like a pull or two. He loosened his grip.

"Did you like that?"

"Actually, could you pull a little harder?"

He did, and she screamed louder.

"Up," he said forcefully.

She stood up and sat next to him, then laid her legs across his lap. He took hold of her lower back and pulled her towards him. She crossed her arms around his neck and they kissed.

Maybe we should drink alcohol, she thought. *They've got to have a bottle or two stowed away somewhere.*

Lucas slipped his hand up Emma's shirt to unhook her bra, but nothing was there, only more skin.

She made it easier for him by removing her t-shirt, while he unbuttoned and unzipped her jeans. She removed them the rest of the way and took his hand. She stood up and yanked him off the couch.

This is it!

He followed her mindlessly down the hallway to a small, decrepit bedroom that suddenly became a throne room.

He pulled off his shirt mindlessly before entering the room. She turned on the bedside lamp and Lucas shut the door behind himself, making the lamplight the only glow in the room. She sat on the bed, legs spread, and stretching her pussy.

Lucas didn't need to worry about getting hard now. He shed off the last of his clothes and joined her on the bed.

"Will it hurt?" Emma asked. She guessed it would happen either way.

"Don't know. Depends on the person, I guess."

He slipped inside her easy, but once he was in he lasted maybe ten minutes. In those ten minutes Lucas tried to remember everything he'd seen in porn. There was a clock mounted to the wall, which he used to time himself. Despite what the clock said, his nervous gut made it feel like hours.

They lied in bed, naked, both swatting at a fly that came flying around once in a while. They made a sort of game of it. She'd swat at it, then it was his turn. First person to hit it was the winner.

Flies are attracted to smelly odors. And their sweaty bodies weren't helping.

"I think we should've used lube," Emma said abruptly. "I mean, I was wet, but still."

"Yeah. I'll pick some up the next time I'm out."

"Some people say they bleed a lot their first time. I was afraid I needed to get towels but I didn't want to ruin the mood."

Lucas laughed. "That wouldn't have ruined the mood, bleeding all over the bed would've ruined the mood."

She giggled too, and Lucas watched as her bare breasts moved up and down with every laugh. There was a shining in her eyes Lucas hadn't seen before. Or maybe it was there all along and he simply hadn't noticed.

After losing his virginity, Lucas didn't doubt smoking a cigarette would exponentially increase his pleasure.

Emma's head sank into her soft pillow, so much that he could barely see it. The fly came around again and Lucas swat at it, missing, and almost hitting Emma.

A car engine roared outside.

Lucas sat up, the bed covers falling off his chest. He peered out the window. "What time did you say your grandparents were coming back?"

"I—uh, they must be here early."

Lucas jumped out of bed and collected his clothes, only his pants were in the hallway.

"I love you," he said.

He left with no time to kiss goodbye and redressed himself on the way out of the hallway. Emma's clothes were scattered across the family room. Her shirt and pants were by the couch. Socks? He couldn't find them, but they could be explained for in the event her grandparents found them.

He gathered her clothes and looked for an escape route.

The front door made a clicking noise and the locking mechanism rotated. He could almost hear his heart pounding.

The backyard was no good. The hallway was closer. He ran down the hall with silent strides and into Emma's room.

"I need to leave out your window," Lucas said, throwing Emma's clothes back on her bed. She was already dressed in new clothes, all except her discarded necklace.

He unlocked the window and slid it open. A cool breeze blew into the room.

"I think your necklace might be somewhere between the couch cushions," Lucas said before exiting.

She said nothing. Emma's grandmother's laugh soared down the hallway. Lucas slipped out and into the bushes, flattening them. He waved his way out of them. The branches caught hold of his shirt and tore at them slightly.

The opening of his pants snagged on the bushes just as he was leaving them. He didn't think to bend down and untangle them. His adrenaline was too high — no time for think. He twisted his leg but it seemed inextricable.

With one more pull his pant leg cut loose, tearing at the opening. He regained his balance and ran to his car. Thank God he didn't park in Emma's driveway.

It was dark. Thankfully, no neighbors were around to see him.

Some guy sneaking out of a girl's window, his car could've been called in to the cops.

Still, he kneeled down and ran to the car in a ridiculous squatting position. He opened the door just enough to slip through. Lucas slid into the driver's seat and started the engine.

Almost out of here, he thought. And he drove off to his house.

Just as he'd seen his cousin arrive as he was leaving, his cousin was leaving just as he was arriving.

Lucas rolled down his window, expecting his cousin to congratulate him. Daniel's smile made him a little embarrassed. He almost didn't want to tell him anything. He'd certainly omit the part where he snuck out the window.

Lucas cut the engine and stepped out of his car. Daniel walked up to him, still beaming.

"Finally lost your V-Card huh?" He slapped him jovially on the back.

"Yeah, well…. you know how it is."

"That was pretty fast. I feel like I just got home."

"Yeah…. well…. you know how it is."

"Don't worry bud, I didn't last long my first time either."

Lucas looked at his massive cousin's face. "Where are you going?"

"Me and some friends are having a bond fire."

Lucas eyed the twelve pack Daniel loaded into his car. It was already opened, and what looked like from Lucas's distance, three beers were missing. "Did you have a little fun already?"

Daniel shifted his massive body, blocking Lucas's vision of the twelve pack. His face turned serious. "I'm okay to drive," he said, looking affronted.

"I trust you," Lucas replied. "You're a big guy, I'd say it'd take that entire pack to get you wasted.

Daniel's laugh was booming. It was a genuine laugh, not one made just to make Lucas feel better.

"Listen," Daniel said. "Something funny happened to me today at the bank. I'll tell you about it when I get back."

"Which is?"

"Don't know, maybe tonight, maybe tomorrow."

"Okay."

They waved goodbye and Daniel stepped into his car. His car seat was the lowest Daniel could possibly make it to compensate his large stature.

He reversed the car, waved one more time, and drove off.

His friends had already started the fire when he got there. He'd followed a park trail to meet them. He wasn't worried about the fire spreading out of control. They'd done this before, lots of times.

The twelve pack was starting to get heavy. Then, up ahead through the trees, he recognized two of his friends. The other two were a mystery to him.

He recognized Tony, the man who'd invited him. Tony was a popular guy despite having somewhat of a baby face. Daniel often thought he was full of himself, but after meeting him, he turned out to be a likable person. His girlfriend, Zoe, was sitting next to him, laughing at some joke he'd told her.

This wasn't a birthday party by any means. No one even knew he'd just turned twenty-one. He figured, because of his large frame, they'd all assumed he was.

They were throwing logs into the fire, feeding it. Where they got the logs, he had no idea. The fire swallowed the heavy wood as it crackled. The extra kindling lit up the night around them, revealing Daniel's face.

"Hey," Tony said.

Everyone turned their attention to Daniel, who was foreboding introductions.

Tony rose from the overturned log he sat on and walked to Daniel.

"Hey bud," Tony continued. He led Daniel to a tall gentleman, smaller than Daniel, but still tall. "This is Sam."

Sam looked the oldest of them by far. In fact, he

looked too old to be hanging around any of them, but Daniel didn't care to point it out. He shook with him.

"Nice to meet you," Daniel said.

"Likewise."

"And this is Trevor," Tony continued.

Daniel shook with him too, they sat down, and Trevor switched on a portable radio. The volume was low but noticeable, not loud enough to hinder a conversation.

"So you'll never guess what happened at the bank," Daniel said.

"What?" Tony asked.

"I accidentally bumped into some old guy and he starts screaming his head off, right there, in the middle of the fucking bank. I tried to help him but he started screaming louder, so I just walked out."

"You'll probably end up on the Internet," Zoe said with a jocular tone.

"Yah, I'm sure it's in some database somewhere," Daniel said as he grabbed a beer from the pack, he threw it to Tony, who not expecting it, had to make a little dive in his seat to catch it. Daniel unloaded the rest of the twelve pack and threw it to the rest of the group.

"Something else happened today too," Daniel continued. "My little brother lost his virginity."

Zoe made an awww noise, Trevor, Tony, and Sam, on the other hand, cheered and high-fived each other.

"Little brother's growing up," Daniel said as he opened the can of beer. It made a hissing noise, then foamed a little out the opening.

"Do you remember your first time?" Zoe asked.

"Of course I do," Daniel replied. "I was seventeen, and at this girl's house party. Her name was Lilly, she actually asked me to the girls ask guys dance. I said yes too, but that was before I lost my virginity to her." There was a dead silence, all eyes were on Daniel, even the crickets had momentarily stopped chirping. "So she threw this house party. I really think she used it as an excuse to get me drunk. I'm not a lightweight though, so it took a few hours at least. She took me upstairs to her bedroom, locked the door, and we fucked. I didn't have a condom on me, she told me she was on the pill, don't know if that was true. Although it's not like I've got some kid walking around somewhere." He paused for them to laugh, they didn't. "Anyways, the whole thing lasted maybe about twenty minutes."

No one talked, but the crickets continued chirping, the frogs joined in with some croaking. There had to be a pond nearby.

"I remember, my first time," Zoe said, anxious to begin her regaling. Everyone leaned closer in their log seats. "It was with Tony here, we met senior year. When we first met, he was kind of nervous, he kept talking really fast. I thought it was kind of cute."

"Actually," Tony said. "I really just needed to use the bathroom."

"Charming. As I was saying we met senior year, we did it that same day. I knew he was the one for me, and we're still doing it three years later. I convinced him to skip class and we drove in my mom's car to the edge of the school parking lot where no one really goes except the bad or the really nerdy kids. No I didn't have a condom either, and to be honest, I didn't care if we had one. People always told me you couldn't get pregnant your first time."

"That's not true," Daniel said.

"Well, I guess we got lucky."

"Weren't you nervous?" Sam asked.

"About having sex?"

"About getting caught in a school parking lot," Sam clarified.

"No, I knew no one really came back there, and there were no cameras either."

Trevor looked at Zoe disapprovingly, shaking his head. Then he looked at Tony. "So I take it that was your first time too?"

"Hell no! I was sixteen. It was some girl I met at

summer camp. My parents always sent me there because they didn't care to have to watch me over the summer. There was this really hot girl, Tiffany, nice ass, nice tits. I'll admit, she was kind of a whore, but I didn't give a fuck, I gave *her* a fuck. And that's about it, I can't remember all the little details or how long I lasted or anything like that."

"Did you ever see her again?" Trevor asked.

"Nah, we didn't exchange phone numbers. My phone was probably lost or broke at that time anyway. When I went back the next year, I didn't see her."

Daniel looked at Sam. "Now it's your turn."

Sam fidgeted in his seat and took a long, head bent back drink of his beer, bracing himself. He crushed the can and threw it somewhere into the darkness behind him.

"Well," he said. "You might not believe it, but first the woman I slept with was one of my high school teachers." Everyone's jaws dropped at least a little. No one was drinking anymore. Sam continued. "She was really pretty. You see, there were a lot of trouble makers in our class. They made it really hard for her to teach. One day I stood up and defended her, I don't care to tell you her name, as far as I know she's still teaching."

"What?" Zoe yelled, then stood up. Everyone shooshed her. "I will not be quiet! You're just going to let her get away with that? What if she's fucking some high school kid right now?"

Sam shrugged. "I was eighteen at the time so it was probably legal. As I was saying…."

Zoe lowered her guard and sat back down. Tony rubbed her back, placating her.

"I stood up and defended her in front of the whole class," Sam continued. "Some people laughed at me, I didn't care. After class was over Mrs. — I mean, my teacher kept me after class. It was the last class I had that day and she offered me a ride home. I already had a car but I knew what she meant. She took me back to her

253

place and we did the deed. Then she took me back to school to get my car. I have no regrets."

There was a silence between them. A gust of wind blew through the trees, and the fire danced a little.

Being as Trevor was the last person not to speak, everyone peered at him, waiting.

"Well how am I supposed to compete with that?" Trevor said defensively.

Everyone laughed. It bought him some time. After their laughter died down, they continued staring.

"It's nothing too crazy," Trevor said. "There was this girl I'd known a really long time. We'd been friends for about four years, I think. We screwed at my parent's place. We dated for a while after that. I still talk to her sometimes. Nice girl."

No one pressed Trevor any further.

The night went on without anyone bringing up any matters more serious than losing their virginity. They finished the rest of the beers then slept in their tents. It was not a legal camping site but they'd slept there once before.

Sam decided not to sleep with the rest of them. He walked along the path he hoped went to his car, with only the light of his cell phone to guide him. If the battery died he had maybe some fuel in his zippo lighter.

The trees grew thicker as the path came to an abrupt end. Something was wrong. He changed direction and took another path.

Dark thunderclouds rolled into the night sky and Sam had an ominous feeling in his chest.

Not now, please, not now, he thought.

It was raining. First coming in light showers, then in a sudden downpour. He hadn't heard anything on the news of it raining that night, although the weather reports had been wrong before. More than one of his outdoor childhood birthday parties had been rained on.

Sam almost found himself regretful for leaving his

friends. They'd brought tents and he didn't have so much as a hood to pull over his head. A twig snapped behind him. His heart pounded in his chest. He turned around. Daniel was walking toward him.

There was a flash of light, followed by thunder. Sam shouted over the sound of the rain. "Daniel, right?"

"Yeah, it's me."

"You're not staying either?"

"No, I'm going to my car."

"Which ways your car?"

Daniel held a hand to point its direction, like he was sure of it. He looked around and pointed confusedly at different directions.

"I'm lost too," Sam admitted.

Another flash of lightning came and illuminated something behind Sam. Daniel pointed behind him and Sam turned around swiftly. There was a sign with what looked like vague directions to the different paths. The sign was poorly positioned out of the way, behind a small bush and in front of a large oak tree.

The sign told them to go diagonally left to the park. There didn't appear to be a path diagonally left. His feet kept moving in that direction, and sure enough, there was a narrow path leading through the park. Another bolt of lightning branched down, revealing a group of weathered picnic tables in a clearing next to them.

As they walked deeper through the path Sam recognized landmarks and trees they'd passed going in. They found a giant oak tree, and a half-built fence made of wooden posts that were beginning to rot.

The stars looked down at him, glowing brightly, there were too many to count. Sam tried to find the big dipper or some other constellation that might help with directions. After a few minutes of randomly looking for them in the sky, he gave up.

There was a large grass field over the hills. They hiked up to it. Goal posts used for soccer games gleamed under the streetlights. It had to be the park just next to the road.

After crossing the field and meeting at the sidewalk, Sam and Daniel said their goodbyes and split off in different directions. When Sam couldn't find his car he thought maybe someone had towed it, then remembered he'd parked just a few blocks down.

His car had a line of cars parked both in front and behind it. He searched his pocket and pulled out a car key, which he pointed at the cars. Sam pushed a button and the headlights of his car lit up, cutting through the darkness of the night.

The rain turned to a drizzle as he crawled into his car. His clothes were wet and stuck uncomfortably to his leather seats. Sam turned on the interior lights of the car and looked at his reflection in the rear-view mirror.

The rain had flattened his hair and his bangs drooped down his face.

Sam was afraid to check the time on his dashboard clock. He had work tomorrow morning. What would he say to his boss if he slept in? "Sorry, I was out partying with some people way too young for my age and thought it'd be a good idea to help them polish off a twelve pack."

Thankfully he'd set an alarm each morning. Still, he didn't want to know how much sleep he was going to lose. He would feel it in the morning.

He stepped inside his large bachelor apartment. The room was in desperate need of furniture, which made it look bigger. Not a single clump of dust could be found, he was sure of that. Sam always found the time to clean and straighten his apartment. If he couldn't, for some reason, he'd be sure to hire someone to do it for him. It wasn't unusual for an attractive girl to stop by unexpectedly and want to spend the night.

Sam clapped his hands twice and a bright light flickered on, filling the room with an almost blinding clarity. He had Andy Warhol replicas lining his far wall. It looked overdone for a one-bedroom apartment, almost the size of someone wanting to start a family.

The kitchen sink was a pure chrome color, reflecting images from twenty feet away. His dishes were never smudged for long because he tended to them after every meal, even if he was on a date. The idea often popped into his head of installing an STD detector to guard his front door. He'd laugh when he'd think of it, but he was half-serious.

How many of his weekly guests would set it off?

Sam dragged his muddy shoes on the welcome mat, walked across the hardwood floor, untied his shoes and kicked them into a neatly filed line of other shoes. He hung his rain-drenched coat on the hanger bolted to the wall.

I can't keep doing this, he thought.

Why did he have to party on a work night? Had he not learned to avoid that sort of crowd since his college years? Would he remember this thought tomorrow? Probably not. His alcohol would drown these thoughts away. Wash them down the drain. He would surely party again. The cycle would repeat itself.

Sam took a shower, redressed in his white briefs, and fell asleep the instant his body stopped moving.

Chapter 10

The alarm sitting on his nightstand buzzed to life. Every morning he expected it, and every morning it made his heart jolt a bit.

He sat up straight, stretched his arms above his head and made himself breakfast. It was toast, eggs, bacon, and a glass of orange juice. The usual American breakfast.

Sitting crooked on his glass dining table was an advertisement for a chocolate lab puppy. He'd often thought about buying a dog. It was only a fantasy because his apartment didn't allow dogs or any other type of pet. He could maybe sneak a lizard or a goldfish, a dog however, was unthinkable.

The front door opened. He didn't need to look, he knew who it was immediately.

"Don't you have a job yet, Evie?"

"I came here to look at the want ads in your paper."

She came walking into the kitchen with a rolled-up newspaper in her hand.

"Don't you get your own paper?"

"I do, but it doesn't come with you."

Sam knew he should be flattered. He also knew he didn't have time to be. He expected that she wanted a back-and-forth conversation of cheesy compliments and job-hunt encouragement.

"I'm sorry I don't have time to talk." Sam stood up and walked across the kitchen. He grabbed a clean coat off the rack. "Lock the door on your way out."

Sam started for the door then turned around when Evie didn't answer him.

She stared at him, expressionless. "Okay."

"I really would stay— "

"But unlike me you've got a job."

Sam's expression hardened with an indignant look on

his face. "That's right."

He walked out his apartment. He thought he heard a faint voice calling him back to his apartment, then decided it was probably his imagination.

Sam walked into the vacant elevator and rode it to the first floor. It dinged opened, four people walked in, he walked carefully around them and left the elevator.

The automatic gate opened and Sam drove out of his apartment complex. Normally by now he'd have a cup of coffee either in his hand or in the cup holder. *Normally*, but Evie had pissed him off too much to even think of it.

Stupid bitch thinks she can come by anytime she wants. And judge me! he thought.

Sam stopped at an intersection that separated him three blocks from his office. Fourth and Burlington was always a bitch to cross. And you couldn't even think about running the light because there was a flash camera stalking the intersection. Sam couldn't deal with that. His employers are very attentive of their employees' personal lives.

A homeless man stood idly by the intersection holding a sign that said, **Need money for food. Anything helps. God bless.**

David rolled down the window and leaned over the passenger seat, waving a dollar bill in the man's direction. The homeless man spotted him, then walked towards him showing a huge grin.

But just as the man approached the car window, a truck flew by and struck him, leaving a trail of tire marks well into the intersection.

Screams were heard from down the street. People from the sidewalks ran to him, and some came running from their cars.

They gathered into a crowd of two large groups around the body. Sam stumbled out his car and the light turned green. But no one cared to honk.

A nearby mother grabbed her daughter's face and

pulled it into her thigh. The little girl didn't resist. She didn't want to see the accident any more than her mother wanted her to.

"Is that man going to be all right?" she cried from inside her mother's pant leg. Her voice was muffled but still audible.

"I don't know," the mother replied.

The man driving the truck swung open his door and rushed to the homeless man, panting. The two large clumps of people divided momentarily to let him in, then closed up again.

"Are you alright? I'm so sorry man, I'm so damn sorry. Please be okay," he said.

The homeless man rocked back and forth, holding his sides. But he wasn't screaming with agony…. he was laughing. His smile showed two, maybe three teeth missing, and the rest were turning yellow.

He laughed so hard his face was turning pink. It seemed as if the truck didn't kill him, he'd suffocate from laughing.

"As if my life couldn't get any worse," he laughed. "All I wanted was one lousy dollar."

The truck driver took out his wallet so fast he almost dropped it. Then he turned it upside down and sprinkled every dollar it held onto the homeless man.

"Here, take it," he said. "It's all I have with me, but if you give me a minute I can stop at an ATM and—"

"You idiot!" someone said. "He doesn't need money right now! He needs an ambulance!"

The homeless man stopped laughing. His face was pale, and blood was creeping across the pavement. People standing close stepped back to save their shoes from getting messy.

"I'll call for help!" yelled the truck driver, almost as if it came from guilt rather than concern.

Sam looked around. Several people were already talking frantically into their cellphones, their ears pressed tightly against them.

Sam wanted to leave the scene. There was a job he needed to go to, unlike this man, who didn't have so much as a house cat to depend on him. Cars were slowly driving by the crowd of people. What could they do? The light was green, and the homeless man had plenty of people watching him.

A siren blasted from a distance. Cars pulled to the side of the road to make room for the ambulance, then pulled back onto the road. It stopped about twenty feet from the crowd of people, who at this point looked like a solid wall, making it almost impossible to see the homeless man through them.

Once again, the crowd opened up, this time leaving an open gap for the paramedics to load the homeless man onto a stretcher.

Would he live? Sam thought. *He had no insurance. Anyone could see that.*

A minute later traffic flow improved and people from the crowd were returning to their vehicles, Sam was one of them.

A second siren rang through the street. It was a cop car that didn't appear to be driving as fast as it should be. It parked on the side of the road on Fourth Avenue. A short blonde-haired officer stepped out with a clipboard.

The truck driver was sitting on the curb of the sidewalk, his hands in his face, probably crying. Sam shook his head and left before he watched any further.

There were plenty of witnesses to talk to, he thought.

Driving back was torture. He'd almost believe the homeless man being splattered was a dream if not for the radio talking about it constantly.

Sam reached to the radio and turned the channel to something else, anything else.

Why'd he have to try and help?

If he hadn't offered him a buck at that exact time the homeless man would still be alive.

But to what? Sleeping under the roof of a box? Eating

out of trashcans?

What would one dollar do to make a difference?

Suddenly he remembered the homeless man lying in a puddle of his own blood, rocking back and forth helplessly on the ground. "All I wanted was one lousy dollar."

Sam did care about other people, although his busy lifestyle sometimes made that impossible. It seemed to him that whenever he tried to help he only made things worse. So why help at all? He didn't know.

The only thing Sam knew for sure was that he had one hell of a story to tell.

Then another flashback. It was him at the bond fire, reminiscing about losing his virginity. Why'd he tell them such a personal story? He hardly knew them at all, the exception being Tony. Maybe he'd told them that *because* he didn't know them. He figured he'd probably never see them again.

Maybe it was the peer pressure that made him confess. Maybe that was why he tried to help the homeless man. Not direct peer pressure, but societal peer pressure. People are always saying to help the less fortunate. All the billboards and PSA commercials, he couldn't forget them.

What would one dollar buy him anyway? Certainly not a meal, that's for sure. It would most likely end up to his Crack fund, which is why he'd ended up there in the first place. He remembered a good look at his teeth, three missing, the rest yellow.

No Sam, he thought. *You're just trying to psychologically make sense of what you saw today and you're putting unfair judgments into your head. You didn't run that man over.*

Still, it didn't help to give him a dollar.

Sam pulled into his employee-reserved parking space, parked, then jumped out of his car. He wondered if anyone from work was already talking about the incident.

Sam straightened his tie, then walked inside.

On the way to his office, a young, eager looking man was walking as fast as he knew was allowed in such a place.

"What's the rush?" Sam asked him.

"I'm headed to an interview. I'm early, but you know, when you're early you're on time, when you're on time you're late, and when you're late you're screwed."

"I didn't know we were doing interviews today."

The man's eyes lit up. Sam took it as a sign the man wanted to use him as a possible reference, something Sam didn't plan on doing.

"You work here?" the young man asked, his eyes wide and hungry.

Sam extended a handshake. He met with it. "Sam Beckett, accounting."

Sam smiled, the young man thought and hoped it was sincere. Sam's handshake was firm, confident, full of energy. It was the handshake of someone who didn't need a job interview. The young man respected him, even if he'd never see him again.

"I'm Jude, hopefully your next internal consultant."

"Well I hope so too, you seem like an eager kid. I think I started working here at your age. Well, I won't keep you. Good luck on your interview."

At the end of the hall Sam turned left, Jude turned right. His foot almost bumped into a girl sitting on the floor with her back against the wall.

"Sorry," Jude said quickly but apologetically.

The girl didn't look at him, she only made a whimpering noise. Jude had the urge to look at her face, he almost wanted to grab her head and look at her forcefully.

"Are you alright?" Jude asked.

The girl looked up this time. She looked beautiful, but broken, like a partially torn painting, beautiful to look at, but unable to be sold.

"I'm fine I guess, it's just…. I'm claustrophobic."

Jude gazed down the hall. He hadn't thought about it, the hallway was long and narrow. He could understand why someone claustrophobic, or maybe a small child, would be scared of it. He looked back down at her. Her eyes looked glossy, like they were hiding tears in them.

"You wouldn't by any chance be going to the job interview, are you?" Jude asked.

"I am."

Jude took a deep breath and considered his time. "I'm going there too, do you want a little help getting there, these halls are a little confusing. I actually came down here once to get a feel for the place."

"That'd be great," she said, but did not get up.

Jude guessed she was too scared to stand on her own.

If she can't even stand a long hallway how's she supposed to hold a job here? Jude thought. *She'd have to go through these halls every day.*

Jude pulled her up, she was heavier than he thought. He looked at her trembling legs then wrapped his arm around her shoulder in case she would fall down. "Close your eyes."

She did. Jude thought she'd protest and insist she was mature enough to handle it. She proved him wrong.

"It's not as long as you think," he said. "I'll tell you when it's over."

Their expensive shoes echoed throughout the halls, no one was around to see them. Everyone was either working or in the room waiting to be interviewed. Jude guessed he should keep her mind off the narrow hallway.

"So what position are you applying for?" he asked.

"Consultant."

Startled, Jude almost lost hold of her.

"What's wrong?" she asked.

"Sorry," he laughed. "That's the position I'm applying for."

"Well I'm sure there's room for both of us."

Jude knew there wasn't. The consultant position had

only one opening. Still, if he didn't get the job maybe he'd still get a friend out of it. If she didn't get the job, he'd consider helping her find another one, in his spare time, of course.

But would she be as nice to him? He wasn't sure he wanted to date a girl as claustrophobic as she was. He'd known her for only minutes and already he was finding her a little…. strange, to say the least.

They turned another corner. The new hallway was just as narrow. Jude considered asking the girl what she'd do to get to the office, or maybe she'd planned on overcoming her fears after she'd gotten the job. There wasn't another route, he was sure of that from when he scouted the office a week ago.

They turned another corner and halfway through the hall was their appointment.

"We're basically there," Jude told her. "You might want to open your eyes, unless you want people to think you're…." Jude thought carefully over his next word. "Odd."

She laughed and he shrugged his arms off her. The girl didn't look around the hallway. Instead, she opened the door and went in first.

The room seemed expensive. There were chairs with armrests, and not a one of them fit more than a single person. There were framed paintings hanging on the walls, and house plants. In the center of the room was a knee-high glass table with an organized stack of magazines on it (several of the interviewees had already taken the liberty of reading them). Against the wall was a coffee machine, and next to that, a water cooler.

The girl walked up to a counter. Jude followed her.

"Is this where we sign in for the job interview?" she asked.

The woman behind the counter looked up from her computer screen, but barely. "Name?"

"Jane Hadley," she said enthusiastically.

The woman clicked her mouse a few times. "Sit down

and wait to be called."

She did, and Jude walked up next.

"Name?" she said just as coldly as before.

"Jude Best."

"Sit down and wait to be called."

Jude did. He would've sat by Jane but she'd sat on an edge seat next to someone else. Jude sat in the only chair left. Apparently, the interviews hadn't started early.

Most everyone there was dressed similar to him — ties, slacks, belts (even if they clearly didn't need them), shiny shoes, styled hair, and collared shirts. The room smelled strong of everyone's combined cologne and perfume.

Soon after, a man stepped from the office they were all waiting to enter. Jude looked at the clock on the wall. He was exactly on time, right down to the second.

"Okay," he said. "We're going down the list alphabetically. Kyle Anderson?"

A man stood up. Jude couldn't tell from his position but Kyle appeared to be the tallest one in the room. He followed the interviewer and the door shut behind them. No sound could be heard from inside the room.

Someone inched their way closer to the door. He cupped a hand around his ear and leaned toward the door, then frowned when he realized it wouldn't work.

"Can't blame a guy for trying," he said.

Jude crossed his legs, rested his ankle on his knee, and watched the clock. There was enough silence in the room for him to hear it ticking. It was almost maddening.

Then someone spoke. He was the only one sweating visibly through his shirt. "What do you guys think, do I look hirable?"

Jude eyes swept the room. He was the only one looking at him. "Uh, yeah sure."

The man frowned. "You don't sound confident."

"You need to stop worrying what I think and trust yourself. If you have the job experience, you can get hired."

The man was shaking. Someone non-medically trained could've mistaken it for a small seizure. He swallowed and ran his hands through his hair.

"Try drinking some water," Jude suggested.

The man exploded out of his chair. Jude had never seen a rocket launch, but he guessed it looked something like that. The man hustled over to the water cooler. The lady at the counter eyed him suspiciously from across the room.

He took a dipsy cup from its holder and filled it with water. For a moment, Jude thought he was going to pour it on his head and let it drip down his shirt. He was disappointed. The man drank the entire cup in one large gulp. He turned to get more but suddenly, the door opened.

"George Barkley?"

The man at the water cooler flinched at his name. The other interviewee walked out of the room, his face expressionless. The now sweat-drenched man took his place in the interviewer's office.

People looked around the room, staring at each other awkwardly.

The interview probably isn't that bad, Jude thought. *The worst part is the waiting.*

He squeezed his eyes shut.

Geez, Jude what do you expect? The room will be dark except for one interrogation lamp blaring in your face? He injects you with sodium pentothal? You tell him every skeleton in your closet? Piss your pants? Get a grip on yourself! If you want this job for goodness sakes get a grip on yourself!

He opened his eyes again.

The ticking clock was driving him mad, and Jude's belief again was that they were trying to torture him, break him, weed out the stragglers.

Bubbles were rising from within the water cooler. Jude could almost hear dogs barking outside, but he was sure it was his imagination.

"Jude Best?"

He looked up. It was the interviewer surveying the room for him. He stood up and walked toward him. Jude offered him his hand but he had already turned around. Jude followed him into the room. It *was* dark, there was no interrogation lamp, however, and the interviewer was smiling, not injecting him with truth serum.

He grasped the armrests of his leather swivel chair and lowered himself onto the seat.

"I'm Dave Perkins. Sorry we don't have time to get acquainted, but we're on a tight schedule."

"I understand. You've got a lot of important decisions to make, a lot of people to manage."

He smiled. Jude could almost see his face in Dave's perfectly white teeth. "That's right."

Jude knew Dave could see past his counterfeit flattery.

Dave broke the silence. He leaned back in his chair lackadaisically and began. "So what experience do you have in consulting?"

"I managed over twenty people at Sears. All of my employees— "

"I'm going to stop you right there. Is that you're only experience that relates to being a consultant?"

"I currently have an associate's in— "

"Okay," Dave said as he stood up from his chair, it rolled back after losing his weight. "Thank you for coming, we'll keep in touch."

Will we really? Jude thought.

Dave guided him out of the room. He tried to keep his face impassive so that no one could see his failure. He started out the door when Jane stopped him.

"Wait," she said. "Could you wait for a little while?"

"What for?" Then Jude remembered Jane could hardly walk down the hall without him.

"So we can talk."

"Sure."

Jude sat down in his original seat. The lady at the counter looked at him strangely, wondering why he was still there, but said nothing.

Dave opened the door and everyone looked. "Carl Denton?"

One by one the interviewees walked out and Jude began to wonder if anyone failed as miserably as him. No one had walked out as quickly as he had but there were still people left.

"Jane Hadley?" said Dave.

"Good luck," Jude whispered, loudly enough for her to hear.

She walked in, and the sound of the door shutting behind them was the most nerve-racking noise Jude had ever heard. He wasn't being interviewed anymore, yet he was terrified for Jane. He guessed that probably meant he liked her, weird as she was.

He waited, and she came out almost as quickly as he had. Water was rising in her eyes. She swallowed to wet her throat. Jude stood up and walked to her, while Dave retreated into his office.

Jude wrapped his arms around her and he led her out of the room. Jane did her best not to wail in the presence of other human beings. But for some reason, Jude, she was comfortable with.

The hallway now seemed like a distant phobia. Her new biggest fear was not getting a job she desperately needed. She sympathized for Jude too but felt even worse for herself.

Who knows? Maybe Jude could be worth giving a chance. She didn't like Jude instantly, so what? Every worthwhile relationship she'd ever had didn't start with infatuation.

"I know you're crying right now," Jude said. "I'm sorry. There's just no way your interview was as bad as mine."

Jane could tell he was trying to make her laugh, she knew she should appreciate it, but she didn't find it funny.

"He said I wasn't right for the company," Jane sobbed.

"Said I 'lacked experience', he wouldn't give me a chance. He didn't even let me finish my interview."

"Same thing happened to me. I would've figured I'd get a little more respect, at least a full interview."

Jane broke away from his arms and walked without assistance.

The walk outside was faster this time now that Jane could use her full eyesight.

"Which car is yours?" Jude asked.

Jane pointed to a silver Mercedes. "That one." She was still crying, although her tears were starting to dry.

Jane unlocked her car. Jude opened the door for her and she scooted into the driver's seat. Jude leaned against the open door.

"Listen," Jane said. "I have to go right now but I'd like to see you again sometime. Hand me your phone and I'll give you my number."

Jude handed over his phone, she pushed some buttons then handed it back. Jude added her to his contacts list. He wiped a leftover tear from her face, said goodbye, and left to his car.

Jude and Jane. He liked the sound of that. His car was on the opposite end of the parking lot. As he approached it, he heard a car honking. It was Jane. She was driving and waving at him. It was hard to believe only a moment ago she was crying. He smiled and waved back.

After crawling into his car, he watched Jane drive away. He could always tell who a person was by the way they drove a car. She was graceful, stayed within the lines, used turn signals, and before her car turned into a tiny silver dot in the horizon he could barely make out Jane politely letting another car merge into her lane.

Still, Jude couldn't stop thinking: *She drives a Mercedes!*

In his mind, he needed the job much more than she did. A good job first, *then* he'd get an expensive car.

He knew the job would most likely go to someone who knew or was related to the owner of the company, making the interview pointless — nepotism.

Jude's phone rang. He answered it, set it to speakerphone, then started driving.

"What's up?" Jude answered. It was Brady.

"How'd your job interview go?"

"Awww, cute. You remembered."

"So?"

"I can almost guarantee I didn't get it."

"Looks like I owe Matt twenty bucks."

"That being said," Jude interrupted Brady laughing at his own joke. "I came out with some girl's number."

"No shit? Is she pretty?"

"Yeah, I mean…. she was too scared to even walk down the hall. I think she was claustrophobic. I felt really bad for her so I helped her walk to the interview. She doesn't think she got the job either. We both talked and she gave me her number. She drives a Mercedes."

"A rich girl huh?"

"That doesn't matter, I shouldn't have said that. I don't know, it wasn't much, but it was something."

There was a loud honking and a car drove past him, half-driving in the bicycle lane. Jude realized he was so pulled into the conversation that he was drifting into the next lane over. He turned the wheel and his car jerked back into its lane completely.

"I'm coming over," Brady said.

"No don't! Brady, you don't have to do that."

"Too late!"

The phone hung up.

Brady was already standing at the door when Jude arrived. He was texting something with his phone, then he heard Jude's footsteps and lifted his head.

"Hey buddy," he said.

A twinge of happiness grew from the pit of Jude's stomach. The next best thing to do was to complain about anything and everything until he no longer felt bad about failing his interview.

Brady pocketed his phone, his attention fully turned to

Jude. "You gonna let me in?"

Jude took out his key ring and separated his apartment's key from the rest. On that ring he had his mail key, his car key, and work keys. He wasn't really supposed to take them home, but it was the best place to keep them, and no one ever called him on it.

He opened the door and went inside, followed by Brady. A dim light drifted into the room through the closed shutters. With one finger he flicked up the light switch and everything became visible. It wasn't a bad apartment for someone his age, but certainly something he wouldn't brag about to the ladies. One bathroom, one-bedroom, paper-thin walls that didn't mute even normal conversation.

"The place still looks the same," Brady said, stepping past Jude to see it better.

"I didn't know you were coming," Jude replied. "I would've tidied up."

Brady made his way to the couch leaning against the wall and sat himself down. He put his feet on the coffee table before him, a wide smile swept across his face.

"Make yourself at home," Jude said sarcastically.

Brady frowned. "You don't seem happy to see me."

"I just bombed an interview, I'm not happy to see anyone."

Brady stood up and stretched. He looked at Jude again to see if he'd changed his mind. He hadn't.

"I won't stay long. So tell me about this girl."

Jude could tell he was being sincere. Brady was the kind of person everyone has in their life, annoying and intrusive, yet lovable and genuine when the mood called for it. He was normal except for the fact that he was a germophobe, Brady wouldn't allow even his mother to touch him, so he claimed. The only person to touch him was his girlfriend, and they didn't do anything sexual until she was tested for STD's.

"Her name's Jane," Jude said. "She seems cool enough. I mean…. I met her curled up in a corner too afraid to go down the hallway but— "

"What?" Brady's face was flustered.

"I told you, over the phone."

"Yeah well…." He waved his hand defensively, almost comically. "All I heard was Mercedes."

"The hallway *was* pretty narrow, I can easily see how someone claustrophobic would be scared. She was really nice though. We were both applying to the same place, same position in fact, and when I came out of the interview she stopped me and asked me to wait for her. She came out almost crying, it was as bad as mine."

Brady's interest was completely invested in his story. He was so involved at that moment someone could've picked his pocket and he'd have no idea.

"And?" Brady said impatiently.

"And I walked her to her car, right before I closed the door she gave me her number. When I walked back to my car she honked at me, it was kind of cute."

"And her tits?"

"Big ones."

"Are we talking oranges or grapefruits?"

Jude laughed. "I'd say a C cup at least."

"You call that big? My grandma's are bigger than that, granted they're a bit saggy nowadays."

They both laughed, Jude did it more out from the awkwardness of the conversation.

After the laughter died Brady's eyes drifted around the room, seemingly trying to find something else to talk about, one more reason to stay in the apartment before taking a filthy bus.

"So did you make any new changes to the apartment?"

"You already said 'the place still looks the same.'"

"Oh, right." Brady rubbed the back of his neck.

Jude could tell he wanted to stay, but he wanted to sleep. Maybe he'd have a wet dream involving Jane….

Jude walked toward the door and Brady reluctantly followed him.

"I appreciate you coming," Jude said conclusively. "I'm sorry, I just want to take a shower and lie down."

"Are you gonna text that girl?"

"Maybe, not right now though."

"Kay." Brady stepped out the door.

"I'll see you later," Jude said reassuringly.

"Right." Brady walked off.

Jude shut the door behind him and stared solemnly at the closed door. Brady had after all, tried to help. He called him at the perfect time to either congratulate or console him on the outcome of his interview. Jude thought however, it was the wrong time to talk to anyone.

He turned around to the quiet empty room.

Almost everything he learned was through the paper-thin walls of his apartment. He could hear exactly what his neighbors were saying, every—last—word.

To the left of his apartment were Mr. and Mrs. Coen. The Coens, he'd simply call them. Mr. Coen was an investment banker and Mrs. Coen, he thought, was a teacher. But he wasn't sure.

Mr. Coen would sometimes come home and complain about his job, government bailouts, stock values. Mrs. Coen would sit there and listen to it, taking it all in like Mr. Coen's personal stress sponge, and occasionally saying, "That's awful," until finally Mr. Coen would tire himself out.

Sometimes they'd have sex and he'd step onto the balcony to smoke a cigarette, trying not to listen. He'd wonder if they knew people could hear them, if they got off on having an audience.

On the right side was Mrs. Bogart. She was a widow, and an old one at that. She was mostly quiet, except when she watched late night reruns of Jeopardy or The Price Is Right and she'd yell at the television. She was on what his dad had called a vampire schedule. Sleep all day, up all night.

Jude suddenly imagined his apartment upgraded, courtesy of the pay raise from the new consultant position he didn't have. It was refurnished with all new leather couches imported from Italy, new glassware, speakers with extra loud bass, wine bottles, and a sixty-inch high-definition flat screen TV hanging from the wall above the fireplace.

He squeezed his eyes shut and when they reopened his apartment turned back to what it was. The Coen's to his left, Mrs. Bogart to his right, and him stuck forever in the middle.

He walked to the bathroom, shed off his suit and tie, giving them away to his laundry basket, then showered. The day had only begun but a good hot shower made him feel better in the middle of any crisis. The water crept lazily down his spine, his skin felt smooth.

Ten minutes later he turned the nozzle and the water stopped coming. He dried off and threw on a t-shirt and shorts. The moment his face fell flat onto his bed he heard a buzzing.

Instinctively, Jude grabbed his pocket and felt the lump of his phone. It wasn't buzzing.

He got up and wandered around his apartment, searching for the source of the noise. It would vibrate frantically every couple of seconds, which didn't give him enough time. He searched and hoped the buzzing would continue.

He stared at the couch. The cushions seemed slightly more spread apart than they usually were. He reached his hand between them and pulled out a cell phone. It was Brady's.

Jude ran out his door, hoping to catch him, but also knowing full well Brady would be long gone.

And he was.

After a moment's stare he felt stupid waiting for no one, then went back inside. He placed the phone on his coffee table and walked back to his bed for a much-needed rest. He'd slept well the night before, hoping it'd help his interview. However, after knowingly failing it, Jude felt too weak to think straight.

As his body was relaxing, his mind unwinding, a knock on his door jerked him back into alertness.

Brady!

"I'm coming!" Jude yelled. He grabbed the phone and opened the door, and there was Brady. He forced his way back inside.

"So you do have it! Thank you!"

Jude couldn't remember Brady taking out his phone a second time, probably another one of his excuses to stay, he guessed.

"I was afraid I'd lost it on the way to the bus stop. Where was it?"

"Between my couch cushions. When I saw it was there it was too late to catch you."

"I understand," he said, taking the phone from Jude's hands. "Thank you."

"No problem." Jude started leading Brady back to the door. When Brady's back was turned to walk outside Jude patted him lightly on the back.

Brady winced. His heart beat rapidly.

"Sorry," Jude said quickly. "I forgot you don't like to be touched."

"It's okay," Brady said, unconvincingly.

Jude closed the door. After Brady was sure he was out of Jude's vision he wiped his back in the place Jude had touched it.

There would be enough germs on the bus, Brady thought.

He walked off the grounds of the apartment complex and onto the street. The bus stop was close. People as poor as him were lined up, smoking cigarettes, ignoring the people around them.

Brady walked to them, some of the people looked too big not to bump into. He wondered how they'd step through the bus doors. They looked like they would be sitters, Brady, on the other hand, was a handrail kind of guy.

Who the hell knows what kind of festering parasites have sat in those chairs before him?

When Brady neared the bus stop the bus screeched to a halt and the twin doors folded open. People stepped onto the bus looking like they wanted to complain about even having to bend their legs.

Brady waited until the last of the bus riders had taken their seats inside, then walked in to join them. No one seemed happy to see him, or to be there themselves. A woman holding two plastic shopping bags in each hand sat down heavily. Instead of easing down her weight forced her to collapse onto her seat. Her legs kicked into the air and she put her shopping bags on the two seats around her, like she was saving them for a friend who would not come. A woman sitting nearby scooted away, making room for the woman's shopping bags. She leered at her indignantly, but the woman did not return her gaze.

Brady didn't know why but he thought the encounter was funny. The twin doors shut and Brady held the rail coming from the ceiling and connecting to the floor.

The bus took off and gradually merged with the flow of traffic. With nothing better to do but look at the scenic roads of downtown Los Angeles, Brady surveyed the people packed into the bus.

A short old man wearing a hunting cap sat across from him, reading a newspaper. It covered most of his face.

There were lots of elderly people too. One of them coughed into his fist, though his face was too far from his hand to make a difference.

Brady was a minority on the bus, almost in every way.

An older woman wearing a sun hat with a pink bow wrapped around it, spoke to the woman sitting with shopping bags. "Did you go to the supermarket?"

The sitting woman looked up, said nothing, then looked back down.

The old woman spoke louder. "Did you go to the— "

"Yes," the woman answered curtly.

The old woman looked away as if she was ashamed. Brady couldn't bring himself to watch further.

Five minutes later they came to an intersection and stopped abruptly. Even grasping the handrail Brady bumped into a nearby woman, who was also standing.

The woman turned around and looked briefly at the man who had bumped her. He looked to her like he was wearing the clothes of someone on laundry day. Baggy jeans, an all-orange sweatshirt. Clearly, he threw on the last of his clean wardrobe.

"Sorry," he said quietly.

She nodded.

They stopped again at a stop sign and she bumped into the knee of someone sitting down, who shifted in his seat, lightly touching a speed freak drug addict.

The addict was shaking a little, despite his layers of clothing. His eyes twitched to the man who'd bumped him, glaring as if he thought he'd take out a knife and stab him.

It'd been twenty hours since his last Crack cocaine smoke, and three hours since his last beer. He was paying for it dearly now, and it would only get worse from there. Maybe he'd ask someone on the bus for change.

No, he thought. *People on the bus don't have jack. Why else would they be riding the bus?*

The people around him weren't saints, but they weren't Crack addicts either. He doubted anyone would know where he could score. He closed his eyes and drew a slow deep breath, but his throat felt thick. His muscles were weak.

People sneezed, coughed, hocked, and cleared their throats. He wanted them all to shut up. Only he was allowed to do that stuff, only he had problems to complain about. Out of all the people on that bus with skeletons in their closet, he had the most, the biggest, and the ugliest.

The man was shaking and he couldn't help it. He had to hold his own arm to control himself. Even still, he brushed against the girl sitting next to him.

She was much too young to be riding on a bus. If it weren't for her clothes she'd look completely out of place.

The bus made another stop and she bumped into a young man in his twenties. He looked at her, she said sorry, and he looked away.

They were now where he wanted to be. The bus doors folded open and he left before the next wave of bus riders could enter.

He wasn't sure exactly why he was in such a hurry. Compared to where he was about to go the public bus seemed like heaven.

His next destination was his cousin's house. They were having a family reunion despite the drama always occurring there. His family had more problems than he could count with all his fingers and toes, and he was sure they'd have a fresh load of problems when he got there.

He already felt sick to his stomach just thinking about it. The thought of his Aunt Margie leaving the TV stuck on the depressing news made him feel worse.

As if they didn't have enough problems to worry about, he thought.

The cloudless sunny weather did not fit his mood and it certainly didn't fit the picture he had of his cousin's neighborhood. A thundercloud spewing hail, wind blowing forty miles per hour, that was the picture he had when thinking of his cousin's neighborhood. He wouldn't be surprised if he heard yelling clear from down the street.

He always wondered why he went. It was the same thing every year. If he wanted to see fighting and domestic abuse he could just turn on Cops. Maybe some of them had been on that show. He could picture Uncle Wally on the roof, drunk, half-naked and screaming obscenities.

The neighborhood was drawing near and he was searching for an excuse, *any* excuse, not to go. But where would he go if not his family reunion? He had no car, no money, and no friends. On a lucky day he could scrounge up enough money to hail a taxi, and if he was feeling dangerous, hitchhike.

All of this didn't compare to a good meal that would probably be waiting for him at the reunion. Given his family's track record it would be dinner with a show.

The sun was setting as he walked to the house. He waved to the different neighbors he recognized in the neighborhood, every one of them waved back. He guessed they were feeling sorry for him to come around his cousin's house again.

His Uncle Wally was sitting in a rocking chair on the front porch, drinking from a bottle of what he guessed was beer. It was wrapped in a brown paper bag in a lame attempt to discretely drink in public.

"Hey, Toby!" Wally called to him.

"Hey Wally!" Toby called back.

Toby remembered the last time he didn't greet his uncle quickly. Wally saw him in a superstore once and called his name from across the store, when he didn't acknowledge him Wally called his name even louder. Anyone who heard it stared at him like he was drunk. It's certain people, like Wally, that people can read like a book, judge them in an instant without ever talking to them. Wally was that predictable.

He rocked himself off his chair, stepped off the porch, and gave Toby a bear hug, his beer still in his hand. When Toby tried to pull away it only made him hug harder. He didn't stop until Toby's back cracked a day's worth of stress, then he let go and Toby dropped to the ground.

"Good to see you," Wally said. "Go inside and grab a beer."

"I'm twenty," Toby replied mildly.

"Oh live a little, everyone's waiting inside for you."

Toby walked off, his footsteps made loud thuds on the wooden porch as he stepped away.

Wally sat back down.

You think this family is bad, Wally thought, as he took another sip of his bottle. *You should've seen my family growing up*.

After slamming back the last of his beer, Wally stood from his rocking chair, grunted loudly, then walked inside to join the others.

The house was as stuffy as an attic. Dust filled his lungs as he closed the door behind him. He coughed and looked at the too large family crowding the too small house.

His brother Andrew sat on his favorite leather chair like he owned the damn place. To make things worse, his bare feet were resting on Wally's poor excuse for a coffee table. His shoes were next to the chair, his socks stuffed into them. Wally wanted to walk behind the chair and push it forward so that Andrew fell out of it.

Wally's daughter, Angelina, stepped before him with shining eyes.

"Daddy," she said.

"Huh?" He looked down at her.

"Ginger says I can't be a president."

"Well," Wally said. "President is more of a boy's club. Why don't you go play with your little dollies, okay princess?"

Angelina stomped on the ground then pouted out of the room. Andrew looked at Wally reprovingly.

"Ain't that just like a woman." Wally said, then winked at him. "Always complaining about something."

"That *woman* is your own daughter. Why don't you try the supportive father technique?"

Wally's smile quickly faded from his face. He didn't know supportive.

"Why don't you mind your own fucking business and raise your own damn kids! Do you even know where they are right now?”

The people around them didn’t stop what they were doing to watch their conflict, they’d gotten used to the yelling. It was like background noise to them.

Andrew tried to see if he could spot one of his kids. He realized that wasn’t possible from his comfortable sitting position, so he stood up, slipped on his socks and shoes, then left.

Wally turned around to watch him leave and came face to face with his oldest daughter, Becky. Her face looked like it was trying very hard to restrain a concerned expression.

“Have you seen Bobby?” she asked.

Wally put a hand on her shoulder. “Don’t know. Why don’t you try the bathroom? Someone’s been in there an awfully long time.”

With nothing left to say, Becky left the room. She strode down the hallway and knocked on the bathroom door. No one answered, but Becky could vaguely hear the window slipping open. After a moment’s silence, the door opened.

Bobby stood in the doorway, he did not look relieved, he looked surprised, and guilty. “Yeah?”

“Why were you in there for so long?”

“I really had to go. Get off my back.” Bobby tried to step around his girlfriend, but she wouldn’t budge. “Other people might have to go too you know.”

“You didn’t seem to care about that half an hour ago, when you went in there.”

“I told you, I really had to go!”

There was a faint, yet unmistakable scent of garlic on his breath. Becky could remember a girl eating garlic chips earlier at the party. She didn’t know her, but didn’t question her presence due to her vast family size and other acquaintances coming through the house.

“You were making-out with that whore, weren’t you?”

“What whore?” Bobby tried to look surprised, it

wasn't convincing.

"Don't you lie to me. I smell garlic on your breath, they kind of smell like those garlic chips, the same ones that girl was eating, that — *whore*."

Bobby didn't say anything. He stood still, apparently thinking of his next move. Perhaps he would try using the window as an escape route as well.

"I know you've been showing your friends photos," Becky continued. "Showing them how hot I *used* to look, before I gained all this weight." Becky pinched the fat of her waist to emphasize her point. "I know I'm not as hot as when we first met, but you're an asshole, and there's no two ways about it."

"You *are* hot, baby, I've just been really stressed, what with getting laid off and everything. Would it be too much to ask for you to make me feel like a man? And for you to act like a woman?"

All the color drained from Becky's face. She hadn't expected him to say that. She knew he didn't mean it, he *couldn't* mean it. She wanted to cry, but the tears would not leave her eyes in front of Bobby.

She set off down the hall.

"I'm sorry baby!" Bobby called. His words did not sound genuine.

You will be sorry, she thought.

Becky looked around the house to form some sort of plan. She would be swift, yet painful. Leave no survivors.

Her eyes fixed on a good-looking boy helping himself a bowl of trail mix.

Charlie!

She grabbed his hand and dragged him off to a quiet corner.

"What's wrong?" he asked, in a not so hushed voice.

"It's Bobby, he's cheating on me and I need you to pretend you've been cheating with me too."

Charlie's mouth opened a little. One minute he was talking to the family, having a nice conversation about football, the next he was being asked to lie to a friend about sleeping with his soon to be ex-girlfriend.

"I don't know…. Bobby's an old buddy of mine."

"That's why it'd hurt him the most. What he did was wrong. Can't you at least have the balls to admit that?"

Charlie swallowed. He opened his mouth, then heard a voice say, "What's going on?"

Charlie and Becky turned their attention to the source of the voice. It was Bobby.

"Charlie and I have something to tell you," Becky said bracingly.

Charlie looked away, back at the rest of the family, wishing he was them, and trying to distance himself from the situation in front of him. He was only barely listening.

"Charlie and I have been cheating on you."

"What?" Bobby screamed. His voice bounced off the walls. "That's stupid! You're just lying to get back at me. Well congratulations, you've thoroughly pissed me off! But I know better than to believe that, Charlie would never do that. Right, Charlie?"

But Charlie wasn't paying attention. His mind had left two minutes ago.

Bobby smiled, seemingly satisfied from Charlie's lack of attention. "See, he's not even listening. He won't back you up. Not a soulless she-devil like you!"

"Oh she's got soul all right," Charlie said abruptly. "She showed it to me last night."

Bobby's face turned a deep red. Charlie had only seen it that red once before, and that was when he'd been sunburned on a beach trip. It was an obvious contrast to his body's usual pale white skin.

"Oh yeah? Well you can forget me doing anything for you, Charlie! My own best friend, un-fucking-believable!"

"Why would you do that to her?" Bobby asked, his voice much lower and more controlled than Bobby's, almost condescending. "She's not a trophy girlfriend, but she ain't half bad."

"Are you actually going to stand there and defend that pig? She ain't shit. You take her now and she'll only turn from a pig into a cow! What do you have to say to that?"

Charlie's body froze. Becky, on the other hand, looked like she'd tear her own hair out.

Charlie started to open his mouth, then shut it quickly.

"Thought so," Bobby said, then started out of the room. Before he could take three steps, Becky pounced on his back, screaming, and forcing all of her weight onto his shoulders, hoping to knock him to the ground.

Charlie wanted to pry Becky off but watching Bobby struggle was too damn funny. He couldn't bring himself to stop laughing long enough to intervene.

Two other guys (who didn't find it so funny) pulled Bobby and Becky away from each other.

"I never want to see you again, Bobby!"

"The same goes for you, Becky!"

Bobby disappeared somewhere in the commotion of the rest of the family, while Becky stayed with Charlie. She turned around and went head first into Charlie's chest, burying her head in it so that she could hide her tears.

They held each other tight.

Maybe I should date Charlie, she thought. *He's cute and there's no doubt I've been infatuated with him for a long time.*

So what if it was infatuation? Every worthwhile relationship she ever had began with lustfulness. She didn't believe in love at first sight, and she had a sure feeling in her gut, neither did he.

She couldn't flirt with him now, if she did, he'd expect it was only a reaction to her breakup. She couldn't even stand to let him see her cry.

Becky broke away and left for the bathroom, leaving behind a very confused Charlie.

She locked the door behind her. Anyone in desperate need of the bathroom would have to wait.

Becky sat on the toilet lid and cried into her hands. Tears seeped through the cracks of her fingers and ruined her cheap makeup. And it was all Bobby's fault.

She didn't know how long she sat on the toilet. She wished she'd ran water in the sink because whoever was close enough to knock on the door would hear her crying.

Becky sat up and wiped her eyes with her sleeve.

She opened the door and her little brother Danny stood just outside the doorway.

"It's all yours," Becky said. They could not avoid bumping each other as Danny squeezed through.

He went, washed his hands (which was a big accomplishment for someone in his family), and left as quickly as he came.

His dad was talking loudly enough to be heard from across the house. He had a beer in his hand (when did he never?) and his other hand was balled into a fist, although it didn't look like he intended to use it for anything violent.

He was talking to his Uncle Andrew by an old war painting. Danny bet his dad wished he could throw Andrew into the painting to join the rest of the blood losing revolutionists.

"Now when you get one of those fancy college degrees that no one else here can afford," his dad said. "Then you can call me your equal."

"Dad?"

Wally turned to face Danny. He had to look down to see him. "What?"

"Can you tell me a story?"

Wally looked both confused and annoyed. "Well…. what kind of story?"

"I just saw Becky crying in the bathroom and I have no idea why. Can you tell me a story of why women get sad?"

His father's face lit up like a Christmas tree. He even put his beer on a nearby table stand with a not so fancy doily spread across its surface. He asked his wife not to use it but she said, "If you let me do nothing else, let me decorate the house."

"Sure!" Wally said to Danny.

Wally sat on his dad chair, Danny joined him sitting crisscrossed on the floor.

He took another sip of his beer, then stared down at his son. Danny stared back, staring intently as if he was about to tell another one of his stories of when he was Danny's age, and why the women he knew got sad. The smell of liquor on his breath was all too familiar to Danny.

Wally's stomach expanded as he eased into a comfortable sitting position. He leaned back, and grunted.

"You see Danny, when I was about your age my mother —"

A hand tapped on Danny's shoulder. "Tag, you're it!"

It was his cousin, TJ. They'd always been competitive and TJ took advantage of Danny's eagerness to stay and listen to his dad's story.

He expected him to say, "Sorry, I can't leave. You win."

Instead, Danny stared at him for a moment, stood up, and chased after him.

They ran around the living room table as Wally called after them. "No running!"

They ignored him and ran as fast as ever. They ran between people's legs, around tables, under tables, over tables. Their game was cut short when TJ ran into a man he'd never seen before.

"Sorry," said the boy who ran into him.

"Don't worry about it," the man replied. The kid's worried faces told him they didn't believe him, so he smiled, and the kid's worried looks faltered. The boy's eyes shifted to a figure that stood behind him. "I'm fine, really," he assured the two of them.

Without another word, the two boys walked off. The man turned and met with a slender pretty girl. She didn't seem like the rest of the crowd.

Her hair was tied into a ponytail and her tank top suggested she'd just worked out. The white shorts she was wearing stood out in comparison to her tan skin.

"Those two are always running into things," said the woman. "Someday they're going to break something important and I'm going to have to call the police as Wally chases them around the house."

"Who're you?" the man asked.

"Jill."

"Like Jack and Jill?"

"It's short for Jillian."

"Oh."

"And yours?"

The man thought for a moment he'd forgotten his own name, like it didn't even matter. "Jack."

"She giggled."

The man remembered he only thought of Jack because of Jack and Jill. He smiled and played it off as if it was meant as a joke he'd planned all along. "I'm Ned." He used the same smile left over from when the boy ran into him.

"I've never seen you here before."

"I'm a friend of Oliver's."

She nodded tentatively.

"Do you know Oliver?" he asked.

"I'm sure I've seen him, people are always running in and out of this place."

A yell from the family room cut through the house, even through all the commotion.

"I've had it with you! You're a whore and I'm leaving for good! I don't care how much you cry!"

"I'm not a whore!"

Ned and Jill walked with a crowd to see the incident. Ned recognized Becky, but the boy she was talking to was a mystery to him.

Probably an old boyfriend, he thought.

Then there was a screech of pain, not from Becky or Bobby, but from an old man in the center of the room.

Everyone turned their eyes on him as he clutched his chest and crumpled onto the carpet.

"Sir, did you throw your back out?" Ned yelled as he rushed to him.

"He's having a heart attack you idiot!" Jill yelled.

Ned looked at her, surprised. "Do you know CPR?"

Jill's face flushed. "No, dammit! We need to get him to a hospital!"

"I'll drive!" Wally said as he bumped his way through the crowd.

"Hell no you won't," said his brother Andrew. "You're drunk as hell. You'll both die on the way to the emergency room. I'll drive."

"You always wanted the most attention!"

"This isn't about you and me! He's dying!"

"Will you two just shut up?" Jill screamed so loud that Wally, Andrew, and several others had to cover their ears.

"She's right," Wally said. "You drive."

Wally, Andrew, and other able-bodied adults carried the old man outside and into a red Chevelle parked by the front lawn.

"We've got to follow them," Jill said to Ned as they watched them load the old man into the car.

"We can take my car."

Ned led her to his car and they waited for Andrew to drive off in his. Several other people from the reunion had the same idea and climbed into their cars as well.

A car door opened and the same man who yelled at Becky earlier hopped into the backseat.

"Mind if I tag along?" he said. "I can't be in the same car as Becky."

Ned wanted to say no, but Jill answered before he could.

"Yes, of course."

Then another door opened and two kids hopped in. It was the same kids who ran into him earlier.

"May we ride with you?" asked one of them politely.

"Yes, hurry up, close the door," Jill said.

The boys did.

"Great," the guy who yelled at Becky said. "There's at least ten words I can't say now because of them."

"Shut up Bobby!" Jill said.

Andrew's car took off. Other cars pulled onto the road, so did Ned's.

"How far is the nearest emergency room anyway?" Ned asked to no one in particular.

"Twenty, thirty minutes tops," Jill replied.

It was night. Ned turned on his headlights and copied the turns of Andrew's car.

They lost them at a red light they didn't make. The car came to a stop and the preceding car's break lights cast a red glow onto their faces.

"Darn," Ned muttered, trying to censor himself in the presence of children.

"It's okay, I think I know the way," Jill said. There was an ominous silence between them, then Jill continued. "You know I never apologized for how rude I was to you earlier, when I yelled. I do that sometimes when I panic."

"Some of the most rude people I've ever met ended up being the closest people in my life."

At this moment the old man could be dead in Andrew's car and there was nothing Ned could do about it. If there was one thing he wanted to do for Jill it was let her see the dying man he suspected was her grandpa.

Chapter 11

The hospital was brightly light and Ned imagined watching the ceiling move by through the old man's eyes as he was being rolled into the operating room. The doctors wouldn't allow visitors as he was under, so they waited in the waiting room.

Ned held Jill's hand as they waited. The people from the family reunion filled most seats in the room. Jill still hadn't met all of them, and she wasn't about to finish.

It was two hours later and no one had left. The silence was almost maddening. Jill couldn't bring herself to read one of the celebrity magazines waiting on the table. It all seemed so unimportant.

A nurse came by and spoke quietly to the room at large. "Mr. Cambridge is in room 508, he's in critical condition. We don't think there's much chance of recovery. I suggest you say your goodbyes now while you're all here to support him."

The family took elevators to the fourth floor then walked to Mr. Cambridge's room. Together, the reunion relatives took up the entire hallway, making passage through them impossible. Anyone wanting to pass had to take a separate route.

Whoever wanted to say goodbye went into the room, everyone else (mostly people who'd never met him) waited outside concernedly. Ned was one of those people.

As a tall man was entering the room, he squeezed by Jill, who was leaving, brushing against her slightly.

As he entered the room, Mr. Cambridge's sick face forced a smile. "Brandon," he coughed.

"Yeah dad, it's me."

"I'm so happy to see you."

"Dad, listen. I know there's not much time left, so I have to tell you I'm going to ask Isabelle to marry me."

"That's great," Mr. Cambridge said, then coughed again. "But I've got to ask you one question." Mr. Cambridge's words were soft and weak.

Brandon leaned closer. "What is it?"

"Are—you—happy?"

"Not completely…. close enough."

"Will Isabelle make you happy?"

Brandon paused. He held his breath. "Yes."

"Brandon?"

"Yeah dad."

Mr. Cambridge looked at the ceiling, almost as if he no longer thought anyone else was there.

"I'm not leaving this earth, not until all my organs fail. I need to know why I existed."

"Are you in pain?"

"Well, yes. But I can't close my eyes, not for good, not until—" He coughed violently, then groaned.

"Dad, I can't stand to see you like this."

"Don't be sad Brandon."

"You can't tell me that. How could you tell me that?"

"Do you believe I'm a good person?"

"Of course I do," Brandon said incredulously, and sincerely.

"Then I'll be making room for more good people. My time is up. You have to understand that. It happens to everyone." He coughed again. This time his coughs sounded as if they were filled with liquid. Then he continued. "I'm just glad I spent the time I did with you and your brothers and sisters."

Brandon put a hand on his father's shoulder.

"I love you dad."

"I love you too, son. And you know what? I don't think I'll know why I existed. I can't know because I won't be around to see the aftermath, the lives I affected. Somehow, I feel like somewhere along the line I served my purpose. You get it?"

"Yeah dad, I get it." There was a single tear in Brandon's eye. It was the first time Mr. Cambridge had seen him cry since he was fifteen and his first girlfriend broke up with him. He comforted his son then like his son was comforting him now. Like father — like son.

"You know it's funny, I know you're in the room, I can feel you, but the only thing I can think about, is the light hanging above my head."

Brandon pulled his hand away.

Chapter 12

It was fittingly cloudy during the funeral. Everyone from the reunion came to pay their respects. People cried, flowers were laid, it was an open casket funeral. Mr. Cambridge looked peaceful, much like he had when he died.

When people talked about him, they used safety words like passed away, left us, moved on. Brandon kept his word and married Isabelle. He never quite knew whether he had wanted to, or if he did as some sort of deathbed obligation. Either way, he was happy.

Chapter 14

After everything that happened, life moved on. The world didn't stop for old Mr. Cambridge. People cried and grieved. To some, he was the most important person in the world. Most people, however, would never even learn his name. It wouldn't matter to him though, he was dead.

What Mr. Cambridge would never know is that his organs were donated to a man who would later become a US president. Some would regard him as the best US president in history.

And it was all because of one old man who knew somehow, in some way, he'd made a difference. Like the imperfect smudge on a beautiful painting that somehow made it look unique.

Thank You

Thank you for reading this book. If you feel you've received a sufficient level of entertainment from this work, please consider writing a review to help others find the same level of entertainment.